D0641017

AN
AUTOBIOGRAPHY
OF SKIN

AN
AUTOBIOGRAPHY
OF SKIN

Lakiesha Carr

PANTHEON BOOKS New York

This is a work of fiction. Names, characters, places, and incidents either
are the product of the author's imagination or are used fictitiously.
Any resemblance to actual persons, living or dead, events,
or locales is entirely coincidental.

Copyright © 2023 by Lakiesha Carr

All rights reserved. Published in the United States by Pantheon Books,
a division of Penguin Random House LLC, New York, and distributed
in Canada by Penguin Random House Canada Limited, Toronto.

Pantheon Books and colophon are registered trademarks
of Penguin Random House LLC.

Library of Congress Cataloging-in-Publication Data
Name: Carr, Lakiesha, author.
Title: An autobiography of skin : a novel / Lakiesha Carr.
Description: First edition. New York : Pantheon Books, 2023
Identifiers: LCCN 2022036145 (print). LCCN 2022036146 (ebook).
ISBN 9780593316535 (hardcover). ISBN 9780593316542 (ebook)
Subjects: LCSH: African American women—Fiction. LCGFT: Novels.
Classification: LCC PS3603.A774254 A95 2023 (print) |
LCC PS3603.A774254 (ebook) | DDC 813/.6—dc23/eng/20220801
LC record available at https://lccn.loc.gov/2022036145
LC ebook record available at https://lccn.loc.gov/2022036146

www.pantheonbooks.com

Jacket illustration by Valya Urm
Jacket design by Kelly Blair

Printed in the United States of America
First Edition
2 4 6 8 9 7 5 3 1

For Alfreddie, Ernestine and Clarence,
My holy trinity.

There are things that a woman sings, and only a woman knows the full meaning. You may sing for men as well as for women, but only a woman knows your full meaning. I am not a feminista. I only think a woman should be true to who she believes herself to be. Or who she wants herself to be. Or who she imagines herself to be. I don't know what I mean, or whether I'm true myself to any of that. I don't think there are many of us who are true to our possibilities.

—GAYL JONES, *The Healing*

My face feels like a living emotional relief map, forever wet. My hair is curling in anticipation of my own wild gardening.

—BOB KAUFMAN, *Afterwards They Shall Dance*

PART I

Some women wait for themselves around the next corner and call the empty spot peace but the opposite of living is only not living and the stars do not care.

—AUDRE LORDE

Yesterday Was a Dream,
Today Is a Miracle

The night, as most nights, was like a dream.

At 10:00 p.m., once I fed the dog the last of the scraps off the stove. Once I cursed the cat for scratching up my mama's antique furniture, then welcomed him back into my arms. Once I slicked my hair back into a thin ponytail, wrapping it up tight in my mama's old scarf. Once I stayed in the bathtub a lil too long, letting the heat of the water do things my husband stopped doing years ago. Once I oiled my body down and up and down again with cocoa butter, I reached for my housecoat hanging delicately against the door—leopard print and silk—wrapping it around my bloated body, not caring if the water or oil stained or bled through.

And as if a ghost, soundlessly, I floated to the garage and had a cigarette alone.

Mostly I listened to the blues. Lightnin' Hopkins. Bessie Smith. Bobby Womack, if my mama was heavy on my mind which was most nights, but especially tonight. So I listened to the blues and nursed a lil Crown Royal poured thin over crushed ice. The kinda ice I used to crunch and eat out of nerves, and now just out of habit. I smoked my Virginia Slims, pulling that cool menthol taste to the back of my throat before pushing it out—a thick plume of smoke.

Creating that smoke is what I liked to do. A lazy sort of cloud that held in the air long enough for me to see the future, revisit the past, the everything at once found within that haze. I let my thoughts drift, curl and bend as the smoke did; full with memories before tapering out and disappearing. Or, as I guessed, becoming something else. Vapor. My daddy used to tell his congregation that life was like a vapor—here today and gone tomorrow—and so they best get right with the Lord soon. As I sat watching the smoke blossom like a flower from my lips, growing and weakening again; slowly giving away with each second, I couldn't help thinking: There goes my life. I took another long pull, watched the ash stiffen then drop to the cold concrete floor and thought: There it goes again and again.

Sometimes I reached out for the smoke, tried to grab it and rein it in but like the life I was living, it always seemed just beyond my grasp.

If I became tipsy, I might sing. Not because I could or should but just because. A low hum. A gentle cry cause sometimes I only felt happy when listening to the blues. Until I changed the record player to something electronic. Something full of shock and wonder. The funk. That beat that lifted me up somewhere heavenly, then gently delivered me back to Earth. That's what music did for me. It was an escape, the sweetest escape there ever was. Until I remembered my body, my senses, my reality called home. Where late nights in the garage seemed a sanctuary. A safe place where I could mourn the life that never was and make temporary peace with the present.

Tonight I did all of those things.

In my bedroom, I walked to my bath, the most beautiful space in my whole house. Decked out with zebra and lion prints; a jungle, the most feminine boudoir where I housed my relief. A long day's exhale. A sigh of regret. There I stood before the mirror nude. There I watched the soft brown flaps of skin fold upon one another, creating stacks and stacks of endless flesh around the middle parts of my body. There I closely examined the fine lines and deep ridges carved like rivers into my face, where it told a story of longing for the unknowable. For the replacement of all that felt lost. Of everything life seemed to take from me, demand from me with the expectation of grace. My eyes were dull, gradually dimming with age. Like a fire whose amber coals glowed a deep burgundy in the dark until exhausted, then smothered to soot.

Needless to say, I was lonely. And my breasts showed the fact; their gentle dips against the top of my abdomen hung like plums gone soft under a hot summer sun. Ripe without appreciation, ignored to rot while gravity had its way. My thighs were thick like tree stumps, and that's how I felt. Tall. Brown. Topped with a crown of hair gone thin, and thinner still, especially along its edges where in certain spots my scalp revealed smooth and soft bald spots. And yet I still felt desirable. Comforted with the warm burn of whiskey in my belly, my gaze took in the absoluteness of my womanhood and for a moment I still felt deserving of something good, someone who might love me. All of my hidden parts that somehow never made their way to the surface of my personality—day after day after day.

Sometimes in the quietness of the early morning hours, just before dawn, when the sky was a dark purplish blue, I felt hopeful. Optimistic. And then once my high began to come down, and the faint sounds of my husband's snoring across the hall made their way into my own room, I was left with fatigue. And so it was then just as tonight that I went to bed; a mess of cheetah-spotted down comforters and black cotton sheets. I slipped under the covers, still nude, grateful for the coolness of the fabric against my skin. To feel at all something welcoming. And then I watched my stories: *Young and the Restless, Bold and the Beautiful, General Hospital, CSI, NCIS,* and all of the other crime dramas where dead bodies the color of cold milk wound up in unusual places and cold white people with serious faces and grim speech sought to find the cause of their demise.

The hours passed. And just as the sun revealed itself in orderly fashion, and the sound of school buses running like steam trains rumbled through the neighborhood and the light bickering of children seeped through the thin windowpane of my bedroom, I pulled my body into myself. Pulled the covers over my head and shut my eyes tight, willing darkness and sleep to come until it finally obeyed.

This was my night. Not so unique. Not so special. But always consistent.

At 10:30 a.m. when the phone rang it was my client Diamond calling to tell me she'd be late for her appointment. Not that this was a surprise. Still I acted impatient, scolding her lightly.

"Girl, can't you ever be on time?"

To which Diamond only said, "Now I wouldn't be me if I was on time, right?" Then she laughed, high-pitched and girlish in a way that made you love her even if you barely knew her.

"Nah, I don't suppose so," I said, relieved that I'd have time to wash my face, dress, even have a cup of coffee and sober up before she got here. Because for Diamond, late could mean two to three hours, and while ordinarily that should and would piss off the average person who at least semi-valued their time, I was grateful. Though I wouldn't show it.

Because not only had I overslept, but Diamond's tardiness meant I could charge a late fee. And that meant a lil extra change in my pocket. Not to mention, Diamond was my only client for the day.

"I'll see you when you get here," I said and rose out of bed.

Time to start the day. New day, same thing?

Now if anyone asked, with a lil liquor in my system I might tell you very easily:

Who do Diamond be? Shit, I've asked myself continually. Big and brown as I is. Thick in places where she ought not be, thus she comes for her colonic annually and I be like—shit, get it all girl! Reflexology for dem feet. Lean back and relax, set them parasites free from your gut! Digestive system harboring the disease, with this cleansing we do harmonize your inner chemistry. Get your body on point. And she be like, yeah yeah do that! Whatever it costs I'll pay. Pass some of this gas and make my belly go flat. Drop least five pounds every time upon your table I climb and my man like it that way. Flat belly, full ass. Black men don't ever change. You know the game! And I be like, true true. That'll be $60 today.

But who is Diamond? What kinda lady is she? Chocolate. She chocolate with voluptuous lips, a broad nose that makes it seem like she can smell everything, smell the world if she tried. Though she tries to minimize its size with MAC makeup that's a bit too light for her complexion. She pretty short too. No more than five-foot-three always wearing them high heels to stretch further into skies. She got them black eyes, what they call dark dark brown, but really they look black, and honestly I feel that should be okay but don't nobody else seem to agree. Sometimes she comes in here with green or blue contacts and I be like, Damn Diamond! You shining girl!

She said she used to be a dancer but now she got three kids—ages eight, five and two And I'm always shocked to remember this each and every time I see her because she looks no more than twenty herself.

Once I asked her as I was warming the water, a rare day she'd arrived early and caught me unprepared and I made small talk of the nosy kind then said, "Diamond, how old are you, chile?"

I'm older and fortunately age allows us to be rude, direct—what my mama called blunt and to the point. Diamond laughed that laugh, tugging down her black leggings and reaching for the yellow terry cloth robe I give all my clients.

"Why you ask that, Miss Nettie?" And with that, I knew she had to have been older than I ever figured her for. Maybe as old as thirty-five? Forty? You could never tell these days when everyone seemed determined to act and dress every age but what they were. Not that I was much different. But if I wanted to get a real answer, I realized I was going to have to couch it in a compliment.

"Girl, you come in here not lookin' a day over nineteen! I have to ask."

Then I laughed, tried to laugh all high-pitched like she does but years of nicotine wouldn't let my voice climb that high. Still, it worked and she told me with a sheepish smile and eyes alive that she was twenty-seven.

"Oh okay," I said. "That's a good number."

"Is it?" she asked, climbing up on the table and scooting her bottom to the edge as though she were at the gynecologist.

I removed the plastic tube from its wrapping and felt for the entryway into her body. Softly, gently, I inserted the rectal nozzle, keeping my eyes focused on her face. "Relax," I said, more out of habit than necessity. "Twenty-seven is a good number."

Diamond once told me she used to dance at this strip club in Atlanta called Baby Dolls. Baby Dolls where all the women wore wigs and weaves that stretched down their backs and blue or green contacts and looked everything but like baby dolls with their scars that showed, even with heavy makeup beneath the bright stage lights. Young girls still, but wounded by life, they had bullet holes in private places like their upper thighs and pelvic regions; cuts on their faces and arms. Nothing like no baby doll I ever had nor would have wanted. But she said the strip club was good to her. She made close to a thousand dollars a week, which was extremely good money back then in Georgia.

She told me this lying on the table, letting the hose remove her impurities and watching them float by in the septic tank, an aquarium-sized bowl where clients could see the progress of their colon cleansing. I remember cause her eyes had gone quiet, almost as dull as mine when she told the story of the girl she used to be.

Baby doll.

"Picture this," she said. "A small, dank club in downtown Atlanta, not far from the CNN Center and dem Olympic fountains where kids played when the weather allowed.

"I was seventeen, but lied and told the manager I was eighteen cause my friend had managed to get me a fake I.D. Not that I needed it. The younger you looked the better, the younger you actually was even mo' better. I was a petite thing. No real titties or ass, but I was firm in the ways young girls are cause nature still got hope in 'em. So I was hired."

"Damn shame," I said, sucking my teeth but careful not to let my face show judgment. She only hummed, "Mhmm . . ." and kept going.

"So I danced there for three years until I met Rodney."

Rodney was her baby daddy and eventually her husband almost ten years and three kids later. They'd married at the justice of the peace a year ago and Diamond had come in for a colonic, claiming she needed to look extra good for her wedding day. I'd done it half price as a wedding gift and she'd invited me to the courthouse to witness the act. I told her I'd come but I overslept, even though the ceremony wasn't until 2:00 p.m. But, such was the life of a woman who didn't sleep. Who spent her late nights watching fictional characters and chasing smoke with her fingers.

Another day I'd asked her if Diamond was her real name or her stage moniker, and without so much as batting an eye she'd simply said, "Oh no. My mama named me Diamond. My dance name was Princess Cut. But everyone just called me Princess."

"But why Princess *Cut?*"

"So everybody would know I didn't play."

And we'd laughed and laughed and laughed until she farted hard enough to blow small waves of bubbles throughout the tank. Then we laughed more.

Most weeks Diamond was my only client. Business was real slow. And while she was never on time, which went strictly against my rules—rules that said if you were more than twenty minutes late, there was a $10 late fee. Rules that said if you had to cancel on the day of your appointment you'd still be charged the full amount. ($60 for a regular colonic, not including a lymphatic drain or reflexology services.) And if you canceled with notice, well that still meant a $20 fee. This was all to say, I attracted relatively dependable people. Except for Diamond, who was reliable only in that she was determined to eat what she wanted and then expect me to pump it all out. But, hey. I couldn't complain, or lecture and risk annoying my most consistent customer with the truth. Besides, I needed the money.

Gas money. Little lunch money. Some cigarettes and Crown Royal money. A few extra dollars so I could play my $5 match at the game room.

It was 1:15 when Diamond finally arrived today and she was her usual chipper self. Watching the silky weblike threads of her parasites pass, she told me again the story of how she got the small burn at the base of her neck. How the thin cut running alongside her left ear was the result of broken glass flying during a fight at Baby Dolls. And before we were done, she gently lifted the skin around her belly, pointing at her C-section scar and told me how when the weather changed it still itched where they took out her middle child. The one with the birthmark over her left eye and so everyone laughed and called her Sula. Not because they understood the reference, but because once a woman at church, a librarian no less, had jokingly called her that while cupping the girl's plain, round face inside her hands. Diamond and Rodney had eaten it up and called her that ever since because as she later told me, "It seemed fittin'." I didn't exactly understand the reference myself but the first time I met the child, a very meek, quiet and homely-looking something with a spirit not at all resembling her mother's, I couldn't help thinking, *Yeah . . . Sula.*

I had no idea what the child's real name was.

I listened to all of this, traveling the length of Diamond's skin and absorbing the stories it told while watching the insides of Diamond's body tell its own tales. I rubbed her feet down with cocoa butter, then gently removed the tube from her bottom with one quick move. Wrapping it in a paper towel all the while she spoke with her eyes now closed, I threw it in the trash can, and smiled though she didn't see me.

Patting her twice against her leg, I said, "We're finished, baby. You can sit up now."

After giving her a mixed drink rich with vitamins meant to replenish her electrolytes, I walked her to the door, laughing though distracted with the ways I intended to spend the soft twenty-dollar bills she'd crushed in the moist fold of my hand.

"Diamond, you take care of yourself, baby."

I stood letting the weight of my body fall lazily against the doorway and watched her wobbling to her car on orange stilettos.

"I will, Miss Nettie!" Her two-toned face was flushed with the effects of purification, glowing just enough to make her look like I imagined her seventeen-year-old self might have, before the scars, before the wounds. In the afternoon sun she appeared a baby doll. My baby doll.

She looked back, smiled and got in her car, a gold tooth in the middle of her mouth catching the light and briefly shining as bright as her eyes. As she drove away, she waved and honked her horn twice.

When I closed the door behind her I breathed a sigh of relief, and sadness and wonder. Then grabbing my keys off the bar, I headed to my car.

It was 2:45 p.m. Time to go play my match.

At 2:50, I sat in my car, a red '98 two-door Lexus with sorority plates on both ends and cheetah print dice hanging from the rearview mirror. I looked at my gas tank. Watched the arrow refuse to rise above E, watched the tiny gas light lit in all its bright yellow glory. Realized I'd already been driving on E for at least two days.

"Dammit!" I said, hitting the wheel until the whites of my palms turned a milky pink.

Shit.

At 3:00 p.m. I started the long walk up and out of my neighborhood, the sun ablaze, my shadow thick and black against the sidewalk. I told myself I was getting exercise. I even walked as though that was my intention. Each foot in front of the other, eyes averted to the ground with short glances to the sky. A flash of cloud and blue to remind me I was alive. Awake. To convince myself I was on the ground and not floating away to somewhere distant and scary outside myself.

Because after all it was three o'clock and soon the school buses would run because school would have let out and those same bickering children would pass me on the street, their tongues and fingers sticking out windows, the bus just as loud and angry as the morning revealed. I wasn't ashamed. This was not the first time I'd had to walk, crossing over several neighborhood streets before reaching the main drag, the concrete artery that would take me two miles straight up the road to the Little Taco, a convenience store slash gas station slash taco hut slash—shhh—game room.

At 3:35 p.m. I walked in only slightly sweating, my body having long ago reached a point of cooperation, my heartbeat only slightly elevated.

Inside, Raud said hello without smiling. The store was musty and quiet save for the muted sounds of Fleetwood Mac's "Little Lies" playing over the sound system. And as if on cue, I acted as though I was going to buy something other than more cigarettes.

This was the dance. This was the part where I glided down the aisles looking at old peanuts and candy bars, juice and soda whose expirations long ago passed. A dusty flashlight that likely never worked, a single nail file wrapped in plastic that'd been opened already, barely visible in the corner of the packaging. Stale chips and sour pickles in glass jars that looked like swamps. The worst kinda algae green.

I made eye contact a few times—which meant no more than twice—with Raud who stood there, all brown and long like beef jerky; lean and looking far too serious for his age, which I estimated as no more than twenty. I was always guessing ages. I noticed he only truly looked at me, stared at me with a sort of bewilderment and softness on rainy days. Those times when I'd walked in as soaked with wet as a steeped tea bag. One of the rare times I was soft too and smiled with embarrassment.

At those moments he always smiled back with the most perfect teeth, and a small tilt of his head. Like he had some manners and remembered that despite the circumstances I was his elder and thus due a certain amount of respect. And even if he didn't have it, he treated me so. Almost like we were doing something honorable other than our usual dance.

When I reached the counter he said, "The usual?" And I replied, "Yes."

Stooping down and looking under the counter, he popped back up with my Virginia Slims. Menthol. 120s. Silver stripe.

"One or two?" he asked.

"One," I said, thinking about the gas needed at home. And then, without making eye contact, I said, "So what's goin' on back yonder?"

"It's quiet. Not much flashing."

Now Raud knew this encouraged me. He knew that fewer jackpots throughout the day only increased my chances of hitting something. The people filled the machines up and I came to reap the reward. When I was lucky. And today I felt lucky, right hand itching since yesterday. Even Diamond had mentioned something looked different about me. Not my hair. Not a new nail color. Not even weight loss. *Just different.* She couldn't put her finger on it. But I could. My right hand had started itching over in the night sometime between *The Bold and the Beautiful* and *General Hospital.* I felt lucky. Real lucky. I had those three twenty-dollar bills burning up my pocket and was ready to make something happen.

"I guess I'll go see how Miss Bertha doin' back there."

That was my code. For whom I wasn't sure. It wasn't like he didn't know what I was doing. But somehow playing it off as if I was only there to visit, indeed check on Miss Bertha, an older lady who walked from the housing projects at the opposite end of the street, made sense to me. In any case, Raud silently accepted it every time with a courteous nod towards the back door leading to the game room.

Grabbing my cigarettes, I followed his nod's direction and thus concluded our dance.

Inside the actual room. That shoe-box-sized place I called my second home, though it was dim, smokey and blank without emotions, except the pulsing energy of win, win, double red, double purple—jackpot! You could hit as much as $2,000 which was good money for any game room. When I couldn't make it west on I-35 towards Oklahoma to the Choctaw reservation casinos or east on I-20 to the Louisiana casino boats, the game rooms were the best alternative.

Ever moving, ever changing, you had to be in the know to find out where they were. And even then, there were some weeks when you still had to find them. Once the cops busted a joint it was a wrap until the operation regrouped and relocated elsewhere. About six months ago we were meeting in a gang of warehouses not far from the Little Taco. From the outside it looked like a group of storage units and you'd have to walk to the correct door and knock three times before someone would come around from the back and let you in, and that's only if they knew you. But once your face became a familiar fixture, you were treated like family. And then you were inside watching the machines flash double double orange with hearts and circles and various hypnotic colors and symbols jumping across screens. You were playing $200 or more some days, losing even more some days. Drinking cocktails and eating chicken wings because oftentimes they fed you at the game rooms and plied you up with liquor. And before you knew it, you were addicted to everything about the experience. Like with cigarettes or porn. Like with sweets or good music. You couldn't get enough and after a while you started to need it to help cover this bill or that bill. Or at least that's how it went for me.

So the game room at the Little Taco had become a special place for what it gave to me, the ways it fed me. My brokeness. My loneliness. Those blues waiting for me every night in the garage. Those times when my husband didn't care enough to ask *How are you today?* And before long, I didn't really think enough to say *I love you. I really do.* The game room family, my $5 match replaced all of that. And Miss Bertha had actually become a highlight of my day.

Sitting there on the barstool, nothing but bones and gray hair, rotten teeth yet she still smiled, real hard and welcoming. There was never a time when I'd seen her without some kinda loopy grin whether she was winning or losing. And best believe she had plenty reasons to frown. To be angry. Still she didn't and I admired her stamina. Had come to love her since we met years ago at the game room inside the old neighborhood rib joint. For my birthdays she always made me a pecan pie, said if I shelled the pecans, she didn't mind doing the rest. I loved her.

She had $30 when I walked into the small room, holding it tight within her right hand, her left knee shaking just enough to bump the machine she played. I walked up behind her and gently placed my hands over her eyes. "Surprise!" I whispered at her narrow face. "Who you think it is?"

"Girl, if you don't stop playing!" She rocked her lean body to both sides with a grin that showed a few healthy white teeth in the back of her head. "Stop playing girl, can't you see I'm winnin'?"

"How much you up?" I asked, glancing at the numbers and colors the machine showed. Red and purple were the best. The highest jackpots always came in royal shades and her terminal, like a video game, was flashing a neat $245 at the top of the screen. She was up, clutching her bills in her bony fingers while pressing the green PLAY button like a drum.

"Look," she said, pulling from her skirt pocket two crisp hundred-dollar bills. "Mama been lucky today!" And this time when she smiled her breath smelled of brown and white liquors with a hint of pineapple.

"Dang Miss Bertha!" I clutched at her money, feigning as though I meant to take it—her and I both knowing I didn't. "Gimme some of that!"

She laughed.

"Gone now girl before you mess up my concentration. Your machine is free!"

I looked behind us and noticed she was right. There against the wall, my favorite old faithful stood vacant; barstool with its torn black pleather material busted open like split fruit looking like it was waiting on me. And I remembered my $60 in my pocket and remembered my itchy right hand.

When Delilah, the game room clerk who doled out drinks—cheap wines, beers and whiskey—walked through, I stopped her with a smile and drawled long and slow, "Heeeey Dee!"

Dee only paused, smiled then winked before turning around and disappearing back into the storeroom walls where they kept drinks and cash to re-up the machines and cash out. Without having to ask she returned with my usual drink, Crown Royal with a splash of Coke.

"Thanks babygirl," I said, relieving her of the cocktail, careful not to spill.

"How you doing today baby?" She held her tray against her wide hips, popping her gum. She always did that and every time I heard the soft pops between her teeth I thought of what my grandma used to say. When you can pop the gum like that it meant you had cavities. I sipped my drink wondering how many rotten teeth she had inside that mouth. A sound that many days sounded therapeutic, almost relaxing and comforting to my ears despite the story it told.

"I'm good," I said, sliding a twenty-dollar bill inside the machine's opening.

"Good, good," she replied, gently rubbing my shoulder. Dee was a white girl who made you forget it. A Tennessee native, she had all these skull tattoos dotting her arms and occasionally showed up to the room with nasty bruises that we watched turn a sickly yellow over time before fading. It was no secret that her man fought on her, but we all knew she fought him back. Some days she'd crack open a Bud Light and laugh, saying, "You shoulda seen him." And we believed her.

My eyes were fixed on the screen, body tense and focused on the win. Never mind paying attention to Alvin, a crippled Vietnam vet who reeked of marijuana and rubbing alcohol every time I saw him, sitting on the other side of me playing just as intently. On the other side of Alvin was Floyd, a real cool cat known for hitting $500 or more on any given day, known for his plump shape usually tucked behind a brown trench coat that he wore no matter the weather, and dark tortoiseshell glasses. Floyd played it cool. As cool as anyone who lived in the game room, as most of us did. He didn't drink though Alvin often tempted him with E&J, his drink of choice, or a beer. Alvin brought his own, pulling a silver canister from inside his coat pocket, the same worn army green jacket with embroidered military patches. 1969. 1971. 1973. The patches alongside his arm a timeline of events only he understood.

But Floyd didn't drink. He didn't drink but he often won and so everyone watched him, trying to decipher his tricks. Was it the time of day he played? The machine he played? The amount of money he played? No one could call it.

I began my ritual chant, double double orange, double double purple. C'mon. Gimme something. Anything.

I glanced over at Floyd who liked to stand at his terminal rather than sit. For a moment I considered doing the same, but the walk had taken a toll on these thick, tree-stump legs. The lack of sleep and alcohol did the rest. I placed my high booty in the middle of the stool, thick sides spilling over the seat and felt grateful and content watching the money flowing like electricity, lighting up the game. The cool of the whiskey felt good going down.

In the back, the music was different. Al Green sang the soulful blues, *I'm so tired of being alone . . .* and Alvin was singing as though he could sing. Loud. Scratchy voice rough yet sweet. Sweeter still the more I drank. And did I mention I felt lucky? $40 in and I was rolling purple sevens, but not enough to hit anything big, just enough to keep me playing.

By the time Dee returned with my third drink, I was tipsy and singing *It's cheaper to keep her . . .* and down to my last $20 after hitting a double orange that briefly saw me up by $150. I didn't care. I was something you might call happy. Across the way Miss Bertha swayed with a slight bop to my crooning and another woman, a face I'd only seen a few times, skinny as can be and caramel colored with her hair piled high upon her head like a basket, snapped her fingers. Her long nails artificial, multicolored and punctuated with pink hearts at their tips. "Heeeey hey!" she called, and I could tell she was feeling it too. The music. The game. The liquor. She held in her other hand what had to have been her fifth beer of the afternoon. I had been counting. She stood at another terminal beside Juan, a Mexican man who wore a black cowboy hat and brown Stetson boots. He stood playing with one hand with his other arm tied around her waist, casually enough to suggest possession, still light enough to give her room to move.

And move she did. The more I sang, the louder I became, the more she popped her skinny fingers and cried out, "Sing it sistah!" I liked her immediately.

Without noticing, Alvin walked up on me and gently rested his salt and pepper beard against the tops of my shoulder. "Alright gal," he said. "Don't you imagine you oughta get while the gettin' is good?" To which I only snapped my fingers too and wrapped an arm around his waist. Swaying. Swaying like waves. Inside my own groove like over in the midnight hours when the combination of mood and alcohol gave me some relief, some peace and escape from my body.

"Leave her alone!" Floyd called. "Can't you see she feelin' it? She gone man. Let her be!"

I only smiled and hiccupped.

"Yeah, get away from her Alvin!" Miss Bertha said, speech slurred and hoarse from her throat. "Don't you know a yella nigga bad luck?" And with that she stood up and walked the three, maybe four steps over to us. She almost tripped over her own feet before catching Alvin's arm and bringing him down with her momentarily before finding her balance.

Giggling, sounding something like Diamond, she said to me in my ear, still audible enough for Alvin to hear, "Told you a yella nigga ain't shit!" I only grinned and removed my arm from Alvin's waist and placed it tightly around hers.

"You know it's cheaper to keep her," I sang back directly in her face. Truly happy now. Truly.

"Aww now Bertha, don't start that shit with me today!" Alvin said.

But Bertha only pulled back and called over to Floyd, "Say Floyd! Tell Miss Nettie over here how a yella nigga won't do shit but take ya money and bring you bad luck."

"My name Emmitt and I ain't in it," he called back, not once removing his eyes from his game.

"Now Miss Bertha, you know Floyd too close to that nigga red color to agree with you," Alvin said laughing and holding his chest like there was something there to hold on to.

"Aww hush up Alvin!" Miss Bertha said. "It ain't no fun if you agree with me."

"Well, I knows I ain't no bad luck," Alvin said. "My mama didn't make no such thing."

"Well anyhow," Miss Bertha replied. "I don't suppose yo yella ass would recognize it if you was."

"Now Bertha," he said, growing serious in his tone. "You know you wrong. How would you feel if I called you a dark—?"

And just like that the world ended. Everything came to a halt before Alvin could even finish his sentence. The music stopped. The machines went silent, everyone's faces drawn tight with tension. No one moved or seemed to breathe for what must have been no more than three seconds but felt more like thirty minutes. From the back storeroom, Dee peeped around the door, green eyes peeled, pupils dilated. Just like that the moment stood frozen. Time stopped until Miss Bertha, blacker than the darkest moonless night, turned her face slowly, slowly, slowly with the sorta drama only a classic Hollywood film could fully appreciate, and faced Alvin straight on.

We watched her full lips turn up into a smile and it was like the universe resumed motion and molecules moved, vibrations sprang out—bouncing faster and faster still. "Nigga," she said, "you ever call me even anything like that and those'll be the last words your black ass utters on God's green Earth."

The room erupted in laughter—tension built and tore down within a span of seconds. The music came back and Alvin said, "Oh, now I'm Black huh? I got to damn near insult you to be considered Black huh?" But everyone only laughed, and Miss Bertha laughed too and said, "Well, hell, we all black in the dark. I figure you might as well be a nigga somewhere. If not in this place, at this hour."

And I could tell Alvin wanted to say something but the jukebox struck up a Bobby Blue Bland song and Dee handed him another Coors Light, sweating through the thin paper towel wrapped around its cold body. He popped the top, took a long swig and instead began to dance in the middle of the aisle, between flashing machines—the lights acting as a strobing disco ball.

"I ain't got time for none of you," he said, doing a lil two-step, jutting his one good leg out to the beat. "I served my time for this country," he continued, closing his eyes and settling into his groove. "And I was lucky enough to make it back. Shit, I'm a Black man. I'm lucky to be alive at all! I'm a man, baby. The realest kinda man you'll prolly ever meet!"

I stood up and took his yellow hand into my brown and fell into step with his rhythm. Moving my feet in time with his. Drunk in the late afternoon. Broke in the late afternoon. Happy in the late afternoon with my game room family. And as Alvin reached around my back and let his hands wander down and grab my ass like it belonged to him, I only said, "Of course you are, Alvin! Of course you are."

In the distance the sound of school bells went off and I heard Floyd's voice yell, "Yes! Yessir! Double double purple baby! Jackpot baby! How you like me now!" And still the bells sounded and the lights shone even brighter casting a neon glow upon Floyd's smiling face.

Alvin whipped around, holding me close to his body and smelling heavy with smoke. "Don't tell me that joker done did it again! Hot damn!"

"Hell yeah I did it!" Floyd jumped with new energy and excitement. "Drinks for everybody on me!"

That's when Juan, who'd been playing and sipping his beer quietly through all the drama, stood up, releasing his lady friend, and went to peer around Floyd's bouncing shape. He was almost a whole three inches shorter than Floyd and was thin inside his starched denim jeans and red button-up. Looping his fingers inside his belt, an oversized buckle with the head of an Aztec warrior, which I knew because under the man's head it read in silver lettering AZTEC WARRIOR. He smiled and said, "You did good," nodding with approval. "But my friend, drinks here are free."

But Floyd couldn't hear him. Didn't hear him. He was too busy dancing now, holding his trench coat open as though he intended to flash somebody, only to reveal a plain and worn purple cotton sweat suit. Looking at him I couldn't help thinking he looked something like Barney, the kid show dinosaur who loved me, who loved you, who loved the world!

"Go head Floyd," I called, stomping my foot and spilling the last bit of watered-down drink in my cup.

"Well hell, I'll get everybody ten dollars towards some gas. Only unleaded though, none of that fancy shit. Go head! Line 'em up out-doors! I'm good for it."

A light clicked on in my brain, and I sobered up real quick, remembering my car sitting at home on E. *Shit!*

"Ain't no gas right now," Dee said from her corner. "We out right now. Waiting on the refill."

"Shit, me too!" the caramel-colored lady said, tossing an empty beer can into the nearest trash can.

"OK, OK," Floyd said, undeterred. "What do y'all got?"

"Tacos," Dee replied, handing the caramel woman a fresh can.

"Oh hell nah!" Miss Bertha hollered out. She spun around on her chair like her booty had a swivel on it. "Them thangs got too much salt and grease—run my pressure up!"

"I'll take a taco!" I said.

"Me too," said Juan.

"Me too," said Alvin, scratching at his balls and finishing the last of his drink.

"I like dem thangs," said the caramel chick. "Thas how I make mines."

"Alright! Tacos for everyone!" Dee called and headed towards the kitchen.

"All y'all must have a death wish!" Miss Bertha said, sucking her teeth and holding her bony arms upon her bony hips but Alvin reached out and pulled her into his chest where they stayed in a close slow dance to BB King until the food came.

We ate as a group, dripping hot sauce and grease down our chins and on the machines and on the floor. Drinking more liquor until everyone was good and full. By the time I stumbled out into the evening air it was after seven o'clock and Raud had been replaced by Amir.

"See you tomorrow Miss Nettie!" he said, plucking at his cash register. "Be careful out there!"

There was no dance or pretense with Amir, a teenaged boy with a clumsy way of being in the world. No dance. With Amir it just was what it was and he seemed to make no judgments.

"Bye baby," I called back. "See you tomorrow if the sun shine and the creek don't rise!"

"What?" Amir said laughing and laughing. The light sound of his voice carried me outside and back into the streets.

The night air was cool on my face. I watched my steps move again as shadows, in and out of darkness with the streetlights, the car lights behind me creating what I imagined an aura, illuminating the outline of my body as I made my way home. I felt strong and powerful. Like my truest self. The taste of onion and cilantro still heavy on my tongue. When I hiccupped again I tasted garlic on my breath and was satisfied at least that it covered the Crown Royal. Feeling the liquor was enough. No need to let it overwhelm me with its presence, revealing itself through pores, bloodshot eyes *and* breath.

I was counting the cracks in the sidewalk, thinking about each dollar I'd lost and not giving a damn. Not giving one damn because at least I'd been free. Maybe not lucky. Not today anyway, but perhaps lucky in my own way.

I was thinking this when my cell phone vibrated long and hard through the canvas of my purse and a car full of white boys pulled up alongside me; a red four-door Nissan, the very red I liked most, like a shiny candied apple. Their pale faces were a translucent haze, a blur not unlike my smoke, and when I squinted my eyes a bit more I noticed that it was smoke, moving and weaving its way around their quiet faces. The marijuana was strong and good. Not like the dirt my husband smoked. I answered my phone, still staring at the red car, idling now curbside as I continued walking.

"Hey now!"

"Hey yaself!" It was my best friend Peaches. "Where you at? I been calling you since three this afternoon."

I noticed one of the boys in the back seat rolling down his window and sticking a head blossoming with soft blond curls out the passenger side, motioning with his hand for my attention.

"I'm headed home from the grocery store. I had five clients today and barely had a minute to eat chile. I'm bout to go in the house now and fix Ernest something to eat and try to get off these feet."

I kept my eyes forward, made the white boys follow me to where the streetlamp shone again bright and yellow against the pavement.

"Sounds like you walking now," she said, and I could hear the confusion in her voice.

"I am, girl! Tryin' to get these groceries in the house." I stopped my stroll and stood trying to muster up a laugh and when it finally came I was certain it didn't sound authentic. But I was also sure Peaches wouldn't question me. She remained quiet except for releasing a light "Hmph."

She was always quiet about these things.

I liked to think it was because of how we grew up. That country upbringing where little Black kids saw all but said nothing. Where children were seen but not heard and so we never learned to speak, and especially when it mattered. Sure, occasionally over drinks or big meals someone might lean back in their chair, someone might cock their head to one side during the card game, someone might move the dominos about the hard surface of a table and say, "You memba how dem white kids chased me from school all the way downtown and beat my ass in the square? Not a single soul helped me."

Or,

"Hey y'all memba when the Black school played against Robert E. Lee and before the second quarter even started dem boys was knockin' heads tryin' to kill each other? Memba how the folks ran out the stands and we was all scrappin'?"

Or,

"Y'all memba how Aunt Baby's boy got shot up by the police over on 1st Street in front of the Baptist Church on the Sandhill? Always told that lil nigga to stay off 1st Street after dark."

Someone would say these things and laugh deeply, bitterly and as unauthentically as I was now with Peaches. And then inevitably someone would laugh in response and say, "Hell yeah! How could we forget?" then someone would say we shouldn't have integrated. Integration was a mistake. To which someone would say, "Hell yeah it was! We lost our schools. We lost our teachers. We lost our culture!" And everyone would mostly agree except for that one fat Negro in the back, the one who always got the cards and dominos greasy whenever he played; he'd always pipe in on a contrary note with "Shiiiiiit, say what you wanna say. Dem white folks was good to me." To which we'd all say, "Nigga thas cause you played ball!"

The truth was simple though we seldom spoke of it. We were but a generation of integrators, assimilators, nine-to-fivers working jobs, twenty years plus, hanging on to the idea of retirement like some sweet dream, the American dream, the real American dream that said after slaving, after going to work sick, tore down, doped up, depressed, stressed and angry all the damn time, we might still have a little freedom at the end of our days. Some time to go sit down and rest the entire sum of our person and reap the benefits of what we sowed.

We were the generation who raised kids we hoped would have better than us, know better than us, figure out how to play this system smarter than us, and maybe even one day take care of us. So we sent them to schools and work to succeed only to have them return (if they went at all) to us with weary eyes or worse—contempt. Our kids didn't want to be like us, didn't want to live like us, and so they didn't. Some didn't live at all. And if they did, it wasn't for long.

We were a generation who watched our parents' Black bodies get beaten down struggling for something called civil rights. We were the generation who watched our children's Black bodies get shot down struggling for something that they didn't quite understand and neither did we.

We were a generation who'd fought but never learned to talk, to speak up, and so how could we be expected to teach our kids how to exist, how to be heard without committing to an identity outside themselves—a job, a house, the right clothes and car, the right hair, the right color, the right life.

I knew better. I knew there was no such thing or destination no matter how hard we worked although I had no offspring to pass this wisdom to. Still I knew it. Deep down the truth burned till liquor or distraction dulled its flame. All this shit was an awful game. We carried this knowledge like secrets, and treated each other's indiscretions much the same.

And Peaches was the kinda friend who wouldn't join you in your shenanigans but also wouldn't snitch, so I knew she wouldn't say a word or push. She seldom did.

Peaches. My pal. My partner. She was my only real friend, especially when I examined my life in hindsight starting from childhood and ending when I lost my mother which was much later but might as well have been childhood. I imagine any adult never fully becomes an adult under a mother's eyes and stops growing altogether after a mother is gone. So in some small way I'll always be twenty. An orphan in the world save for Peaches, and her daughter Ketinah who might as well have been my child too.

The white boy in the car was hissing at me now like an albino snake. Psst. Psst.

"Yeah Peaches, so let me call you back when I get settled in the house." I reached down off in my purse for anything that might act as a weapon. I'd been lazy and left home without my pepper spray. I recalled changing purses and looking plainly at the blue can nestled in the side pocket yet not thought to transfer it.

Shit.

"Yeah OK girl," Peaches said, and I could hear the tension in her voice. When you spend your lives hiding behind emotional masks, walls and defenses, your body learned well the sensitive language of nonverbal cues. I could hear Peaches clearly, and most of all, I could feel her worry.

"I'll call you before I have my last one," I reassured her. It was our ritual. We always had our last cigarette of the night together and caught up on the day's events. But before she could respond, I closed my phone, hand tight around a lone pencil with a sharp tip I'd rummaged up.

"What y'all need?" I hollered, standing firm and projecting my voice towards the car in that deep, hard way years of living in my neighborhood had taught. Firm. But not scared.

"Can you tell us how to get to Toliver Street from here?"

Under the light the boy looked small and stoned. His face skinny and naturally elongated by the slenderness of his frame. His eyes probably as bloodshot as my own. Music crept out of the car—a thump, thump baseline too fast and hollow to be worth a damn to the ears, much less the heart, where I thought music was supposed to start and finish. The other young men stared straight ahead as if I were not there, and it dawned on me that they were nervous. My strength returned.

"What kinda business y'all got over on Toliver?" I asked even though I knew the business well. One of my partners at the game room had a house over on Toliver, a stretch known for white shit. Cocaine. Heroin. Ecstasy. Name it. If it was white it was making its way up and down Toliver, and somewhere nearby white people were chasing it. Kinda like how Pacman gobbled those white dots while ghosts chased after him. And I mean, weren't we all doing just that? Chasing some relief. Some high. Some fantasy while steady on the run from our ghosts? Demons past. The thought made me smile and I could see this eased the boy's anxiety.

"We're just going to see a friend," he said and smiled.

"Mmhmm," I hummed and feeling more confident stepped closer to the car. "Keep going straight. When you see the liquor store on the right, start looking for Toliver. If you see Popeyes chicken you know you went too far."

"Gotcha," he grinned. And seeing his teeth, perfectly aligned but dull and stained, I couldn't help thinking, now I know he got enough money to get them thangs cleaned. "Hey," he continued. "Can we give you something for your trouble?" He was still grinning, looking younger and younger until he might as well have been a baby. No more than sixteen or seventeen.

"Gimme something like what?" I took a step closer, my chin jutted out towards the car and tipped on my toes peering further into the car, curiously. "Whatchu got?"

A buzz always made me bold. Drunkenness made me foolish. I was feeling grateful for both, knowing I only had five raggedy dollar bills in my pocketbook. Indeed, one of them was delicately held together by a thin strip of Scotch tape with the words YOU NEED JESUS written in all caps along one side.

"Come and see," he said, still grinning, the mischief bringing his blue eyes alive in a way I'd seen before. I sharpened my eyes into a steep glare, real real cold much like how my mama used to do when all of a sudden she was no longer playing and meant serious business.

"Aww hell nah . . ." I started but before I could finish a voice screamed out from the opposite side of the road, "You aiight, Miss Nettie!?" The man's baritone voice was like a boom that carried over like waves in the ocean, getting stronger before receding.

"Miss Nettie!" His voice now heavy and mean.

I looked up squinting again across the way and saw Melvin, one of the many neighborhood drunks, decked out in his usual brown dickeys, dingy white wife-beater under an old, soft leather jacket. His malt liquor was wrapped in a brown paper bag in one hand, his walking stick in the other.

"That you Melvin?" I called.

"That me!" he called back, leaning hard against his rainbow-striped cane.

I heard the white boy in the driver's seat mumble something like "Dude, fuck this. Let's go." The music still thump thump thumping like a heartbeat. The blond's smile had disappeared and found its way into agitation. I reared back on my heels, taking him in again under the light and thought, yeah, now he looks more like himself.

"I'm good baby!" I hollered back. "These boys done got turned around and I was just straightening 'em out. Ain't that right?" I said, nodding my head at the blond, giving him the out and picking up his grin where he'd dropped it.

"You sure baby cause I got my stick!" Melvin stood erect and raised his cane in the air, shaking it towards the night skies. The absurdity of the rainbow-striped cane with its glitter catching the streetlamps light made him look absolutely maniacal.

"Fuck this!" the white boy in the driver's seat said, and pressing down on the accelerator caused the car to shriek and send another kind of smoke from its tailpipe before roaring down the road. Those blond curls hung waving in the wind, his face growing red and more red as he moved further away and out of sight. A kind of warm, pink red I'd come to associate with young white men over the years. The kind that used to scare me. The only red I didn't like.

As soon as I could see nothing more than their dim taillights down the road idling at a stop, I burst out laughing. A real laugh.

"Good lookin' out Melvin!"

"Anytime baby," he slurred and now he sounded like the Melvin I knew and loved.

I looked at my watch, swimming in a film of perspiration around my wrist. It was 7:45 p.m.

At home the windows showed no signs of life. If not for the small glint of light escaping from beneath the garage door where it was slightly cracked it looked as if no one lived there at all. As I walked up the driveway, the motion detector light popped on. I passed through the spotlight and walking towards the garage was met with the soft musty scent of weed. Dirt is what I called it. Nothing like the smell of the white boys' goods.

I leaned down and knocked against the yellow plaster to get my husband's attention. The faint sounds of Earth Wind & Fire played, and smoke wafted as though from a chimney in winter. I knocked again and called out.

"Ernest! Let the garage up!"

"Jeanette?" he called back with more question in his voice than any man who'd been married more than twenty-three years should have.

"Who else would it be?" I yelled with irritation. The walk had worn down some of my buzz and the adrenaline rush from my encounter with the white boys left me tired. But mostly I was just irritated with Ernest, that he was even still awake. With the smoke, moving like clouds of dust across my face, stinging my eyes. His voice was heavy and slow and so I knew he had been drinking too.

"Wait just a minute!"

I waited, listening to the sounds of his big body stumbling about, making its way to the door opener at the wall. I stood up as the door began to lift allowing the funk of weed and sweat to burn the insides of my nose. Ernest was still in his work clothes, blue pants and blue button-up, the tiny red emblem of the Amtrak station on the front shirt pocket. His eyes were lazy and bloodshot, pupils fully dilated.

"Damn Jeanette, I was wondering where you was when I seen your car here."

"Now where would I be?" I walked in and plopped down in the chair situated next to him, only the stereo separating us. My feet were tired. A dull ache had come over them each, and now I was sure my high was gone.

"Well I know five dollars ain't have you playing that long. What time you leave?"

"Shit Ernest!" I said removing my shoes and rubbing my feet. "I didn't get up there till bout five."

"Well why didn't you take your car? You know it ain't safe for you to be walking at night."

His concern mellowed me out some. I leaned back in my chair and looked him full in his face, pausing before answering. I took in the deep burgundy of his features, his arms and hands. His hair was graying around the edges of his hairline, his temples especially coarse and white with age. Even the stubble around his mouth and chin shown pale hairs. And the large hands holding fast to the whiskey and joint, those large calloused hands that hadn't touched me in months were dirty, nails grimy. His eyes glazed and vacant looked as cloudy as the ice in his glass. He looked old. And I wondered if I looked as old as he did; tired, long body sprawled out in the lawn chair. And I also wondered why he hadn't thought to call and check on me if he'd been so concerned.

"Gimme a sip of that," I said rather than answer and reached for his glass.

"Nah." He pulled back before I could connect. "I'll go make you one but this one's mines."

"Ugh." I groaned. "You so stingy with everything. Ain't ever known a man as stingy as you!" I sat back in my chair and crossed my legs and arms, but Ernest only chuckled and said, "Shit you don't be sayin' that when I pay your car note every month. Or the light bill. Or the water. Or . . ."

"Don't act like you doin' me no favors!"

"You mean I'm not?" He laughed again. "Cause we can bring all that to a halt real quick."

"Hmph." I sucked my teeth.

"Hmph, my ass." He stood up, stumbling against his chair before catching his weight. "Have yo ass walking all the time and everywhere." He smiled at me and turned to walk in the house.

"Crushed ice, Ernest! And use the glass I like!"

"Yeah yeah," he muttered. "You think after all this time I don't know how you like your drink?" I smirked and sucked my teeth again.

Ernest laughed and made his way inside, shutting the door and leaving me alone. I had a craving for a cigarette but I'd already smoked my pack down to its final six and I knew that wasn't enough to get me through the night, much less the next day. I looked across the top of the stereo where Ernest had the remains of his marijuana scattered upon one of the speakers, his wrapping papers nearby. For a moment I considered pulling out one of his grape-flavored cigarillos, anything for a pull of something to calm nerves that were already starting to jump.

Ernest did that to me. It was so rare that we spent time around one another with his early morning shifts at the train station that sent him to bed just as I was getting home most nights. Our routines and lifestyles had created a rift neither of us knew how to address. Without alcohol or weed, some form of intoxication, we had forgotten how to be in each other's company. Forgotten how to speak save for shooting the shit or answering those pedestrian questions that had become the norm for a lot of married couples.

Him: What you got to eat?

Me: Go look on the stove.

Him: You need some gas money?

Me: (stubbornly and slowly) Yes.

And so it went.

I leaned back and inhaled the smoke left lingering in the garage, wanting it to lift me up through contact. I didn't smoke anything but cigarettes but Ernest had been a smoker ever since we met. By the time he shuffled back out, I felt only slightly buzzed and still agitated by the difference.

"Here Jeanette," he said and reached me my drink. I took a sip and immediately gagged.

"Ew!" I frowned, and considered spitting it out. "Ernest this Coke is flat! Did you put the top back on tight like I told you? Goddammit!"

"Flat? Ain't nothing wrong with that Coke girl. Besides, too much carbonation give you gas."

"Ernest!" I put the drink on top of the speaker and wiped my mouth as though I might remove the taste with my hand. "I can't drink this shit."

"Well I'm not bout to make you another one. And you ain't bout to waste that one neither." He reached for the drink and took a deep gulp. "Aww hell, ain't nothin' wrong with this." He took his lighter and lit the end of his blunt till it burned cherry red. I rolled my eyes and stood up in disgust.

"I guess if you want something done right, you gotta do it yourself."

"That's right," he said, coughing through a strained laugh. "Go head, Miss Independent Woman. Walking the streets at night. Take yo ass in there and see if you can get it right." He took another pull, holding the smoke in his chest before releasing it. "See if you can find me something to eat too cause ain't nothin' on the stove."

I rolled my eyes again, and made my way inside the house and to the kitchen. Then turned back around sharply and peeped back out the door.

"I need my glass!"

"Goddamn Jeanette, can't you drink out another glass for once?"

"Give it here!" I said and snatched it from his hand, not caring that I sent brown liquid flying. Pretending as always not to notice his hand with the missing pointer finger that he'd lost as a boy. After all these years I still hadn't grown used to the hard brown nub.

When Ernest was a boy he'd worked the cotton fields alongside his mother and eight siblings on a plantation in Louisiana. He claimed he never realized it was a plantation until he'd become a man at thirteen, not too many years before losing his finger. He was shaving down a log with his oldest sister, it was almost dinner time and he'd been in a rush to eat. As one of nine kids, and one of three boys, the little food that was there tended to go fast and long days spent outside picking and plowing built a ravenous appetite. He'd paid the price for his hunger and anticipation when one quick push and pull of the saw sliced right through his finger, so smoothly and so very quickly that it took him a moment to realize it'd happened. If not for the piercing scream of his sister, if not for the blood, so much blood, he wouldn't have noticed. He was numb, the only very real thing inside his body was the pulse of his stomach turning into ache. But even losing a finger didn't compare to the horror of learning he'd lived and worked on a plantation. I couldn't remember the exact details of how he'd learned his home was on a plantation, even having heard it so many times over the course of the years. But I always recalled his confusion and absolute devastation at the fact.

I remembered how he said the oak trees seemed to grow thick around his chest as if he might suffocate and the old colonial-style house on the hill had loomed like a ghost that chased him in his dreams for years after. Filled his boyhood imagination with visions of death and slavery, and whippings. The whole of the land had come to represent a graveyard to his young eyes where he swore he saw other young men of his age long gone yet still haunting the grounds with thrashings about their brown backs and rope burns around their necks. He'd been traumatized and both frightened and angry with white people. Scarred till this day and it remained a sore spot I chose to pick when he made me angry enough.

Field hand! I'd call him. Field hand! And sometimes, very briefly, he'd look mad enough to strike me though I knew and trusted enough to know he wouldn't. And perhaps that's why I continued to do it. For all his flaws, Ernest respected women. He'd been raised by one and groomed by six others, all older than his fifty-six years. Strong boisterous women, take no bullshit kinda women. And so that's how he'd come to expect me to be, never realizing I was as soft and fragile in his hands as the cotton he used to pick. But just as he'd resented the tender feel of the bud, he'd refused to acknowledge the similarities that resided in me. He'd ignored my soft places and so with time, and with him, I'd grown tough. Bitter. Mean about the mouth. And this is how we communicated and lived with one another.

In the kitchen, I transferred the drink to a plastic cup and handed it out the door to him without looking. "Here," I said, waiting for the weight of the cup to leave my hand. He took it without making a sound, without protest or preferences. I went about preparing my own drink now, glancing at my phone for any missed calls before heading back out to the garage.

Ernest was high. Super high because the drink was barely holding on to his four fingers and his body was in a deep gangster lean, folded over the blue and white ends of the chair. The Temptations sang on the stereo, *Just another lonely night.* I kicked his chair and shouted his name. He jumped, his body jerking from the shock of the blow.

"Damn Jeanette," he moaned. "Why you so rough?"

"Go in the house if you sleepy. Don't sit out here and fall asleep in the chair."

Ernest bucked his eyes, blinking hard before noticing the ashes in his lap that had fallen from his blunt, now going dead from neglect. "Nah, nah . . . ," he said. "I ain't sleep." He brushed the ashes to the cold concrete floor and put the blunt in the ashtray sitting on the ground beside his chair.

"Jeanette," he moaned again, eyes closed. "You got something to eat?"

I took a drink from my glass enjoying the strength of the Crown Royal on the rocks. "Nah, what you want? Hand me some money and I'll go get you something. What you want?"

"Shiiiit. I don't even know."

I relaxed in my chair, knowing this wouldn't be going anywhere soon. Not when he was like this, the combination of fatigue and alcohol and weed having its own unique effect on his personality. Watching him now was like seeing a familiar show, one of my stories even. I knew how the scene would end, as predictable as any episode. See . . . there he went now:

"Jeanette, you know what them white motherfuckers did today?"

I said nothing and instead lit a cigarette.

"Jeanette, you know what that white motherfucker said to me?"

I said nothing.

"So then I said . . ."

Nothing.

"But you know I wanted to knock that motherfucker in his mouth."

"Of course you did, baby. Of course."

I was high now and floating away somewhere willingly. Leaving my body and watching white strands of shit and parasites depart my insides with each "white motherfucker" Ernest uttered. And I kept floating and floating to a place far away in my mind. A place full of 7s. Purple 7s. Red 7s. Orange and green 7s. An entire rainbow of perfection and jackpots. A saturation of something I didn't know what to call except I knew it was good. Better than what I was, better than how I ever felt sober or intoxicated.

"Jeanette, did you pay the cable bill this month? I don't want them motherfuckers callin' me charging me up bout shit."

I floated.

"Goddamn I'm so ready to retire. I'm tired of carryin' all this shit on my own."

Still I floated.

"Ahh shit, what time is it? Let me take my ass to bed."

And ignoring him, I continued to float, drowning I suppose in the warm and sweet daze of inebriation and music. I went to a place where life grew quiet and quieter until it tuned out everything and there was nothing. Nothing. No one. Not even my mama who I missed more than anything. More than myself.

My mama was to me a secret, something private, and the older I got the more I realized the value of privacy. With age it was difficult. The body gave away everything first. The mind was second, and perhaps the last to go. I held on to both with everything I had. Never mind a drink, or nights in the garage. Colonics were an exorcism and with each body I performed on it might as well have been my own. But my mother was a matter of the heart. Something extraterrestrial. A creature who'd given birth to me during the height of racial violence though I'd never heard her speak of it in this way.

I pulled a long drag from my cigarette.

My own ultimate secret was my grief. A grief I'd never let go of—my mother's death was an anniversary I'd celebrate publicly until I turned fifty. Then celebrate quietly thereafter alone with a drink in the garage alone. Music. Cigarettes. The blues. Alone.

A child orphaned at twenty, and yet it was never old enough for someone like me. Tall, broad like my mama. Brown skin. Brown eyes, dull. Unlike my mama who always seemed so alive until she wasn't. Until she'd died on this very day.

My chest grew weak with the weight of unleashed tears and I took a long sip from my drink.

"Jeanette," Ernest moaned, lifting up out of his chair, eyes closed. And at that moment, my phone vibrated in my lap. It was Peaches.

I figured she was still worried. I knew she remembered the day, though she'd never say as much.

"Well girl, you ready for your last one? And don't bother lyin' to me, I know what you did today. Did you at least get lucky?"

Lucky?

I watched Ernest disappearing behind the closed door. I watched the smoke from my cigarette like a lost spirit trying to escape, twist and twirl in the air.

"Nah. Not today," I said. "Maybe tomorrow though."

PART II

I have been in Sorrow's kitchen and licked out all the pots. Then I have stood on the peaky mountain wrapped in rainbows, with a harp and a sword in my hands.

—ZORA NEALE HURSTON

Lost Your Head Blues

Troy's mama said Maya didn't really know how to do anything but have babies and she wasn't that good at that. Even getting pregnant had been a challenge for her.

Doctor said her womb was weak which made it difficult for her to carry full term. "You see," he said, pointing at a chart with lines that jumped and folded at various points. "Your estrogen levels are here." She watched his fat pink finger travel to the base of the page.

"When it should be here," he said, dragging his finger mid-level at the graph where it idled.

To Maya's eyes all the lines looked like a heartbeat's register. Where the heart bottomed out there was no chance, where it leapt there was hope.

"And your uterine lining is here," he said, now holding his fingers apart, leaving little space for the fingers to breathe. "When it should be here." He spread them apart, a gaping hole.

She received the news on a Monday morning with quiet devastation; face drawn up into a tight bud that refused to blossom and give anything, much less a reaction to the news. It was 75 degrees out with a slight chance of rain, or so the weatherman had revealed with his own form of graphs and lines jumping about the screen the previous evening.

"Do you understand?" her doctor asked.

Maya understood and told him so with a short nod of her head. She told herself this was life. Still she was angry something so personal was revealed to her on a piece of paper that resembled something she might have studied in statistics or physiology because after all this wasn't merely a class, a fact, some piece of data. This was *her* life.

And she was devastated.

Her grandmama and great-grandma and aunts and great-aunts having long ago told her the womb was the seat of a woman. It was the place from which all things originated.

She remembered everything.

She accepted nothing.

Maya's mother told her to get a piece of selenite and soak it in saltwater under the gaze of the moon for three nights. "Ask the Goddess to help you," she said.

Her grandmama told her to pray to Jesus and read Psalms 91. "Place yo Bible under your pillow while you sleep," she said. "This will protect and uplift you."

She'd done neither.

But still she'd tried and tried. Throwing skinny legs around her husband. Opening herself wide to catch it all. Moving her hips to some ancient rhythm inside herself—desperately seeking to communicate some rebellious message that said *I don't need anybody. I don't need anybody.*

And it worked.

Over time it worked and she produced two healthy boys whose gestation periods left her bedridden for most of her pregnancies. For months, she lay in bed watching little else but cable news and her body growing with smoldering resentment—belly swollen, hips and thighs full with heat.

Twice her husband Troy watched it all play out—very quietly, afraid to say the wrong thing. Afraid of the circumstances in which he found himself. But unlike hers, his mouth was not a flower. In fact, closed or open, most times he felt it was nothing at all. Both at home and work, his mouth simply didn't exist. So most people mistook his silence for wisdom and a patience he'd never known.

Troy only knew that during both pregnancies, when she needed someone to help her to the bath to either relieve herself or freshen the parts of her body grown sour from days of neglect, he was there to provide some weight upon which she might rest; tenderly holding her plump arms, steadying her as she made her way from the bed, his arms fixed around her bloated waist while she peed or washed at the sink. He was there like a baseball catcher waiting with open hands to collect their child should gravity have its way and the baby drop unexpectedly.

Her womb was weak. The uterine lining was fragile.

He remembered these things.

She, too, remembered her body before. But now she no longer recognized herself.

She remembered when the doctor first told her the news and how very briefly she'd caught her reflection within the cool eye of his stethoscope. Her eyes were dim, pupils dilated. Her skin burning where sweat formed above her upper lip and across her forehead where it drew a pattern of wet dots stretching from one temple to the other. She remembered she was thin, hair a curly basket upon her head, and wore a red lip that suggested she was ready for anything.

She remembered these things, the small memories of herself before everything came crashing down.

Time passed. Time moved fast.

She had her babies, each one born preemies whose tiny bodies struggled to breathe and thrive once inside the outer world. Preemies who weren't expected to survive beyond her body. Both times the doctors had her sign resuscitation orders before wheeling her into emergency surgery. Both times she checked no.

But Maya endured.

She'd moved from her bed to the hospital bed, where she remained on her back, legs cramped and curled with clotting. Healing. Prolonged bed rest will do that. Nurses said she was healing. They drained excess fluid. Woke her up early mornings to gently push and pull her body around. Get blood circulating. Tend to the cut along her stomach where they'd gathered her child.

And she lay there trying to heal, ashamed the only thing she wanted more than a healthy baby was to piss by herself. To go into the bathroom, close the door and relieve herself of everything. Alone.

Doctors said her bone density was still good considering. Gestational diabetes resolved itself. Then she got up. Finally. Stretched.

Finally.

Long days and nights sitting in NICU watching each child struggling to live behind the smooth glass of an incubator, sitting in a wheelchair and then finally on her legs.

But her babies were here. They endured too. And everyone was ready to give credit to all but her.

"Told you to listen to ya mama! The Goddess was with you," her mother said.

"Doctor said one thing, Jesus said another," said her grandmama.

Her husband was quiet. Shuffling around the hospital, early mornings after work reeking of smoke and cheap perfumes. His eyes red. He drove her and each child home, nervously fidgeting with the radio. "Radio Disney?" he asked.

She looked at him and said nothing.

Time passed. Time moved fast.

Time slowed down before catching speed again. Maya imagined it had forgotten itself. It had disappeared into the same place her identity seemed to have gone, only while time kept its appointment, recovered quickly from all confusion no matter how brief, she was not quite as efficient.

Because his mama said she didn't really know how to do anything but have babies and she wasn't that good at that.

She had heard her through Troy's phone while he paced around their home. His mama talked loud. Troy thought moving around from room to room distorted the sound of her voice but she was clear. "All that education and she don't work! What she gon' do with herself? Just stay home like some white woman?"

Troy knew Maya heard her. He thought she would cry. Get mad. Say something. But when she didn't, he didn't either.

And what could she say? His mama was right?

She and the babies had withdrawn back to the bedroom, though no longer confined, and the news was on. Always. *There was another Black man killed by the police yesterday.* Maya lay down willingly. When she passed mirrors she looked away because when she looked at herself she wasn't sure what she saw so she stopped trying to see.

Maya felt her body had become a ripe piece of fruit, bruised and soft in places where it shouldn't be. Some exported good that had been grown in a foreign land once called home then sent away and sold. Unpicked until her husband saw fit to touch her, and she wasn't sure she existed until he did. Thus she didn't know any other way to be but open and easy, as soft as she was. Legs wide. Mouth wider. A perfect O shape. And she had read somewhere that God moved in circles, worked in circles—life a cycle, some circular pattern in which she was caught. Round and round. A cog in the wheel of a fast-moving train, a fast-moving something with which she couldn't keep up.

Round and round. Day after day.

By the second child, a year later, her mind had given up and crumbled. Lone from neglect, beneath the clouds, it had been overwhelmed by rain, overgrown with weeds. Too many weeds and her thoughts were tangled. A mess she couldn't sort nor control. Feeding the boys was confusing. Sex with Troy was complicated. Her body began to disappear under his weight. She was fading, no longer captured and held by the train's pace. She was instead the tunnel. She was the void. The blackness and enigma the train entered with no visible exit. It was the only reason she still allowed him inside. She thought perhaps Troy could solve the riddle she was becoming. Or at the very least, merge into it. Become his own vanishing.

He was silent enough. Was he there? Some days it wasn't clear. Or maybe she'd stopped seeing *and* hearing. Couldn't hear him over the kids and the news and the destruction of the world.

There was another Black man killed by the police yesterday.

And then there were the voices other than her own that spoke to her all the time.

The damn voices.

At first she welcomed the company. Something other than the cries or coos of a toddler. She entertained them. They whispered and hummed songs she knew well like, You'll never amount to anything! or, You hate yourself! and, You're a bad mother! What were you thinking?

You can't do anything but have babies and you ain't that good at that.

Maya believed them all.

The voices hypnotized her. It was a trance in which she moved and existed while the babies slept or ate, or didn't sleep at all. While they cried out for her, or for something she didn't understand nor desire to be. The voices preyed on her. Like parasites they sapped at the yolk that was her insides, nourishing themselves on her fear. And so she grew afraid of breastfeeding for fear of passing the parasites. And besides, if there were people living inside her, they were hers. Something that was a part of her.

Even if they were another cog.

She began collecting things. Anything to call her own.

In her closet she kept a box that housed her regrets. She didn't remember when she started ripping the edges of mail—advertisements stuck against the front door. The corner of a bill, napkin, a piece of gum wrapper. She scribbled feelings fast and without thought. *Should have never been with him. My mother has no idea who I am. Library science was dumb. People don't read. Believing in this world was dumb. Going off the birth control was dumb. Nowhere is safe.*

The shoebox sat at the top of her closet, safe in the bland multicolored boxes of all the shoes Troy bought her over the years because he didn't like her going outside barefoot. He wouldn't say this but she knew. She understood. But he didn't understand how much she needed to feel the Earth's face. She needed to know she was standing on something solid for as long as it would hold her.

Troy didn't understand.

"That's white people shit!" he said. And since she didn't go outside much she figured there was nothing to miss and stopped going altogether.

And then there was the condition of her heart. She couldn't decide if it was breaking or broken.

Her heart.

There was a Black girl killed by the police yesterday.

Her heart. That swollen thing inside her chest. She heard it beat. She supposed she understood its function on the most basic physical level. She supposed it was a necessary thing. She listened to its thump thump and supposed it was biology. Science. Another equation she was but part of, endless cogs. Endless motion. She felt very deeply that if she listened very closely to that thump thump she might discover some mystery. A code. The password that might lead to freedom from her current reality. To what she didn't know.

Something else? Something new was enough.

And so she listened, sometimes in the middle of the living room floor surrounded by toys and the noise of her boys.

"Shhh!"

She'd hush them with all parts of her body flailing about the floor in irritation. And the oldest of the two would sit startled by the harshness of her tone, spit hanging from his thick bottom lip, eyes prepared to flush with tears if only she said it again. He was locked and loaded, tears ready to go. The youngest at five months would only continue trying to eat his right foot. The struggle to make his pinky toe reach his mouth was as real and valid in his mushy mind as his mother's troubles so he mostly ignored her.

Bitch! said the two-year-old.

Bitch! said the five-month-old.

"You think I'm a bitch?" she'd scream, jumping up from the floor in tears, lost from the beat of her heart. When in truth, neither boy even knew what a bitch was. But after hearing her yell it at them, they figured it as a name. A name for the woman who sat watching them at times with wide brown eyes. Who cried at times longer than they thought their small bodies capable.

The two-year-old cried. Bitch was crying so he joined her while the five-month-old kicked his tiny right foot toward her, as if seeking somehow to pacify her troubles. But she mistook his kind gesture as an act of violence and only cried harder.

"Baby, you gotta stop sayin' bitch in front of the kids," her husband said. "You gon' teach 'em that word."

Maya watched Troy's lean body stretched across the end of the bed. He held his face in his hands before rubbing his eyes and then the temples of his head. He'd thrown his shirt across the chair beside the nightstand and the coarse hairs, clustered in the center of his chest, lay down still slick with the day's sweat. She let her weight fall against the headboard and it bumped against the wall hard causing her body to jump.

"But," she said, recovering from the momentary shock, "it's the only time their eyes light up for me."

Troy threw his arms in the air as if reaching for something or someone and, finding nothing there, let them fall back against the bed. When he lifted himself up he did so slowly and for a moment Maya admired the way his muscles tightened and expanded beneath his flesh.

He didn't look at her when he sighed, rubbed his face again and said, "Babe, you might need some help."

"Well yeah," she said, eyeing his chest, his abs, his hair. "It would be great if you cleaned the bathroom sometime."

"No, no . . . ," he said and sighed. "I mean like *psychological*."

He threw his arms now in front of him as if gesturing to an audience. Only there was still no one. Only the wall. Only the door and for a moment she thought he might get up, put his shirt back on and leave, even though it was three in the morning. He had only just returned from work but it was always there. These were his hours.

But he didn't. Instead, he stood up and went into the bathroom, never once looking her way. So when she heard the shower and saw the steam seep from under the door, she unfurled herself. Reached deep down under the covers until she fished out the remote idling along her cold feet. She turned on the television to the news and watched until he returned to bed, his wet body illuminated only by the screen's light.

When he lay down, he turned his back to her.

There was a Black man killed by the police yesterday.

He pulled the covers over his head.

I mean like psychological.

It was the only time he had acknowledged something was wrong. She wasn't sure if the pregnancies or his work had worn him down. Once Maya was back on her feet, Troy rushed back into the world as though making up for lost time and she supposed he was. All those long months spent tending to her and then the babies.

He showed up.

When he was home, that's where he was—if only in body. And when he was at work, that's where he was.

And he worked hard, so hard you almost thought it was legitimate. And it was in what it brought.

First year in Houston, Troy managed Thursday nights at a club downtown and weekends in Galveston. He kept working. He kept working; he'd go home and stretch his feet. Listen to Maya. *There was a Black woman killed by police today.* Eat. Rub Maya's back. Shower. The rush of the water a fountain from which he drew inspiration, and he liked the water hot.

Second year: Friday nights at a new club. Ballplayers came. He helped the ballplayers cum. He brought a few women he knew from

East Texas towards the Gulf of Mexico. He was discreet. He made the ballplayers cum and was promoted to the weekend parties.

Third year. His mouth took root. Only it didn't bloom. Blossom. Flower. No matter the water, Texas sunshine unlike any he'd ever known.

Riding home early mornings along the bay, the shoreline a dizzy picture he saw but didn't see. He enjoyed the heat of the sun against his windows but kept focused on the road home.

He ignored the waters, convinced their surface carried the pollution of not oil or waste, but brown bodies lost trying to reach the American shorelines and he wasn't gon' be one of them.

Go home. Find Maya some nondescript shape beneath the covers, network news a blast. *There was a Black man killed by the police yesterday.* Their tiny boy a shadow in the bassinet beside the bed.

When he popped a pill that took him down from the mountain he'd spent the day climbing, he slept. But his mouth. His mouth was a swollen thing inside his head and while he thought, while he dreamt, while he listened to Maya: *They're killing us. Police are killing us!* While he watched women, water, the brown and black bodies. His mouth simply was. It was a brand new thing.

New address. New side of town. New neighbors that spoke through faces that refused to move no matter the emotion, and a steel iron gate that opened and closed with the entry of five digits. So that if Maya wanted to watch bad news, if she and the boys wanted to sleep their days away, they could do so in peace.

Still one Sunday morning riding home, music a blast, he thought he saw her as she was. The person he refused to see. Maya. Somewhere where the water met the sky and the sky met the sun, she was there floating away.

He rubbed his tired eyes, and kept going, focused on the road.

"White people been killing us since the beginning of time!" he screamed at her. "Black people too!" He screamed at her.

Maya cried. She heard him screaming. The pendulum swing from mute to high sound too much for her feeble senses.

This was Troy mad. The only time he was loud.

"This how it's always been for Black folks!" he screamed. "Stop acting brand new!"

Black.

New.

Maya and Troy were becoming that new Black American. That so new Black they had become a new shade. They had assimilated and assimilated until Troy was nothing more but the house and the car; the man who wore the plastic smile and yelled "Hi Bob!" to the fifty-something-year-old white man across the street as they both picked up the morning paper.

Black.

The Black. The Black. The Black.

Maya felt like writing it along the walls.

No one knew how angry she was. The world continued to move and she was but a small thing on it. No one understood how the television taunted her. Shot dead. Strung up from trees. Dead. Walking home. Dead. Coming home from the store. Dead.

She had assimilated until she'd become nothing more than a gasp, a blurry picture staring out the window at the trashmen, watching the can lift and tilt, wondering if that's where she belonged.

Troy was from the streets. Maya was from the neighborhood. Troy worked. Maya did not.

It was an assimilation.

"But you had two parents," he said.

It was an assimilation.

"My parents' house was five blocks from where you grew up," she said.

It was an assimilation.

Money a new thing. A green thing that still couldn't erase the Dead. At the bus stop, stabbed dead. Inside the police car handcuffed—suffocated and dead. Asleep on the couch, police raid: nine-year-old Black child dead.

White men in blue uniforms and pink faces, veins pulsating from their arms and in strange places along their necks and foreheads. Dead. Hate.

Maya saw the hate. She saw the guns. She saw the dead black bodies of children and determined she needed a solution.

Dead.

Her family hadn't endured for this. *Dead.* She became obsessed with the idea that she needed some way of protecting her boys from *Dead.* Some way of keeping them hidden from the pink men in blue uniforms. Pink and blue the very colors associated with babies, perverted and lost to a violence she was afraid to admit she understood, because she was growing to hate them as much as they hated her and her babies.

And she saw the Black people march until they got tired.

Another body.

She saw the Black people march again until they got tired.

Another body.

She saw the Black and white and brown people march until they got tired. The news would light up with the energy of excited reporters' adrenaline until they too got tired.

Another body.

This one more quiet than the rest. Hidden within the news of wars. Hidden within the news of poverty. Hidden within the news of violence. Inside homes and outside clubs. Inside schools and outside corner stores.

The newsman said someone stole something at gunpoint last night and Maya wondered briefly if that thing was her mind while she'd slept through the entire ordeal.

Wall Street white men in nice suits with equally nice haircuts stole everyday. She wondered if they were all in cahoots. Perhaps they'd slipped through the mind's windows, tiptoeing through her thoughts; picking and choosing as they saw fit. But what was fit?

Who was she before? What was she in the beginning? And where was the beginning?

The day Maya and Troy met everything seemed alive. The sun was alive. The moon was alive. They were alive and crossing paths at a particular point in the universe that must have been designated at that point in time just for them. And how could anyone look at it as anything but this? How could this not be true?

What would have been the point if not something divine?

This was Maya. This was Troy.

She wore white denim pants and a white cotton shirt with lines that seemed to carve rivers where her abdomen lay, her cropped top falling just above her belly button where she imagined her navel connected her to the spirit world.

Back to her mother, held within the darkness of the void before existence.

And there was Troy. He had this brown skin and a crown of curls on his head; and when he smiled he had what looked like vampire teeth and gold crowns at the back of his mouth. His tongue was a white people pink. His clothing was baggy—loose-fitting acid-washed jeans that clung to his small waist before giving away and a plain black T-shirt. No words. No writing. No expectations. Just black. His feet looked small within his black Air Force 1s and normally Maya didn't notice such things, but everything about Troy struck her. And she wondered very briefly before they spoke if her thoughts were already too sexual. And if they were, would it show on her face? Her lips? Mouth? She watched him speak and felt guilty for having noticed the color of his tongue and the whiteness of his teeth. Their sharpness.

They met in the middle of the breezeway outside her university library where Maya worked. It was getting dark. The moon already shone against blue skies.

Troy saw Maya in her all white and she looked so innocent, her natural hair a chaos of curls framing her small face. She seemed to be shining. Was she shining? Her brown skin reflected the setting sun and to his eyes she might as well have been a mess of particles, the most perfect chemical combination; some mirage in a desert. Was he being dramatic? He tried to play it extra cool. It wasn't like he was that thirsty.

A desert seemed all wrong as he took her hand upon approach. Was she an ocean instead? Or something much smaller—a lake?

Why had she offered her hand so easily? He wasn't sure but he was shaking it and nodding, watching her smile and her curls shake with the wind as she nodded too.

"Wassup," he said, perhaps a bit too jovially. "You know where the library at?" he asked.

And she'd answered, "It's straight ahead but we closed now. What book you lookin for?"

And still he held her hand inside his own.

"You too late," she said. "But if we have it, maybe I can put it on reserve for you."

"Too late? There's no such thing," he said. And she withdrew her hand and frowned while still smiling.

Was that possible? he thought.

Obviously so because here they were. Smiling, nodding like two fools caught outside while dusk emerged. There was no one else around and Troy was forced to accept how late he was. The campus was empty, save for an old blue Oldsmobile idling in the parking lot in the distance. He felt self-conscious. It was never his intention to get there so late but life was often a thing in which hours commenced without his control, and even when he had control, he seldom had control. He wanted to explain this to her but knew it made no sense before the words formed in his mouth. Instead he simply said again, "It's never too late," to which she smiled and frowned. Smiled and frowned. Her face couldn't make up its mind and he realized she had as little control over her life as he did, at least in the ways that mattered most.

"How do you know?" she asked and he looked like he wanted to say something but stopped himself.

"Some things you just know," Troy said.

And because Maya couldn't think of any proper way to respond she chose not to think at all and instead blurted out, "Like what?"

"Deez . . . ," Troy blurted out before stopping himself again and laughed like it was the funniest thing ever and Maya was still confused but just as curious.

"Deez?"

Troy laughed. He did this kinda corny shit when he was nervous. He felt self-conscious again but there was no way to stop what was already ahead of him. Time had its way and his words, his face had its way without his control. He knew he'd fucked up.

Maya was still frowning, still smiling, only now her smile held questions.

It was the oddest exchange she'd ever had. And still Troy laughed out of nervousness while Maya admired those sharp incisors. He looked like he could eat someone if he wanted to.

"Say, you ask a lot of questions," he said. "You know that?"

Maya smiled. Yeah. She knew that.

When they left each other that evening the streetlights had flickered on then off before struggling to come into their shine and he still hadn't told her the name of the book he was looking for, nor why he'd come so far in search of it or even his name. But when he walked away from her, he did so with her phone number.

And it wasn't until Maya put her key in the door and pushed its frame to walk in that it occurred to her.

Deez . . .

When he called later that night his voice sounded unsure and softer than before when he said, "Hello may I speak to the beautiful FBI agent slash librarian chick?"

Maya cleared her throat.

"Oh no, she's not here at the moment."

He paused.

"She's not?"

"No, but she wanted me to tell you who you can talk to."

He paused.

"Who?"

"Deez nuts wit yo corny ass!"

His laughter was deep and long. He *was* corny. It was so true.

Maya giggled too, feeling quite proud of herself.

"Yo, I didn't think . . . ," he started before laughter took over again. "I just didn't think you was the type of chick to . . ."

"My name is Maya," she said. "Not chick. Not FBI. Not librarian yet. Just Maya and can I just say you fell for that way too easily?" She let her body fall against the insides of the doorway and briefly caught her reflection in the bathroom mirror. She smiled.

And this time when he laughed his voice was soft again.

They talked on the phone that night, falling asleep to the sound of each other's breath and the gentle static on the phone line.

"My mama always pull the phone cord too hard when she mad," Troy said through a heavy yawn. "Cause a shortage."

"You still live at home?" Maya asked.

"Shit, I'm just happy to have one," he said. And there was a long silence that Maya was sure held the end of them before they'd yet to truly begin. Still he called three days later and asked over that static blaring more than ever with white noise and electricity, "What you doin?"

Maya was in her first year of a master's program where she learned the secrets of books; how to organize, categorize, file and apply geometrically sound numbers to their spines. No matter their age, she encouraged books to remember themselves, their truths despite the passage of time. She figured herself a keeper of knowledge though she was no more than twenty-two and still young enough to have dreams she wasn't afraid to pursue.

Troy, too, was a student but of a different kind, having long ago traded the classroom for the streets. When they crossed paths along the breezeway that day they both were obviously coming from different ends of the spectrum—Troy in his black, Maya in her white. Still Maya imagined they created something new by the mere fact they saw each other, found one another and there was no one there to witness it.

It had never taken much for Maya to fall, however gently or unpredictably, in love and so Maya always questioned herself: Was she really in love? Was she too easy?

Not for sex. She'd never been easy with sex. Growing up in a small town didn't afford the opportunity for her to explore herself in that way. Nor was she easy with the time or attention she seemed willing to give; not to anyone but Troy.

Ketinah, her best friend since childhood, had always mocked Maya's romance but Maya could never take Ketinah seriously. Ketinah was just as bad as her. Romantic. Fragile. Two Black girls who grew up in a small town in East Texas with dreams that seemed so much bigger than their bodies, their souls, even as they aged. Who'd even know they ever existed unless they did something big? Something real big? And at the moment Maya didn't feel anything was bigger than loving Troy.

Ketinah laughed, high off her ass, as she usually was when Maya told her she was in love with the boy from the library.

"But it wasn't even the library," Ketinah said, laughing.

"It was the breezeway, but still . . . ," Maya started before Ketinah's laughter took over and overwhelmed the moment.

"You just don't understand," Maya said, sighing. "I think he's just like me, a seeker."

"And does he know that?" Ketinah asked, exhaling marijuana smoke—her breath heavy over the phone. "Does he know who you are? And even if thas true are you sure you're both seeking the same thing?"

Maya was quiet for a moment before gathering herself and responding.

"I mean, do any of us know who we are or what we seek?"

"Aw hell," Ketinah said, laughing and coughing through her smoke. "You got it bad, girl."

Maya frowned. Smiled. Frowned. Then she laughed too.

Because it was true. Maya did have it bad.

Troy was special. Not merely a person or body but otherworldly and sexy and different. He caused her to question existence and because that was in her mind the purpose of life, he became everything she was ever looking for.

Their conversations took twists and turns that were so unexpected that she found herself feeling self-conscious in a way that wasn't unfamiliar to Maya, but this time the person evoking these feelings was someone whom she'd come to trust. Sure she was used to occasionally feeling insecure in her classes; she never felt her vocabulary large enough or that she'd read enough books to keep up no matter if this fear was legitimate or not. But Troy was different. He made her question her body and her thoughts. He'd read many of the books she found most important. The kinda books that questioned reality, posed conspiratorial questions and when they made love it was as if they were testing one another on the metaphysics of it all.

Maya often thought of him and found herself lost within the idea of what he'd become in her life. But, who was she becoming?

Ketinah was right. She was so gone.

Troy might be rinsing the hood of his car on a Saturday, head thrown back to where his face pulled the sun. Music blaring from busted speakers. She'd sit on the cold cement where the water seemed to stop before reaching in and giving up. She was dry and hot and taken by the mere image of him. The way his silhouette seemed to mirror the sun. The way his hands moved rhythmically to the sound of the music and the water's flow.

She'd sigh.

Maya fell in love quickly. It was always this way.

. . .

Maya reminded herself of all the ways they resembled one another and when she couldn't remember, Troy was there to remind her with his everything. Never mind Ketinah's concerns, who Maya loved but realized was also dealing with a broken heart that she was convinced made Ketinah bitter in a way she was not ready to admit.

Besides, Maya felt she knew Troy. Understood him deeply. Took him deeply into herself—with conversation, with an intimacy that was new and an understanding of his life that she was convinced was expanding her consciousness in ways she didn't yet have the words for. Not when her parents asked about the new guy she was seeing. Not when Ketinah asked her questions. Not when she listened to Troy late nights together, talking, listening, talking. Not when they made love, and he touched her there and there and there too. When they cuddled and spoke softly in the dark with the sheets clinging to the sweat of their bodies. They kissed. Pulled from a poorly rolled joint and she listened while he whispered about his life.

He lived at home not because he had to but because he was worried about his mama. His only brother was in jail and his sister had been killed two years ago. Maya listened to Troy explain how he was the primary caretaker of his mother who was known to smoke cigarettes and wear the same nightgown for days before the smell became too much to anyone's senses but her own. His mother had refused to leave the house ever since she lost two of her children.

Troy's father didn't exist.

Maya was amazed by these facts because she could vaguely remember hearing some of the details Troy described on the local news over the years but had only concentrated on its proximity to her parents' home and not the names, never the family to whom it happened.

Troy.

She pulled the joint harder, held the smoke longer within her lungs and listened while he explained how he came to be.

Long nights under white streetlights, Troy had a way with words that allowed him to flourish in the streets that most didn't understand, not by his looks. He was tall, yeah. But skinny. And he made up for the strength but petiteness of his bones by wearing extra-baggy shit that seemed to make him grow in size—big, black, luminous under the night lights. Even his shadow appeared a dangerous thing. He'd sprung up, bebopping around their neighborhood with a black bandana wound around his brown face; mouth slow to move but mind thinking quick. Money moving like lightning between and inside his hands.

He'd once come to her apartment, head bleeding and hand red with inflammation.

"Boil some water," he said. "And get some ice."

She did so without words, her body moving at his directives. Too scared and confused to process the sight much less what might have caused it. She sat the pot on the stove and watched the fire lick its bottom before the water responded. It was a sexual act. She held her gown closer to her body, ashamed of the sensation. The way the fear and adrenaline traveled to her womb, settling before spreading, like the very fire she watched, to her most private parts.

He stuck his hand first in the boiling water and before she could scream "What the fuck!?" he'd removed it and quickly placed it in the bowl of ice she'd prepared while on autopilot. He grimaced. She watched as his skin flushed pink while he tended to his forehead with a wet rag.

"See, you gotta have the fire and the ice in order to heal it," he said. "My grandmama taught me that." His eyes were closed now and she stood watching his face grow calm before the flesh of his hand responded.

"You're crazy," she said.

It didn't change the fact. Her panties were wet and she knew it was a problem.

Always was a problem. Always was the cure.

Their sex was a special kind of magic she'd never known. He took her high. Higher. Higher still. High. Higher still, till she was as afraid of the height as she was of his lifestyle.

No. She was more scared of the sex. Deeper. Richer. Otherworldly.

And she had no one to discuss it with. Her mother had told her early on to never share her sexual life with friends. "They'll only want what you have," she said. "That want will eventually push them towards action and then you'll lose a friend."

So Maya was quiet and afraid and lying to everyone but herself about what exactly she was in, which was, which had been since that day in the breezeway, love.

It happened quickly. It always did. Except this had been the first time.

And Troy was no better. The first time his mama caught him up all night on the phone with Maya, she'd snatched the phone cord from the wall and called him ruined.

"Who stays on the phone all fucking night when they got shit to do?" she screamed.

Troy had been embarrassed and then angry but neither emotion mattered, neither deterred Maya. When he went up the street and called Maya later that morning from a pay phone she'd been on her way to class and only asked "Are you OK?"

She wasn't mad. She didn't clown him for his mama's actions nor question him for still being in the position that his mother could humiliate him in such a specific way.

He'd stuck his hands in the pockets of his jeans and smiled before answering, low but harshly, "Yeah."

He walked back home that morning accepting the fact that he was gone, the kinda man who stayed on the phone all night, and occasionally all day when Maya had to commute to Dallas for the classes necessary to finish her degree then later drove back to East Texas. After Troy got his first prepaid cell phone sometimes they went whole days not talking but listening to one another, the light sounds of their breaths, their moans of discouragement and frustration throughout the day enough to hold them over until they were physically together again.

It was exhilarating to Troy, this feeling, this something to look forward to when he was used to everything seeming so unsure. So unsteady. So much of the same.

Troy wasn't sure how much it was Maya and how much it was him desperately needing something new. Someone who understood and believed in him no matter his circumstances or choices. But every time Maya went to Dallas and came back still just as much in love with him, still curious about the world and excited to discuss it all with him, he felt something warm. Something so excruciatingly hot around his heart that it took his breath away.

She loved him. She loved him. She truly loved him and he loved her too.

And Maya, sweet Maya was so different yet so much the same as him.

How could he not love his own reflection? Maybe he was worth something after all.

Because deep down Troy was as tender as Maya. As rough as he could be, he was comfortable with showing just how tender he was with her.

In the early mornings while she fried eggs, standing with sleep still crusted at the corners of her eyes and wearing a silk bonnet, he'd watch her crack an egg against the cold laminate of the counter, watch the lines form and scatter along its body before she broke it in two and spilled its insides on the face of the skillet. And it was something about the yolk that reminded him of himself. It looked so fragile. He imagined it might even be scared before meeting its fate over the fire where it somehow remained as bright as the morning sun that poured through the windows illuminating her face while she yawned. He'd rest his body against the counter watching the yolk harden. Become solid.

He ate it conscious of the tenderness that remained. He moved it around the insides of his mouth admiring how fragile it still was though changed. Hardened. Fried. He couldn't help but believe that on some level she too was conscious of this; who he was. When she held him during their lovemaking he felt her eyes seeing him beneath his shell and that she still saw him as strong despite what the world was and how he chose to move in it.

Plus she was curious. Always reading and touching books in ways that she caressed him. When she threw herself against the bed after a long day's work in the library, he looked forward to her stories. About the petite Asian woman who shyly asked for help finding the book on sadomasochism. The chubby teenage white boy wearing heavy black eyeliner and chipped black nail polish who asked where the occult section was. "He had all these tattoos of birds: falcons, eagles, hawks that looked like the ink had smeared," Maya laughed.

Troy laughed too.

"You just know the poor kid read too much Harry Potter and now is looking to be finally initiated into the dark arts."

"Did you show him where it was?"

"Hell no! I took him to the Hobbit books. I figured it was esoteric enough to keep him preoccupied for a bit longer. He's not ready for the real thing. God no!"

Troy asked her what she knew about that "real thing" and she only smiled and said, "I read everything."

He never pushed it.

Never questioned it until she became the egg that broke and scattered.

At the time, Troy was happy enough and more tender than he'd ever allowed himself to be with the librarian chick who drank with him, touched him where his skin stopped and never asked questions when he came in with bloody body parts.

When he asked her to go to Houston with him where he intended to move into the adult entertainment industry—south coastal Texas was hot and teeming with bodies ready to share themselves for a dollar—he didn't have to work hard to convince her. She only asked that they live close to a bookstore, and a library within walking distance because she wouldn't have to drive. Driving in Dallas was one thing, but she found Houston much more intense with its sprawling highways and heavy traffic.

"That can work," he said. And because that was enough for her, he figured it was for him too.

Marriage was what he wanted. The kids were her idea.

Maya wasn't sure. Maybe it was the hypnotism of Troy's perfect teeth. Maybe he'd been a vampire after all. Perhaps he'd died one day under the same sun they'd fallen in love under. All she knew was that once she graduated with her master's in library science and he from middling-ass street hustling, they packed their few belongings and set sail to Houston crammed inside her old Honda Accord.

The wedding was a small but baroque affair her parents paid for, content with the tales she'd gradually shared with them over the years. He doesn't have any family, she said, to which they rushed to him with the fervor of a white savior in a feel-good movie, hugging him extra tight on holidays. He works on cars, she said. He has an opportunity to manage an auto mechanic shop, Maya said. And she figured it wasn't really a lie. She'd once read a spiritual book that likened a car with the human body. It was accurate enough, she thought.

Her mother didn't ask any questions, content with Maya's stories as she usually was. A retired law clerk at the county courthouse who taught meditation classes on the weekends at their neighborhood recreation center, she held fast to her own fantasies where God was really Goddess and the truth was relative.

Maya's mother was beautiful and something bizarre that always felt out of reach to Maya. Sometimes Maya felt she only sought out a higher knowledge so she might one day reach a plane of existence where she could better understand her mother. But her mama had her own philosophy that she lived by, gripped tightly, so she lived seemingly oblivious to anyone outside of herself. And despite the fact that at various points of Maya's life her teachers and other folks in their tiny town had described her mother as neglectful, Maya instead saw her mother's behavior as the ultimate freedom.

She did her yoga. Refused to eat meat. She dictated their lives by the movement of the moon—was it waning, gibbous or full?—these things mattered deeply to her mother. She collected strange and abstract pieces of Black art that she hung on the walls of their small home until all the white space was swallowed up. She only drank water and tea. Let her Afro blossom over time into the most beautiful shades of gray and black and white.

Yet beyond even her own black and white, Maya's mother chose to live in the gray. Nothing was ever entirely clear with her mother. There were no concrete answers or ways of being, which meant growing up for Maya was often a confusing and liberating experience, yet still fun.

Maya's father, however, always managed to balance the fine line between higher truths and the day-to-day. He was the one who stayed on the ground, loved both her mother and her—diligently, frightfully. His attention was impossible to shake, his lessons impossible to master because he was always watching and he never missed any detail. No matter how small, or insignificant. He taught Maya everything was All and All was symbolic. He was patient with Maya's mother, loving her at times from a distance yet always holding her close.

Maya grew up watching them dance around the house to an old Ella Fitzgerald and Louis Armstrong jazz album that to her ears sounded ancient. Thus her parents were both proven in her eyes not of this world; unconventional, a tad kooky, not of this world and her father became her ideal. Holding her mother . . . never letting her go, or venture too far into another realm.

On the day Maya and Troy left for Houston her father was quiet when he hugged and kissed Maya on her cheek goodbye. He wished her and Troy well, but he said little while Maya's mother had made a fuss taking their pictures from odd and unusual angles. Let me capture the sun behind you this way, she'd say, and they all moved at her direction.

Maya and Troy were quiet too.

In fact the entire four-hour drive they didn't speak at all.

· · ·

Assimilation is a funny thing. The world doesn't require much authenticity, which is why people both love and loathe those who dare demonstrate it. But assimilation is not so much a process as a choice. And it's not so much a choice once you grow honest with the self about what it takes to survive and thrive in this reality. When you learn how important to that survival it can be to preserve, indeed hide your very own authenticity lest the world judge then devour you whole—with equal parts love and hate.

Troy's assimilation was a slow one only because he wasn't conscious of it. It happened quickly because of this. He had no idea what he was becoming while it happened, and Maya helped him get there.

He had a new gig. His parties were moving to film, and though he'd never cared much for anything Hollywood, the fake or shallow, there was something inside him that responded to the idea of creating something that would last forever.

He bought a tie. His first one. The tie was navy with white stripes that ran diagonally along its body. It hung from his neck like its own government agency. Maya taught him how to tie the noose, draw it tight around his neck. Even though he figured he worked with whores—young ladies with full breasts, round brown, black and yellow thighs with sad but pretty faces—he should be a professional. He should look like the professional he was and hoped to be. Ignore their eyes. Stay focused on the prize. And the few times he convinced himself to look at himself in the mirror he was genuinely moved by his own reflection.

He bought expensive shoes imprinted with European names he couldn't pronounce. Maya ironed and washed his white button-up shirts, bleaching, always trying to bleach out the piss-colored stains gathered under the arms; the only place that revealed the level of his anxiety. But they would not be moved no matter her efforts and so eventually she stopped, realizing she was further damaging the garments he wore while kissing her goodbye, going to work like it was something respectable. He kissed her late in the morning hours, having returned from the job with the smell of cheap body sprays and drugstore makeup clinging to his skin.

And she listened to his stories. Looked forward to hearing about the young Latina who did the threesome with the African girl and the white dude from Idaho.

"She squirted for the first time and didn't know she could," he said, yawning. "It scared her."

Maya's eyes grew big. She'd read about this phenomenon before.

"And then," he continued, "she expected us to pay her more for it."

"Did you?" she asked.

He kicked off his shoes, and asked for her help relieving the pull of his tie. She leaned forward, grabbing the rope with one gentle jerk and it was undone.

"We gave her an extra $20."

Maya had a curiosity about Troy's work that was almost clinical. Detached. She made no judgments. She was content that he was no longer in the streets. No longer bleeding. Besides, she thought women should do what they wanted and needed to do—it was their decision. She made no judgments. There was room for empowerment inside sex work. She'd once confidently debated the subject in one of her women's studies elective courses during graduate school. It was one of the rare moments she'd actually spoken up.

She'd taken on the entire class with her argument: It's possible for women to enjoy sex with multiple partners as much as men. To conclude women resort to porn only as a consequence of psychological damage or socioeconomic circumstance was subscribing to the same bullshit men peddle which is they are the sexually liberated ones with women constantly seeking to oppress and rein their asses in with nearly impossible expectations. Preclude them from being their true, most primitive selves.

The class groaned.

OK, well, name a wealthy woman who's ever participated in porn, asked a skinny white chick whose dark brown roots bled into a dry blonde frizz. Actually, I can name two! Maya said. Oh please, the girl countered. Sex tape leaks don't count. Uh, they do once she cashes the check! Maya shot back. Women are too emotional. Physiologically ill-equipped to handle multiple partners. Our bodies are fragile, argued a white girl wearing glasses bigger than her face. Bullshit! Maya said. We push whole humans out of our pussies. Gimme a damn break! Certainly we can handle a few dicks!

And the professor quickly shut the conversation down.

But not before another Black girl sounded back with Well, why is most porn mostly produced by men? Many of these women are still taking directions from men, made to perform to the delight of men. Besides, you know the average woman don't wanna be pounded on from every which way! The clit don't require all that!

The class laughed in agreement. And Maya was silent, not because the professor visibly squirmed in her seat at the turn the discussion had taken or the language used to do it. And not because Maya agreed. But because, truth be told, sometimes Maya enjoyed a good pounding. From every which direction. She thought of Troy and instinctively squeezed her vaginal muscles, squirming in her own seat. She wondered briefly if her professor shared the thought, some stimulation at the idea, but when she looked into her pale blue eyes there was nothing there but fear.

Maya supported Troy. She believed in him. She figured the porn wouldn't be forever. This was a phase. Some stage of their journey together with lessons to be learned. At the very least, it was an elaborate metaphor in their lives for something not yet realized. She didn't think about the naked bodies he coached every day. Not when he came home early mornings and shared his stories, then showed her body his stories—over and over again. She giggled one morning just before the sun rose when she asked him, "Do you think I can squirt too?" He pushed her legs back above her head and moaned as he entered her.

"Let's see," he said.

. . .

Maya believed in Troy.

On the weekends she read to him from Plato's *On Rhetoric and Language* and he consumed the strategies for persuasion as though preparing for an exam. Coupled with his street savvy he became unstoppable and further drawn into the assimilation matrix. Only he was becoming the most sincere kind. The kind who dabbles before committing themselves wholeheartedly to a life of crime legitimized by the system, choosing in their own ways to remain oblivious to how their work affects the lives of others. The way politicians tell the necessary lies to move forward or stay put, the way pharmaceutical scientists mix, shake, test then confirm drugs they know will kill over time.

Troy, like them, appeared a gentleman. He had the right accountant and soon the right attorney. His fortress was fortified.

He moved Maya from their small one-bedroom apartment to a high-rise condo overlooking the Gulf, and then finally to their Spanish-style home inside a gated community. Organic food store three blocks away. The local library was a ten-minute walk. Maya was happy and patient, even though she still hadn't found a job using that master's degree her parents paid for. When she took her résumé to the library in their new neighborhood there was no availability. The white woman at the desk looked as old as her own mother and spoke with a smile in her voice though her face didn't move. "These jobs don't have high turnover," she said, and pushed the résumé across the shiny mahogany surface of her desk back towards Maya's hands.

At first, Troy thought Maya wanted kids because she was bored. Surely you haven't read all the books there are to read, he said. And that was the first time he saw her truly angry, something he thought her incapable of. Five years together and they had never fought. Up until then she'd expressed any signs of frustration with silence. She'd move away from his arms at night. Withdraw her feet when his were cold and seeking her heat beneath the covers. But that was the extent of it. Had been so until the day he told her she needed another means of preoccupation.

"What did you say?" She was in the kitchen making another one of those green smoothies she force-fed him. Bits of chopped spinach were still stuck to her fingers when she raised her hand as if to stop traffic and repeated, "What did you just say?"

"What?" he asked. He looked up from the couch where he lay poking at his phone. "Come here." He went to the kitchen and reached for her at the sink but she moved away, tears filling her eyes. She went to the bedroom and slammed the door, loudly moving across the floor. Then she stomped right back out to their living room where he'd resumed sitting on the couch trying to make sense of this new thing she was.

The evening sun filled the room with dazed beams that washed her face, creating a blur where her features as he knew them usually relaxed into quiet smiles or complete stoicism. Emotions had been resolved in ways he related to and understood, and then responded to appropriately. But this outburst confused him and he found he didn't have words when she screamed, "You are the most selfish muthafucka I know!"

She cut up his ties.

"I helped string yo ass up and I can cut you down if necessary!" she hollered.

The fuck? he thought.

It was the first time he questioned if he really knew her.

And her voice had sounded a trillion light-years away from behind the closet door cutting up his shit. He slept on the couch that night still wondering what she'd meant. And what more did she want from him? Their courtship had been so quiet. He thought they understood one another. No questions. No need for answers that did not yet exist.

He tossed and turned all night.

He was agitated. So used to the men on the street. The way they moved and communicated. The unspoken was the most powerful and anger usually revealed itself through actions that equaled the taking of something—be it a material thing, be it a life. Be it an intentional or circumstantial victim. It was what it was and there was no greater religion than learning to live with this. Accepting death may come anytime, so be ready, be prepared. And if it wasn't death then it wasn't that serious and even then you couldn't always let it be. *So chill.*

There was no time for feelings lest you get caught slipping. Lest it slow you down in contemplation. Lest the loss and fear kill you long before the body dies.

Troy didn't know how to react to this woman, so different from him in the ways she was raised, still so similar in the ways she navigated the world. She read. She was quiet. She minded her own business.

He chose silence when she finally broke down and cried after destroying his clothes.

They were both seekers, right? By any means necessary, right? Why was she breaking the code?

Her display of weakness both disgusted him and scared him. He'd read somewhere that each person was but a mere reflection of his own self, but he refused to accept the image before him. His lady. Her face wet with tears and words that held little coherency to his ears.

His wife. The egg cracking.

Troy chose silence. He forgave her. He charged her with buying new ties as punishment because he knew how much she hated shopping. And he went to work. Only now he worked longer hours hoping to make even more money because somewhere in the midst of her babbling Maya cooed she wanted a baby and he'd rocked her in his arms like a child and agreed.

They could try.

And he worked so hard, funky and hairy bodies bouncing and secreting things it was sometimes difficult to push out of his mind. Some nights Maya wanted sex, to be the perfect O and he couldn't meet her there. All the while trying to remind himself that she'd never truly known his life. She didn't know what it meant to travel your day not knowing what each hour held. She had never been hungry or violent beyond the extent of her words, beyond their neighborhood, which he was beginning to think was merely an abstraction her books shielded her from. She'd never killed or had someone she loved deeply, depended on unequivocally and believed in, be murdered during early morning hours when the sun was just beginning its ascent and half the world moved about trying to get their day started; while in their neighborhood kids were already dying.

Or wasn't she paying attention?

He'd known so many men who'd died with girls carrying their babies, and he'd watched some of those babies grow up without fathers only to themselves die without ever meeting their child. It was a cycle he had no interest in engaging in. Troy still didn't trust the world, even less since assimilating, but he wanted something bigger, longed for it in ways that permeated his soul; traveled through his veins and thoughts during the days and nights.

When day broke he was still the sun, and the prize was staying alive, getting what he could get. Staying smart. Alert. Keeping pace. His ego didn't require offspring. The legacy was enough. And besides, this wasn't a place he thought babies belonged.

——#——

Maybe they don't belong here, Maya thought.

Because after all she'd had a hard time having her children. Doctors said she almost died with each one and still they had the nerve to cry. Every day. Every night. They wanted more from her, and what did she have left to give? What more could she offer up but *What the fuck do you want from me?* She'd dig her nails into the warm flesh of her thighs until she drew blood. She'd watch it dry, a cool scab moving erotically along her legs.

Or maybe they know what's coming to them, she thought, so they cry. *A Black boy was killed yesterday. Killer acquitted of murder. Killer tried to auction the gun used to kill Black boy.*

They know. They must know.

It's inevitable. Why else cry no matter what I do for them?

And they'd cry. And then she'd cry, matching their screams. Sometimes this would go on for hours. Their stucco home smothered in the sounds of sniffles and yelps, until one day a neighbor called the police, afraid the children had been left alone.

Maya opened the door, her face swollen shut and as red as her melanin allowed. The police saw her robe, soiled and hanging off her thin body barely concealing the soiled gown she wore underneath. She looked at them while closing the door at first in panic then confusion.

"No, no . . . we don't have any candy," she said.

The police caught the door with the palms of their white hands and gently pushed back. "Ma'am, we're the police," the one with the buzz cut said. "Is everything alright?" And for a moment he looked genuinely concerned, his green eyes shot and scattered about his bearded face.

Except by then, the children dehydrated and tired from their own loss of energy were sleeping. In fact, when the police walked in, surveying the tidiness of the space, the cream-colored leather furniture, the green folds of potted plants tumbling on top of chestnut tables and hanging from the ceiling near large arched windows, they immediately decided there was nothing amiss. Babies cried. Sometimes mommies did too. Plus they were hungry, and slightly distracted by the way her gown hugged her thin frame, somehow creating curves where logic suggested they ought not be. And the way the slope of her breasts, bare under the thin cotton of the pale blue gown, shone just so. They made eye contact, some unspoken way of communicating that years of doing police work together afforded them. Then the other one, thick in body and bald, wiped the growing beads of sweat from atop his upper lip and asked for some water.

"Me too," said the other one. "If you don't mind."

There was something about the soft confusion in her eyes. The way her voice trembled when at first she spoke before recovering and finding itself. There was an eroticism to her vulnerability they both responded to. Not at all eager to help, mind you, if indeed that's what she needed, what was in fact required. And never mind the brown babies sleeping heavily with only the thick crust of tears formed inside the corners of their eyes.

If she had a special seduction about her, some unique and unusual way of being, she was oblivious yet still conscious enough to not close the growing gap of her gown where it tied and split, exposing smooth brown flesh at her chest. And had she not seen some semblance of lust in their eyes. The way their lips touched and held their glasses of water, releasing breath from their swollen bodies then swallowing—thick pink necks jumping at their Adam's apples before resuming pace and moving on. And had the look of sex not reminded her of how and why she'd gotten pregnant to begin with she might not have snatched one glass, then the other from their hands not caring where the cold water fell.

"We fine!" she said, marching to and opening the door. "We fine!" she said again, this time more sternly, eyes averted to the brown fibers of the carpet. She focused in on a stain Amari, her oldest, had made weeks ago and kept her gaze fixated there until she felt the policemen move, their eyes searching everywhere but where they clumsily moved. Shame evident in their gaits.

"Call us if you need—" one started, but she slammed the door before his words found an ending. And the sound of the heavy door meeting the hinge woke one baby. He cried. And the sound of his cries woke the other baby and he cried. So she grabbed her face, her body sliding against the cool surface of the door's exterior to the floor, and cried too.

And just like that, they resumed where they left off.

Maya wanted to hug her children, to assure them they were protected but she didn't yet have the answer. Her mother said the Goddess. Her grandmother said Jesus. Her father said reality is an illusion she must transcend because its reflection was that of her own mind. But she'd never wish for dead Black children. That's not who she was. Dead Black people. That's not who she was. She went through her books in search of metaphysical explanations and found nothing other than what finally appeared to her splintered mental state an integral truth. *They've been trying to destroy us since the beginning of time.* But when was the beginning?

When she first began the bleaching it was a quiet thing. It had arrived in the mail a slim jar enclosed inside a small box that from the outside looked as though it were a book. *Blanc Afrique.* Its cover a Black woman smiling with perfect white teeth and beneath her smile a caption that read *Bright Ways, Bright Future.*

A future. It was more than enough reassurance.

This was their beginning. Their time. A new chapter.

And she treated the seriousness of the act very quietly. She treated their small bodies like houses where she rubbed the cream softly into hard to see and reach areas. Those places where dust often collects in houses thick as mucus over time only because it's mostly unseen. She rubbed and hummed one of the few gospel hymns she recalled. Behind their ears. *There is a God.* Within the tender folds of flesh gathered behind their knees. *He is alive.* Inside the brown crevices of their elbows. *In Him we live.* She counted two toes—the pinky. *And we survive.* Along the short lengths of their big toes. *From dust our God.* On their tiny hind necks. *Created man.* Then finally the smalls of their backs. *He is our God.* And before she could withdraw her fingers. Before she could wipe the residual cream from between her own digits with slow, agonizing pulls. Before she could dress each one though they fussed and struggled within her arms. She cried. Each and every time the tears came, with a mouth full of bitter spit, she sang the song's closing.

The Great I Am.

Does this mean I believe in white Jesus? she wondered during her day. And she cried with her boys whose tender skin would grow pink before blooming into a fiery red rash. They groped and pawed at their bodies, not knowing nor possessing the necessary coordination to scratch in ways that relieved the fire. And so she rubbed more bleaching cream with a dollop of aloe vera from a plant she'd bought from a roadside vendor shortly before they were born. It was easy to keep, unlike her boys.

And she resented them. Their lack of appreciation for what she was trying to do for them, her protection and due diligence. Why she was forsaking her mind! Was this not as the scripture mandated? Be in this world, but not of it. It infuriated her and so many days she didn't even want to touch them. Not to protect them or comfort or feed them, nor talk to them in that garbled language they spoke.

What did it mean to be Black and not believe in God? Worse yet, what did it mean to be Black and desire whiteness? A purity and protection associated with the color. Was this a form of worship? Had she given in?

Maya watched her husband assimilate while she enjoyed the privileges it brought, even if that meant she had the luxury of losing her mind quietly and within the peace of her home. She didn't have to venture out into the world. She didn't have to fight her demons and those of others just to make it through the day. And by God, hers were enough.

So Maya both feared and understood the violence she watched on the news. Because if somehow her own thoughts really were a reflection of the world then how could she judge?

She smiled at her conclusion.

Even this idea was biblical.

Troy was home early.

It was Monday. Weatherman said it was 79 degrees, clear skies.

He asked Maya to run him a bath. Some nights he just wanted to sit down and soak. She went to the bathroom. Ran the hot. 5, 4, 3, 2, 1 second. Then the cold. She let the two meet inside her hand until the temperature was as she knew he liked. She pulled the stopper. Watched the tub fill—slowly, slowly before walking to retrieve his towels. Wash towel. Dry towel. She folded them over her left arm then draped them over the toilet's face. Steam began to rise and the tiny room gave way to haze. She stopped to enjoy the smoke and looked at herself in the mirror. She watched her features disappear, the water and fire swallowing her whole and she wasn't scared.

This was the routine. He didn't like bubbles or oils—nothing as fancy or ornate. No, he liked his water warm and still. She knew the temperature as if it were her own. This is what it meant to truly love a man. To know his body as though your own. Perhaps even better.

Maya knew her man. In her mind, she knew her babies too. Small men she'd given birth into the world. She was so sensitive to the fact that they had come from her own body that it allowed her to make assumptions that felt like facts. And who knows? Perhaps they were.

But there was no time to think about those things. Not now. Not while the bathwater reached its peak and the steam threatened to erase all rationale, however lacking or clumsy. Not while the sound of her husband's voice called out to her from another room that to her mind sounded like another realm altogether.

She moved slowly. Slowly. Out of the bathroom and down the length of the hall. He called, and she carried herself towards the sound until she heard the babies' cries. Her youngest, Jaden, yelped and grew quiet before his lungs pushed forth a scream she knew well. Then Amari followed suit with his own variation.

Maya stopped. Paused. Drew a long breath that filled her chest with flames. Then she ran.

There were drums. Later, she distinctly remembered the sound of drums, their beats caused the house to vibrate. There was her husband standing over Jaden who lay with his back against the bed with his legs thrown in the air. Troy held one chubby, two-toned foot and yelled at her but she couldn't make out his words over the drums.

"What?" she screamed. And she cried because the boys cried and this was their routine. "What?" she screamed again. But when he pointed to the baby's inner thighs and opened his mouth again but there was no sound but the drums. His face grew large, his eyes were sweating. She was sure they were sweating because she too felt the heat rising inside her chest. Like rivers of gold, the tears carved themselves through the crevices of his brown skin before puddling at the hairs of his chin.

Troy was crying. She stood for a moment, struck by the image before her. He had finally met their rhythm and joined their collective sobs. They were finally on one accord. A family.

Still he kept pointing. First at her and then the baby's thighs till she looked. Till she saw the red blisters like a string of ant bites along Jaden's tender skin.

She smiled. *Oh, that.* She could fix that. She turned and reached for the baby powder on the dresser but before her fingers could reach its body, Troy grabbed her arm, spinning her back around. And his eyes were as red as Jaden's legs. And his tongue flushed with saliva. And his lips were full and angry.

She recognized it now. Remembered. This was her husband when he was mad.

The drums grew louder. So loud she covered her ears. She felt the oldest baby grab her right leg and when she looked down and met his face she couldn't see anything for the drums. They were blinding her. The scene before her was going black until her husband grabbed her face, forcing her back into the moment. And the pressure of his hands and those of Amari, now around her leg, threatened to cause the heat to burn her alive. But she couldn't burn. There was no time to give in because Troy was pushing her face now, he had a handful of her hair and cheeks and forced her to look at Jaden's legs. And even through her tears, through the drums, through the fire, she could see how the blisters ran up his legs, stopping short at the mound of flesh that was his manhood before resuming above his navel.

She saw his foot where the brown remained before meeting the milky pink flesh then turned red. He's hot, she thought. That's why Troy is so mad. It's burning up in here. She went to pull away from his grasp, causing her own spit to go flying and the oldest son to topple to the floor. He cried even harder and when she reached for him she saw the ant bites running along the length of his underarms. He reached out for her and she reached back to receive him but her husband had her again. His arms grabbed her shoulders so deeply it hurt, and the pain was so sharp it stopped her tears.

"What did you do?" he yelled. "Look at them! What have you done?"

The room was spinning. And she was confused before attempting to answer but he was gone before the words could form inside her mouth. He ran towards the bathroom and she followed. She turned back and saw the boys like pink and red flames upon the bed and sprawled across the floor crying. She followed Troy.

He tore open the cabinet beneath the bathroom sink and ripped through its contents. He stood to open the cabinet behind the mirror, his face a very brief smear that gathered and unfolded against the room's steam. He slammed it shut, only it refused and hung open, bouncing off the hinges' clasp before stuttering agape.

He pushed past her, now moving towards the kitchen. "Where is it?" he yelled, his voice hoarse with tears.

The drums played. The drums played. Maya retreated to the living room, finding the corner that knew her body best and stood there before sliding then collapsing to the ground.

And when he found the bleach inside the cupboard behind all the food seasonings she was surprised. He never cooked, barely went into the kitchen unless receiving a meal. Even when she was bedridden he had food delivered. She had thought it a safe place. And when he held it before her face. When he grabbed her face again and forced her to *Look! Look!* she refused.

She closed her eyes. She let the drums carry her away. When she felt his hand slap her, she still refused. Her eyes remained shut. And she stayed this way until her eyes were opened again by the ice-cold white fingers of the same policemen from days before.

Now she reacted.

Screaming. Fighting with every bit of energy possessed. She felt her arm make contact with one of the officer's necks, leaving a pink bruise that blossomed before turning bright red then repossessing its natural pasty color and she wanted to laugh.

She laughed though her face was wet with tears and maroon now with anger. But when the medics restrained her then placed her thin wrists inside the cuffs, she was lucid. As she passed the mirror hanging on the living room wall above the couch she saw herself as maybe she was: Wild. Untamed. Red and wet. She felt coherent, finally, when she asked, small now and afraid, "Where are you taking me?" And when they pushed her head into the police car she asked, "What about my boys?"

A medic said, "We'll meet you there."

A policeman said, "Can you sedate her now?"

A woman's voice over a sound system that crackled with static said, "Black woman. Violent. Possible 5150."

The full moon peered down and it was as white as those who restrained her. So beautiful it was that she became lost in its glory so that when the needle pierced through her arm she felt nothing. She heard nothing save for the sound, distant now yet still strong, of drums. And she smiled. Smiled big with the excitement of her boys when discovering something new, when it occurred to her that the bass. That boom boom. That syncopation that filled her ears, spilling out into the world, was but the sound of her own heart.

She smiled. Maybe the answer was near.

The police car's blue and red lights strobed against the blackness of the streets and she only thought, "It's time."

The way to beat them, she concluded, was to become as scary as they felt. Be the fear. Let the curls atop her head run as wild as her mother's, dry as the perfect conditions for a forest fire. Become the fire. Reach up when they reached down. Be the mystery, as unpredictable as life. Do not smile. Move the thickness of her lips up and out. Fill the eyes with hot water. Lava. Become a volcano. Become the ocean, the unexplored depths.

Be woman. Be Black.

Maya lay on a cot, wrists bound at the bedpost. It was dark in the room and still night outside. Across from her on the other side of the room she could barely make out the faint outlines of a large figure whose shape rose and descended under the moon's light. She heard a crooning.

They call you lady luck . . . but there is room for doubt!

The woman's voice held a heavy Spanish lilt. Each vowel was as if a song inside the song she sang.

At times you have a very unladylike way of running out . . .

Maya turned over, feeling the leather restraints on her arms cut her blood circulation.

You're on this date with me, the pickings have been lush . . .

If I wanted, Maya thought. If I dared, I could die just like this, she thought. Just another inch in this direction. Toward the moon. It would be a terribly slow death but it would do.

. . . and yet before this evening is over you might give me the brush.

She rose, the restraints pulling her back down before she could complete the move.

You might forget your manners . . . You might refuse to stay.

She laughed to herself. They don't know I've been fastened to beds before. I know this hell.

And so the best that I can do is pray . . .

Pray?

"Shut the fuck up!" Maya screamed.

There was silence. Maya was unsure if like her the Spanish woman was also stripped and tied down. If not and if she wanted to, Maya was sure the Spanish lady could easily reach her and have her way. Punch. Slap. Pull. If she wanted to she could and there wouldn't be shit she could do. As soon as the words were said her body tensed in preparation for a blow—verbal or otherwise. But there was none.

Only silence. Only the moon.

And then, *Luck be a lady tonight!*

The woman sang as if Maya never said anything at all. And because there was nothing worse than being ignored, Maya accepted her defeat. She took it by lying back down against the bed's cold starched sheets underneath the moon's rays and she yielded to her own demand.

She shut the fuck up.

But she didn't turn towards the moon, and she figured this was a small victory.

The next morning it was the same. The sun replaced the moon and in the day's light Maya found herself alone. She assessed her situation. White socks on her feet she didn't recognize. White cotton gown. Her body was completely nude underneath and it was cold. Chill bumps scattered across her body and she felt a burst of mucus in her chest waiting to explode. When she coughed, not once, not twice but multiple times, it was a strange relief. She couldn't stop once she started and only then did a nurse enter the room.

"Do you know where you are?" the nurse asked. She was brown. Not Black. Not white. Something else. Her voice was gentle in that affected way Maya sometimes used to soothe her children when anxious for them to stop being scared or misbehaving.

The nurse looked at her now, finally, and full in her eyes. She reached to loosen the straps holding Maya's arms. "This might help," she said. "Do you know who you are?" she asked as if it were the most normal question in the world.

Do you know who you are?

But Maya didn't know how to answer. Was there an answer? Did anyone truly know? Then because she felt tricked she became agitated. No matter the nurse's soothing voice, or warm hands. No matter the pools of brown that were her eyes—so peaceful, so still as though standing water.

And she might have grown calm under her gaze. Might have allowed herself to swim in those waters if not for the next thing the nurse said, which was: "You're in a psychiatric ward. Your name is Maya and everything is going to be OK. You're OK now." And because Maya immediately recognized that the nurse was lying, she moved that mucus, coaxed it through the tunnels of her chest, and up her throat and spit. Firmly. Completely. And directly in the nurse's face.

"Lying bitch!" she called. "Where the fuck are my kids?"

The Spanish lady was Esmeralda. Esmeralda, which to Maya's mind sounded like emerald. Sapphires. Diamonds of an exquisite kind and Maya wanted to see Esmeralda as such but here she was rambling, her words crashing into one another with little distinction to where a sentence began or ended; the same lilting of her vowels ringing out as though music. Much better still than the Frank Sinatra tune she belted out the night before.

She introduced herself by quietly pulling up a chair and flopping her big body down beside Maya in the cafeteria. They were being fed. Esmeralda had roast beef, potatoes, stewed carrots and three small containers of chocolate pudding. Maya looked at her own tray. Same food though smaller portions. Dry meat that looked like a raisin shriveling under the sun. Potato that looked like wet cement. Carrots like tender orange fingers, aged, withered, tired. One cup of chocolate pudding. She didn't ask for it. It reminded her too much of her boys but when she'd protested the cafeteria lady ignored her.

"I'm from Nicaragua," Esmeralda said. "My family is here now." She bypassed her lunch, went straight to dessert and heaped a spoonful of pudding into her mouth. "But I'm from Nicaragua." She took another bite. "They ask me why I don't have a home, you know?" Another bite. "But I tell them Nicaragua is my home. I have a home." Another bite, the chocolate now coating her thin pink lips and crusting at the sides of her mouth. "I say Nicaragua is my home and nobody believes me so I stay on the streets. I come here for the chocolate though." She ripped open the third container and dug in first with a finger before picking up her plastic spoon and diving back in. "It's not so bad, I guess, until someone takes me home to Nicaragua. Maybe I'll get lucky, huh? Go back home to Nicaragua."

Nicaragua. She said it so many times Maya began to question if she were subliminally trying to call her a nigger. Maya reached for a sip of water. It was ice cold. No ice, but ice cold.

"Are you going to eat that?" Esmeralda asked.

"Eat what?"

"That," She pointed to her pudding with a stubby thumb.

Maya took another sip of water.

"Nicaragua?"

Chocolate pudding. Nicaragua. Bitch you think you funny?

Maya hit her. Not once, not twice but multiple times.

"Has she ever been violent before?"

"No. Never."

"Has she ever shown signs of being unwell?"

Troy thought long about what that might look like. His mama? His father who didn't come around at all? His baby sister who had been pregnant at fourteen and again at seventeen. She'd joined the neighborhood gang at fifteen even though he'd told her "Nah this ain't what you wanna do." She was gone by twenty. Shot to the head. No one knew if the bullet came from her children's father or his rivals.

No one knew or cared to know the truth.

His oldest brother who had been locked up since he was nineteen? They said he'd killed a man. No one knew whether it was true or not.

No one knew or cared to know the truth.

Troy had avoided the gang life, selling drugs instead to gang members who no matter what color or block they repped didn't fuck with him mostly because his product was good and he was quiet. Minded his business. Nothing like his siblings.

Troy shook his head. He knew violence.

"She ain't violent," he said and pushed away from the interview table. He stood up and stretched his legs. The interview room felt too much like a police interrogation room and like always, he ain't know nothing. Only this time he spoke the truth.

"She never been violent," He was trembling and didn't wanna show it so he paced a bit. "She likes books, ya know. That kinda shit."

Does she have any friends?

He was quiet. Thinking.

"Her best friend Ketinah." He looked up at them as though they might recognize the name he called, and seeing nothing from them he frowned. Troy never liked Ketinah because he suspected Ketinah never liked him, and what right did she have to judge him? She'd gone into the world only to return to Texas with her tail tucked between her legs; still Troy thought she saw herself as better for having gone so far away at all.

Ketinah, who his wife was convinced actually saw and communicated with ghosts. And at first Troy found the idea kinda cool, esoteric and mystical like their relationship. But when he'd met Ketinah, her own unique mayhem of curls, skinny, light-skinned and perpetually high, he'd instead determined her both spoiled and delusional. Still he'd asked Ketinah one night when Maya had forced the two of her favorite people to hang out, if she'd ever seen his sister. Troy too was high, slightly drunk from the tequila he'd abused because it was the anniversary of his sister's death.

Her name is Monique, Troy stuttered with weepy eyes, holding the shot glass by the numb points of his fingers and Ketinah had pulled long from her blunt and told him with equally weepy eyes that yes his sister walked behind him everyday looking sad and confused about her place in the world—was she dead, was she alive? It was difficult to tell.

"And she's worried about you," Ketinah said.

Troy became enraged. His sister deserved peace or what else was there to look forward to?

"Fuck you!" he'd yelled at her before throwing his glass at the wall behind her head. And still Maya had been calm, and rubbed his back, told him it was OK while Ketinah eventually crawled and huddled against the corner wall crying softly.

Maya ignored Ketinah and tried soothing Troy but it was too late. When he looked at Ketinah he saw madness, chaos and delusion. He saw his sister, lost and bewildered. The hole still a fresh wound in the side of her head.

Fuck Ketinah!

How dare she speak on his sister? Spoiled bitch! How dare she judge him? He wanted to yell. How dare she have an opinion at all when it was clear she hated all men? he thought.

But he hadn't said anything else, he'd only cried while Maya held him within her arms and told him it would be OK, over and over again.

"But she likes books?" the doctors asked.

"Yeah," Troy whispered.

The woman and man wrote this down as if it were important. And perhaps it was.

Books.

To tell the truth Troy was tired of books and had long ago given up on them as anything but what he figured they were in the world, yet another distraction.

No truths. No facts. No secrets.

Still years ago when he and Maya moved into their first apartment, Troy woke up late one afternoon reaching for her body and not feeling her beside him, rose out of bed in search of his wife. He walked, stretching, yawning through their puny place until his eyes focused on her small body sitting on the living room floor, reading. As usual.

He smiled. He wanted to frown but it wouldn't come, and he was slow to admit to himself that he still loved this about her.

"What you reading?" he asked, sitting down beside her.

They were newly married and strewn about their new apartment on the floor. No furniture. Her dad offered to buy them some as a wedding gift but Troy had shook his head, smiled and said, "We good."

The brown carpet felt thin beneath their bodies and they were reminded of the Spanish tile floors that were there before, according to the leasing agent. The tile was now relegated to the kitchen and bathroom floors while the rest of the space enjoyed Berber fibers with light stains too persistent to be removed left by previous tenants.

Maya instinctively moved towards him and placed her head against his shoulder before sitting up on her elbows. The floor was so hard.

"You really wanna know?" she asked.

He widened his eyes like *girl quit playing* and she giggled before sitting upright, back totally erect though there was nothing there to offer support.

"It's about this goddess who's lost and somehow finds herself on Earth. She's lonely, ya know, and her memories have been taken from her."

He placed an arm under his head and closed his eyes but not before seeing her sitting there in the last of the evening sun; sweatpants and an old cheerleading shirt. She glowed as she spoke. The end of the day had its ways with her and she was absolutely beautiful. He wondered if she knew it. Did she realize she was golden?

"So she's wandering the Earth, looking at all the confusion. The violence. And she assumes she's in hell."

"Shiiiiiiit . . . ," he said. "She got that right." He shifted his other hand down to the warmth of his balls and let it rest.

"But what she doesn't know yet is these are her kids she's watching. This is the home she created." She paused and tilted her head toward the ceiling and her eyes were briefly full of light. "She doesn't realize this is what it means when you've failed as a mother and because she refuses to acknowledge it, she wanders endlessly falling victim to all her kids and man do they fuck her up!"

"Daaaaaamn," he said. "Thas fucked up."

"I know, right."

"So what she do? And who took her memories anyway?"

"I dunno," she said falling back to her elbows beside him. "Haven't got that far yet."

"Shiiiiiiiit," he said again. "She'll be aiight though."

She looked at him fully now, his brown face glistening with sweat. They couldn't afford to run the air conditioner much and the single blade of the rotating fan oscillating at their feet threw air stingily.

"You think so?" she asked.

"Yeah," he said and closed his eyes. "Mamas are tough. Tougher than anybody."

. . .

Do you have thoughts of hurting yourself?

I'm already hurt.

Who hurt you?

Everyone, I think. I'm trying to remember.

Silence.

I see. Have you ever thought of hurting your kids?

Absolutely not. Absolutely not. I'm trying to protect them.

Is someone else trying to hurt them? Has your husband hurt them?

Yes. The whole fucking world is trying to hurt my boys.

What makes you think this?

Don't you watch the news? You see the Black and brown boys kill each other and the white men kill them all. I figure if my boys have white skin, at least they have a chance. A camouflage. Protection. And if I keep their hair close cut, who will ever know the difference? I mean, who really looks at another person closely? Who really cares? Black skin is an easy mark in this game.

Silence.

Maya looked at the doctor.

You don't understand, Maya said, starting to cry and rocking, how difficult it was to get them here! You don't know how hard it was on me! she said, grabbing at her body.

Silence.

She held her arms against herself as if she were the child seeking a mother's warmth, and she was. She was someone's child, but not like her little boys. She sniffed. They belonged to no one. Not even herself.

Bang, she whispered.

Silence.

Maya cried, and stretched her arm out before her body until her hand uncoiled. She watched it grow, then balled it into a fist and then managed to curl three fingers back, her pointer and thumb held high. She pointed them all at the doctors.

Bang, she whispered, pulling the trigger. It's so easy for them to leave me, she wept, throwing her head back. The tears overwhelmed her words and a nurse rushed towards her until a doctor stopped her with his own outreached hand. Stop. And the nurse did.

Bang, Maya cried, weeping. Grasping at her body. Reaching out for her boys. Shooting the doctors.

You don't know how hard it was to have them, she wept. No one will ever know. So hard, she wept grasping at her body. So hard.

The nurse stared at Maya, her hair wild, her tears a river unable to find an ocean. She moved towards her again, innately seeking to comfort, to heal before being reminded again by the doctor not to interfere.

Maya wept.

Bang, Maya whispered. Gone, she whispered.

Bang.

I see, the doctor said. Boys are hard. We should all hope for a girl, right?

They gave her a Xanax and sent her back to her room. Esmeralda had been moved.

The nurse said nothing.

Maya once thought it might be safer to have girls only she was too intelligent to entertain the idea for very long. Wasn't nothing in this world worse than being a woman other than to be a Black woman. You weren't a body. You weren't a voice. You just was and what that was no one cared enough to discover. No one asked the fundamental questions. No one even pondered the question. You weren't a body. Even a body has more respect, though it may lack a name, a spirit, a soul.

She thought of the white women in the movies her husband made with their shiny straight hair and crooked teeth. Their breasts were full with silicone and crowned with pink nipples that spread before melting back into their pink areolas. They could have bad skin, pudgy bellies and flat asses. Thin lips. Thinner thighs. Long red tongues that stretched before them as they peered up with large blue or green eyes; pupils dilated—the only black parts of them other than the men they allowed into themselves.

She thought about them and the ways Troy said some of them

had come from similar backgrounds as himself. Poor. Uneducated. If asked to speak more than ten words inside a script they struggled, then laughed before turning as bright red as the soft flesh inside their pussies. Some threw the scripts down, asserting their sexuality by rubbing themselves. "Who really cares what I have to say? People wanna see me fuck!" And others, even with the acne that makeup struggled to cover and cavities having wreaked havoc inside their mouths leaving blank spaces where incisors should be, would somehow assert their whiteness. There'd be a look. Some small glance that implied these niggers don't know what they're doing. "My manager doesn't even want me fucking Black guys on camera!" one lady screamed, even though the father of both her children was Haitian.

Somehow. Some kinda way, they were always better, if only in memory; some portion of the subconscious so deeply and thoroughly programmed that any person of color seemed to bow when reminded.

Maya only once visited the set of one of Troy's films.

She was curious.

They were between shoots on a long night, when oftentimes they'd make as many as five movies a day. The room inside the tiny warehouse was cold, so cold her skin broke out in goose bumps. On a small table there were generic fruit roll-ups, Ritz crackers, Cheez Whiz and cheap sparkling wine. The stench of marijuana still hung in the air. A white woman was almost at the point of fake orgasm, her legs shook as a young Black man pounded her insides and when she screamed she was coming, Maya could relate to the falsity of it all as of late. *Hurry up! Let's wrap this shit up!*

Afterwards she'd watched as the woman took a towel between her legs as if freshly coming out of the shower. There were none of the usual baby wipes she'd been told were the norm. The white woman wiped her body down before wrapping the white folds of terry cloth around her head, damp with sweat and semen.

Thirty minutes later a Black porn star arrived. Portia Mercedes. Beautiful. Shitty blonde weave. Brown skin scarred and marked up with bad tattoos. She watched as her husband's production assistant replaced the cheese and crackers, the cheap sparkling wine with red hot flamin' Cheetos, ranch dressing and a liter of off-brand cola.

When the production assistant, a slim Cuban kid with full black weed-smoking lips and a frail ponytail, saw her side-eyeing him as he went through the motions he stopped, shrugged and said, "That's what she likes!" And when she saw the Black woman throwing her ass against the same young Black man who an hour ago had fucked the white chick, popped a Viagra, took two hits off a blunt and mounted her with nothing but his dingy socks on, she knew it was time to go. Her husband saw her walk towards the exit and made no move to stop her. Maya looked back at the Black woman and saw her eyes closed, how her breasts jumped with each stroke and heard her scream through gritted teeth, *Yeah! Give it me!*

She got home and rushed to the bathroom, leaving the house key still dangling from the front door. She vomited and then quickly found she had to relieve her bowels. She took a cool washcloth, flushed with cold water, and ran it across her face. It wasn't enough. She stripped off her clothes, not yet relieved of her panties and bra before jumping into the rushing stream of the shower. There was not enough soap.

That's what she likes!

There was not enough cold water.

That's what she likes!

And when she had to hop out of the shower, body slick with wet, and vomit again that's still all she heard.

That's what she likes!

Three weeks later she learned she was pregnant with her first child.

The hospital halls were quiet and dim, the cafeteria long ago closed yet Troy found himself wandering aimlessly through its corridors. Maya's father was in town, and even after all this time Troy was struck by the ways Maya's father showed up while her mother did not. He'd called Troy's cell the previous morning and told him he intended to pick up the boys from the children's clinic where they'd been examined physically and then emotionally by a social service worker before being granted release. "I don't want to give them any reason to hesitate sending the boys back home," he said. "You stay with Maya and let me tend to them. It'll be good for the social service people to see y'all have some help."

Troy couldn't disagree with that. He was ashamed to admit that he hadn't thought far ahead enough to consider what he would do about the boys. He'd never spent a night alone with them. Wasn't sure what they liked to eat. Didn't know how they might react to a home without their mother somewhere in it, accessible to them, no matter her condition. He was relieved when the hospital said it was necessary to keep them for observation. He was relieved Maya's father had arrived so quickly to help but bothered that meant he'd have to see him. Eventually.

He made a few loops around the main floor, idling in emergency waiting rooms where he'd sit for a moment trying to guess the reason for each person's visit. He imagined that they were all there for far more important reasons than himself.

There was an old woman, racially ambiguous which was so often the case in a city as diverse as Houston, knitting from a red ball of yarn tucked in her purse. She'd look up at the television every so often though its volume was down and barely audible. Across the room was a Latina woman whose age he couldn't figure. She had three small children she struggled to manage, two boys who took turns throwing themselves over her lap then placing sticky, candy-stained fingers in her face before squealing and chasing the other. And a baby girl who stood in the adjacent chair, held in the crook of the woman's left arm, watching her brothers with large brown eyes as though confused.

Next to Troy was a young white girl, skinny and wearing what looked to be workout clothes. Yoga pants, his wife called them. She sat with both arms wrapped around her purse and pulled to her chest, legs crossed, shaking one foot so vigorously it caused his own seat to vibrate. For a moment he thought he recognized her. Had he worked with her before? It agitated him that he likely wouldn't remember even if he had. *So many girls. Too many women.*

He sighed, stood up to leave and caught one of the little boys just as he was about to trip over his own feet and fall. It was instinctive. He wasn't sure he'd even seen the child. The boy looked up at him. Troy watched his eyes cloud with tears and wondered if he'd grabbed his arm too tight while preventing the fall. "Gracias!" the woman said, making her way over with the girl on her hip. She grabbed the child and yanked him back to their corner of the room. The boy's face was wet but he never made a sound. Not until his brother stuck his candied hand in his face, pointed and laughed. Then the boy cried so loud that the mother tried pulling him onto her lap to join his sister who sat perched and still watching. But there wasn't enough room on the woman's small legs, so the child settled for a place standing nestled between her legs.

A few more lazy loops around and Troy found himself on the nursery floor where he watched newborns either sleeping peacefully or crying, their faces so red it looked like they were on fire. There was no in-between. Both his boys, born prematurely, had been so small you couldn't see their faces for all the cords hooked up to them supporting their breathing and keeping them hydrated and fed. He had rarely visited them those first weeks because he couldn't stand to see their tiny bodies working so hard to stay alive. When a nurse tapped the window before him, he was startled. She removed her face mask, pointed to the lone Black baby in the nursery, smiled and held her thumbs up. Troy tried to smile back just because but found he couldn't. Instead he backed away from the window and left quickly, afraid the nurse might come out and ask a question he wasn't prepared to answer.

He resumed wandering until circling back to his wife's ward. Too tired to keep walking and too drained to inquire about Maya's well-being since he was last updated, he simply stopped in the middle of the hall, pulled out his phone and dialed his mother. She picked up on the fourth ring just before it went to voicemail.

· · ·

"Mama, you got my message?"

"Hell yeah, and I been down on my knees for dem babies ever since," she said.

Troy sighed.

"See, I knew Maya was bored inside that house. An idle mind ain't nothin' but the devil's playground."

"Yeah well, the kids aiight," Troy said. "Doctors said since they got that new skin, it should heal fast with treatment. Might leave a lil discoloration though."

Troy looked down at the brown of his hands, imagining them discolored, something other than what they were.

Troy's mama sucked her teeth.

"But I just don't understand why that girl thought she had to bleach 'em when at the most she coulda just used some pressed powder. Hit the face real good and the ears and neck. See, problem most people make is they don't get they neck and chest real good. Make it all the same color."

Troy shook his head and sighed.

"Mama, that don't make no sense. Why the hell would anybody be powderin' they kids? And how you 'posed to not show they arms and hands even if you do? They kids!"

"See, thas why they gotta wear long sleeves."

"Mama, we live in Texas! It's too hot for all dat."

Why?

"OK, so you wear you some linen. Y'all can afford you some nice linen. Just not white linen cause ain't nothin worse than seeing makeup laid up against some white clothes."

"Mama."

Why had he called her?

"Worst mistake I ever made was lettin' yo Aunt Bernice borrow a white dress of mine only for her to return it with makeup along the collar and sleeves."

"Mama."

Why had he called her at all?

"I looked at that shit then looked at her and said, now what the fuck I'm 'posed to do with this, huh? You can't get no shit like that out easy with just a few washes."

"Mama."

It was yet another mistake.

"Hol up! M!"

Troy heard the faint bells of the Wheel of Fortune puzzle pieces turn.

"M, guh!"

Nooo, we're sorry. Pat Sajak said. No M.

The wheel spun.

"Mama, when's the last time you been out the house?" Troy asked.

"Wait, wait! I'm tryin to solve this puzzle," she said.

Troy looked up the hall and saw Maya's nurse making her way in his direction.

"D!" his mama called to the television.

"Mama, I gotta go," Troy said. "Imma call you back and let you know what the doctors decide."

"Aww shit, bankrupt. Now see, Black folks oughta know they can't depend on dat wheel. If you think you know it might as well go 'head and solve it cause Imma tell you right now dat wheel rigged against us."

Troy sighed.

"Mama, I gotta go, OK? Imma call you back."

"Oh! Well, OK baby, well just know I'm praying for y'all. Bernice prayin' for y'all. Ya brother said he prayin but Imma pray for him too cause I don't know nothin' bout no Allah but I know what Jesus can do!"

"OK Mama."

Troy paused. In the background the bell chimed again three times and he could see Vanna so clearly in his mind pushing the digits with thin fingers over to reveal the letters as though it were a touch pad phone.

Troy was about to hang up when he saw the nurse notice he was on the phone, turn around and walk back to the nurse's station. He paused again.

Watched the nurse walk away.

"Mama, did you ever have postpartum with us?" Troy stammered and he wasn't sure why he felt so nervous saying it aloud. "With me?" he asked.

"Postpartum?" his mama asked.

She smacked her lips so hard he could hear her gums meeting each other inside her mouth, and Troy knew why he felt anxious. He'd never asked his mama a question. Not with the expectation of an answer and certainly not about her mothering. How could he? How would he even know how to begin to?

"Like sad and shit cause I had you?" she asked.

"Yeah," he said, prepared for the verbal blowback of questioning the unquestionable.

"Well hell naw!" she said. "Wasn't no time for that. I had to work!"

Troy nodded his head as if visible to his mother, as if the question was dumb and he was dumb for asking. And maybe, somewhere deep within he believed any question was dumb because who could rely on life for answers, much less people to provide them? Who looked for honesty even in their weakest moments?

Troy. That's who.

He cringed then frowned, tried to keep from crying but still the tears ran. Ran a little more, so deep from within him, then so far away from him that he was able to watch them go.

Troy sighed again, wrestling with his emotions. And he was about to hang up the phone for real when his mama said his name in a serious way, the tone she reserved for ass-whoopins and bill collectors.

"Troy," she said. "Lemme tell you somethin' bout babies."

Troy sniffled, held it in so he was sure she couldn't hear him crying.

"Gettin' em here is the easy part," she said. "Now losing a child? Losing a child is the hardest thing in the world. A woman don't know what sad is until that happens."

Troy wanted to tell his mama it was never easy for Maya, not one single part, but he was afraid she'd hear the tears in his voice. Crying wasn't something she believed in. He didn't either but when the tears continued down his face, he didn't wipe them away.

. . .

A tall, white woman wearing thick brown glasses and bobbed hair was the one who told Troy they were releasing Maya to go home. He was confused because he'd never seen nor spoken to the woman delivering the news. She noticed the expression on his face and explained before he could ask that she was the attending counselor on duty who made the final analysis and determined continued treatment. The other doctor Maya had seen was a psychiatrist who'd diagnosed Maya with acute postpartum and prescribed anti-depressant and anti-anxiety medications. Since she'd been calm and relatively lucid for the last twelve hours they were confident that's all she needed to help her along. He wanted to ask when exactly she'd proven herself lucid because as far as he knew she'd been sedated and sleeping most of the day. He wanted to ask, What about her hitting the police officer? What about her hitting her roommate? What about the kids? Is she safe? But he simply nodded his head as the doctor reached him Maya's prescriptions and told him she'd be ready in a moment. *They don't think anything is wrong. They think it's normal to want to be white.* His thoughts were confirmed when he read in just barely legible writing on Maya's chart: *Patient was warned of the dangers of using cosmetic products on children who don't yet meet the age for proper and safe application.*

And when he saw a nurse walking Maya's former roommate Esmeralda down the hall, holding her hand and coaxing as though she were a child, *Come on Esmeralda, there'll be more chocolate tomorrow,* he only looked at her and sighed.

The woman who rode in the car with Troy was quiet, her hair a tumbleweed pulled together with a flimsy rubber band best used for tying cards or pens together. It was matted in places and in beds of soft baby curls in other places. Maya's eyes were closed and only opened when the car braked at lights and stop signs. She was so thin. When had she become so thin, he wondered. He'd grabbed the change of clothes he took to the hospital without much thought. A pair of jeans he found in one drawer and an old high-school cheerleading shirt from another. She wore them now, pants slack through her thighs and waist and shirt swallowing her upper body whole. The gown she'd worn to the hospital that night was inside a paper bag provided by the hospital. It rested at her feet like takeout.

He turned on the radio, let the voice of public radio fill the silence. Maya loved public radio. Outside, the summer sun was beginning its descent and on the radio a man said there had been another shooting. A police officer shot a Black child who appeared to wield a gun at a neighborhood park. It was only when the child was dead that police realized it was a toy. Troy lurched forward to turn the station but Maya stopped his hand at the knob.

"No," she said gently. "This is how you'll know I'm not crazy."

At home, Maya's father stood in the driveway smoking a cigarette as they pulled up, his normal conservative attire of slacks and button-ups replaced with faded denim and a T-shirt from Maya's high school days. LOBO DAD was visible on his belly, FIGHTING LOBOS on his back. He threw the cigarette to the ground as they moved to get out of the car, rubbing its butt into the pavement with his foot.

Maya reached for her seat belt and froze. "I'm not ready to see the boys," she said. "Not yet."

"It's cool," Troy said. "I got it."

But before he could shut his car door, she'd stepped out of the car and Mr. Williams was already wrapping his arms around Maya's shoulders, rubbing his large hands across her face and hair where he lingered over one of the matted parts at the base of her neck. She was barely visible inside his embrace until he pushed her back onto her heels and looked into her eyes.

"This will pass," he said. Troy made his way around to the other side of the car and saw Maya, head down, refuse to look at her dad. Mr. Williams grabbed her chin. "Do you hear me? This will pass. All of this."

Maya kept her eyes focused on the ground and Troy was struck by how childlike she appeared. It was more than the tininess of her frame, the cheer shirt and baby hairs that wisped around the edges of her face looking as soft as some of the newborns he'd watched at the hospital. And it was more than the image of her father towering over her, both gentle giant and firm parent. Maya's arms, still held within the tight grasp of her father's hands, dangled there like a child's and when she did finally meet her dad's face it was with wet eyes and a protruding bottom lip. She shook her head as if to say OK, and pushed back into her father's chest where she stood disappearing again inside his arms.

Just like the little boy, Troy thought. Just like him.

"Don't worry about the kids," Mr. Williams said. "They ate and fell asleep watching a movie." And with that Troy noticed Maya's body fully relax.

"I think I need to rest too," she said. She moved to grab the paper bag from the car but Troy beat her by two steps.

"I got it!" he said.

If Maya was startled by Troy's abruptness she didn't show it. Instead, she glanced at the bag and then back up at her father before slumbering towards the door, as if too tired to question either of them or say another word. Mr. Williams smoothed his hand across her back as she walked away and asked Troy if there was anything else that needed to be taken into the house.

Troy shook his head no and closed the passenger-side door. "I got it," he muttered. Two clicks and the alarm sounded on the car and the doors locked in unison. He turned to follow Maya's lead and found himself stopped in his tracks. Mr. Williams's large hands, so gingerly placed and comforting on Maya's body, became a brick wall against his.

"Let me talk to you for a minute, son," he said and smiled, though Troy saw no real smile.

"OK," Troy said, backing away from the pressure of Mr. Williams's hand on his chest. "Wanna go in and sit down at least?"

"Nah, I think we'll be better out here. Let Maya and the boys have some quiet."

Troy blinked. Was shit about to get loud? He was afraid to ask. He felt impositioned, vulnerable in a way he hadn't felt with another man in years. Usually, if there was about to be confrontation he anticipated it in every sense. He was mentally prepared, where it counted most, for whatever was. Now, he felt small. Too small to make much noise though he knew he'd have to face Mr. Williams eventually. He wasn't sure if it was the tears he'd cried earlier that day or his mama's words through the phone affecting him. He felt no better than the wheel, spun and stopped at someone else's hands.

In the past his interactions with Maya's father had been brief; Troy listened while Mr. Williams talked. The conversation seldom turned around to his side and he was thankful for that. He never figured he had much in common with a man who wore khakis and pastel button-ups. Whose skin was smooth and nails perpetually clean. Not even after he adopted a similar look himself.

"It's been a while," Mr. Williams said. "You and Maya rarely come back to our neck of the woods. We haven't had a chance to catch up." He stood now, resting his right leg on top of the car's bumper. Troy watched the car grow depressed under his weight, its body sinking to meet the driveway's face.

Troy reached in his hind pockets and let his fingers settle there. *I don't have anything to defend myself with. Not a thing.*

"Yeah, well," he said. "The kids are so small it's hard to travel with them. And work keeps me busy." He smiled. Tried to smile a fake smile, all teeth and no emotion. Keep it light.

"I can imagine," Mr. Williams said and he looked into the distance, at first at the melting sun and then across the street where their neighbor Bob smiled a real smile and threw up his hand in greeting. Mr. Williams grinned and nodded his head. "How ya doin?" he called. Bob picked two pieces of mail from his mailbox and called back but neither Troy or Mr. Williams could make out his words. Neither cared to try.

"Oh yeah, I've been meaning to ask how work is going for you."

"You know," Troy said. "It's a job. It does what it's supposed to do."

"Oh really? And what's that?"

Troy paused. Watched Bob walk into his house and shut the front door but not before peering at the two Black men across the street with curious eyes. Troy's mind wanted to flutter away with what he might be thinking. It was probably the most Black people he'd ever seen gathered at daylight in their community. Troy fiddled his hands inside his pants and shifted his weight from his left side to his right.

"Takes care of my family," he said. "Provides a nice home for Maya and the boys."

"Is that right?" Mr. Williams said. He looked again out into the distance, at some invisible scene only he could see. "So the shop's doin' pretty good, huh?"

"We manage pretty well," Troy said.

"So tell me this," he said. "How the fuck you managing work so well but don't know what's goin' on inside your own fuckin' house?"

Troy paused again. If anyone were listening they wouldn't have ever guessed Mr. Williams's question based on tone alone. If anyone were watching it would look like two men sharing a perfectly agreeable moment.

"Before you answer that," Mr. Williams continued. "Let me tell you somethin' my daddy used to say to me." He looked at Troy dead in the eyes and did the fake smile again and again Troy wished for a weapon. A real tool. "What's the use of making a meal if you don't know who's shittin' in your house?"

Troy cocked his head.

Mr. Williams laughed. Not a real laugh. Not a loud one. But still he grinned at Troy as though Troy were caught in something he didn't yet realize.

"That's an old folks' sayin'," he said. "But I figure it holds a lot of truth to it."

"Well, don't nobody shit at our house," Troy answered. "'Cept me, Maya and the boys."

"Uh-huh," Mr. Williams said and removed his leg from the car. He stretched for a moment, looked into the distance and back to Troy. "Wanna know what I found today while putting the boys' movie on?"

Troy hated trick questions and whatever patience he had, despite his emotional fatigue, was waning. His options were limited. This wasn't work where he might use the same language and logic he'd learned in the streets when someone tried to jerk him around. The threat of violence was almost as effective as the execution of it. Nor was this the streets where words were seldom passed and action meant everything. This was Maya's father. A man he didn't know, never thought he'd get to know and had no solid feelings on the matter either way. But still, he was Maya's father.

Dusk was easing in and above their heads the North Star already made its shiny appearance. A crescent moon formed against weakening blue skies.

"The bleach?" Troy asked. It was the worst kind of deflection, he felt even smaller for saying it aloud, but it was all he had to erase the tension and bring Mr. Williams back to the reality where his daughter had done what she'd done and he was now here because of it.

Mr. Williams flinched. It was quick, his smooth face crinkled like a wad of paper, before unfolding itself. "Nah," he said slowly and motioned for Troy to follow him with his fingers. They moved towards the front door, Troy's hands still tucked away at his behind and the wolf on Mr. Williams's back growling with pointed teeth at Troy, at the moon. He stopped at the bushes resting alongside the front door and stooped down, reaching for what appeared to Troy's eyes like a book at first. It was only when he stood up, and brushed off the residual dirt on the object's surface that Troy recognized what it was. A movie. One of *his* movies.

Big Breasts, Hot Chests. Even in the dim light, Troy made out the title in large red letters punctuated by a woman's large white titties and a man's rock-hard pecs. He made the flick over a year ago just before Thanksgiving. There was even a scene where he had the actor say "Ain't nothin like dark meat, baby, but I love me some breasts too!"

He thought it was clever at the time.

Troy smiled. Mr. Williams was making it too easy. "Aww, Mr. Williams, every man likes to watch a few movies sometimes."

"Big-breasted white women huh?"

"Sometimes," Troy said and shrugged.

"And what about this?" Mr. Williams turned the box over and pointed at its bottom half. Day was almost gone and Troy could barely see the writing Mr. Williams pushed into his face but his heart sank when he realized Mr. Williams had figured it out.

The Rise of Troy pictures emblem was nothing but the silhouette of a man with an erect penis. He thought it was clever at the time. He'd even made T-shirts, cups and keychains with the image and words The Rise of Troy: Real Res-erection stamped on it. Maya laughed when she'd seen it.

Troy didn't say a word. He made and produced the movies but the operation was financed and distributed by a wealthy Ukrainian man. His name, however, was not in the least bit traceable to any of their dealings.

"What?" Mr. Williams said. "Cat got your tongue? Matter of fact I think I saw another movie called somethin' like that too."

This was also true. *Cat Got Your Tongue* was filmed last fall. It was a lesbian flick and managing all the ladies to get it done had nearly drove him mad.

Troy sighed. He really couldn't think of anything to say and so he didn't. He pulled his hands from his back pockets and folded his arms, as if deep in thought. And finally allowed his body to rest against the wall behind him.

"Shit, boy, I'd say you look like someone got your balls to the wall huh?"

"OK, OK!" Troy stopped him before he could name another picture. *Balls to the Wall* had an all-male cast and they'd been as difficult as the women. "So I make movies. It's legal, man. It's a job like any other."

"Like any else?"

Troy shrugged. Let his arms dangle at his side.

"I'm sorry we lied to you," he said.

Mr. Williams hit the wall right at Troy's face so quickly and with so much force Troy jumped. "Don't throw Maya into your shit! If she did anything she agreed to lie to protect your trifling ass!" He stood in front of Troy with his finger pointing at his chest where his hand once was. "You think I ever believed that bullshit story about a car shop, boy? What the fuck you take me for? You got to get up real early to fool a man like me and you always struck me as the type who like to sleep in. You want shit the easy way!"

Troy couldn't move. His arms dangled and his chest began to hurt just from the heat of Mr. Williams's attention. He was sweating. He felt a trickle of water make its way down his face and made no move to gather it. Mr. Williams wasn't loud. Troy was sure no one could hear his berating other than the two of them, but the way he spoke through clenched teeth and angry face was more intimidating than volume or a blow to the stomach, which Troy wasn't entirely sure wasn't still coming.

"Mr. Williams, I . . ."

"You what? You brought my daughter down here to this goddamn big city! Always sunny except when it rains and floods, right? Always beaches and bullshit! And you left her to fend for herself while you go film people fucking! You left her and your own damn kids to make a dollar sittin' on your ass with a camera while others did all the work!"

Mr. Williams was so close to Troy now he could feel his breath on his face. His spittle met Troy's sweat and merged somewhere at his chin.

"Hell, I knew what you were into, Troy! I know a street nigga when I see one. But I also knew if Maya saw somethin' in you, you might prove worthwhile. But now look at my baby! Look at your babies!" Mr. Williams stuck his finger now firmly in Troy's chest and held it there. "This shit happened on your watch!"

It was the blow he'd been waiting for and it rocked him to the core. When his tears came for the second time that day, they were too hot and too fast to mask or stop. And when he gasped for air because his throat was too tight to breathe and more tears threatened to choke him, he twisted his body side to side against the wall and grabbed his knees for support. He expected Mr. Williams to really let him have it now but Troy didn't care. He was too small and too hurt to care.

For a while, Mr. Williams stood listening to Troy's cries gradually become sniffles. When the boy doubled over in tears he was taken aback. He wasn't sure what he expected, if anything, so concentrated as he was on being heard above all else, until he realized the boy needed to cry, and judging by the way his tears coursed violently through his whole body, he imagined the boy had needed to cry for some time. So he stood patiently, resting his own body against the opposite stucco wall, and he let the boy cry. When the blackness of night consumed them and all that was left were the sound of crickets and the dim glow of the streetlight, they both stood saying nothing. In fact, they were both quiet for a long while before Mr. Williams shifted, rubbed those palms across his face and said:

"You know who introduced Maya to all those books she like to read?"

Troy said nothing.

"When she was a little girl, I read to her about existence. Wasn't no see Jane run, see the dog run in our house. I taught her *I am.* I am because. I will be forever because *I am.*"

Troy shifted his weight and pulled himself up to stand upright again. He couldn't make out Mr. Williams's shape in the dark though he was very close, his voice seemingly emanating from a void. He smiled, though, sad and tender. Maya once told him those exact words when they first met. *I am because. I will be forever because I am.*

"See, I wanted Maya to find truth during her life. To make sense of this reality and transcend it. To learn even more than me. She was a seeker."

"She is a seeker," Troy said, nodding his head. "She is."

"How would you know anymore, son? You haven't been paying attention."

Troy sighed and threw his head up against the wall.

"You know what she told me when she met you?"

Troy didn't answer.

"She said, 'Dad, he's a seeker too. His path just looks different.'"
Troy's eyes welled up again.

"And I believed her because I trusted her." Mr. Williams paused. "I still do. That's why I tell her all this will pass."

In the darkness, Troy held his hands to his face, for comfort. For some privacy while he released fresh tears. But he lowered them, with resistance at first when he felt Mr. Williams pull him by his neck and hands into his chest and invited him to nestle there, crying in peace.

"Ain't nothing new under the sun, and the shit goin' on now in the news damn sure ain't new," he said, holding Troy inside the tightest hug he could manage. "This will all pass, son. All of it. But you gotta make some changes."

Troy thought he would find Maya sleeping when he approached their bedroom. There was a light visible beneath the door, but he figured she'd gone to sleep with the television on as normal. He turned around and went to the bathroom in the hallway, washed his face. He looked in on the children, sprawled across their beds. Amari had the sheets wound around his legs. Spiderman dipped to the ground and scaled walls across his abdomen. Troy was tempted to move closer, try to see again the red burns scattered over the child's body but opted not to. When he saw Jaden cooing in his sleep with the overhead mobile, a spinning bunch of mystical animals, owls, unicorns and lions, illuminating his tiny face, Troy felt content.

Maya lay in the bed still wearing her cheer shirt. On the television, CNN repeatedly played the grainy image of the little boy in the park bewildered and overwhelmed by police and then dead; his small body appearing a black spot on the screen.

"It almost looks like a video game, doesn't it?" Her eyes were transfixed on the TV, its light illuminating her face and reminding Troy how very much Amari looked just like her.

"I think you should get some rest." Troy sat on the bed and started to remove his pants, one lazy leg at a time. He reached for the remote but Maya held it out of his reach.

"I just want to see one more thing," she said.

"What?" Troy pulled off his shirt and smelled himself. He was too tired to shower.

"I wanna see his mom," Maya said. "I wanna see if they'll show her tonight."

Troy leaned back against the headboard, enjoying the coolness of the pillows against his bare skin. He wanted to pull Maya to him but was scared she might not want that. She had that intensity in her eyes, the kind he'd seen for years now and pretended he hadn't.

"She's prolly too upset to be all on TV already," he said.

"Yeah," Maya said and looked at him as if acknowledging his actual presence in the room for the first time. "You're right."

She hit the volume, turning the television down rather than off and inched over to Troy's body. He lifted an arm, welcoming her into himself.

They lay there quiet. Troy let his mind find the relaxation the rest of his body enjoyed; the light from the TV still offering sparks and shadows behind his closed eyes.

"Troy?" Maya said. Her voice was soft.

"Yeah?" he replied.

"What book were you looking for that day?"

Troy moved his legs under the covers. The coolness of the sheets felt like an ocean of sensations. He couldn't get enough of how good it felt to lie down. He flexed his toes and let them go.

"What day, baby?"

"The day we met."

Troy remembered. He could never forget. *Finding Ast.* It was a book about Ancient Nubia and matriarchal societies throughout Africa. He was especially intrigued by the idea God was a woman. His sister had been killed not long before and he wanted to know she might be some-where in heaven with a Mama God. Perhaps a mama who would be there and protect her in ways their mother did not. He could never forget because he'd never found it. The day he met Maya he forgot all about that book.

"I don't remember what it was called, baby." He yawned and stretched his legs again. "That was a long time ago."

Maya shifted away from his arms and leaned towards the television; the mother of the boy now in front of the cameras, dazed, confused. So many tears. Maya cried. The woman cried and when Maya went to wipe her face, she wasn't entirely sure if the tears belonged to her or the mother she lay watching.

"Yeah," she said and closed her eyes. "It was."

PART III

You do not deserve love regardless of the suffering you have endured. You do not deserve love because somebody did you wrong. You do not deserve love just because you want it. You can only earn—by practice and careful contemplation—the right to express it and you have to learn how to accept it.

—TONI MORRISON

An Autobiography of Skin

What was Lena doing when the phone call came in?

Well, what was she normally doing in the hours just before dawn?

Same ole.

Night fell over the room with the sort of silence reserved for darkness. Two silhouettes danced against teal walls, rigid bodies jerking and releasing. Jerking and releasing. Marcel was astride her body, cupping her wiry yellow legs between the lean bulk of his hairy brown arms, his eyes turned toward the loft-beamed ceiling, his mouth stretched taut in an O. As in *Oh baby right there. Oh baby that's it. Oh yeah. Oh yeah* . . .

While Lena's face had been drawn in a straight line, a grimace; a weak moment filled with false baby-like whispers and compliance. *Yes, yes . . . that's it,* she cooed.

When it wasn't. It wasn't the spot. Wasn't pleasure. Wasn't feel good. Wasn't love.

L-O-V-E.

Or maybe it was and she'd forgotten the fact. Or maybe it was and she'd yet to remember that love sometimes meant faking it for the sake of keeping it real. Real being love. Real meaning accepting the very firm ego and flaccid penis that was her husband's. True love being receiving the hard pink plastic strapped to his thin waist that was the dildo replacement for his manhood. Had been so for almost five years.

Oh oh . . . is that it baby?

Yes, yes . . . right there!

Their sex was a kind of game of tic-tac-toe and she was content to let his O's win it every time. Her own invisible X marking a spot he hadn't reached in years, even before the cancer.

So you ask what was Lena doing when the phone call came in?

Well, what was she normally doing in the hours just before dawn?

Same ole.

When the phone rang, she reached for it with the enthusiasm of a child released from the cold confines of the classroom to recess. Quite simply, it was a break.

Whew! Lord have mercy!

Marcel slid off her body with the resignation and authority of a referee granting a time-out.

Whew! Lord have mercy on her!

The call was from California, a whole two hours behind Texas, and so how would the caller have known and, given the circumstances, why should he have cared that he was disrupting a moment in love?

L-O-V-E.

Besides, Uncle Sonny had died while using the toilet just like Elvis, and having no children of his own, his sister's kids were the closest living kin to notify.

Marcel turned on the bedside light, a lamp no bigger than the fullness of his arm; dainty and quaint, casting a yellow glow against his brown skin. He cleared his throat one good time and took the phone from Lena, feigning as if he'd been asleep.

"Marcel, man it's Rodney," the voice blared. "I hate deliverin news like this over the phone. But I figure you was the best person to notify first."

"What happened?" Marcel rubbed his eyes and reached for his glasses as though it might help him hear better.

"It's Sonny," Rodney said. "Heart attack, man. He got up from eatin at the table and they say he fell over in the bathroom."

"Is that right?" Marcel swung his legs over the side of the bed now, feeling the soft fibers of the carpet beneath his feet.

"Thas right, man. He gone, man. Just like dat."

There was a pause.

"So when you think you can get out here?"

Marcel paused.

In the background, in a voice that was sharp and clear, traveling the distance from coast to mid-country, cross wires, and equally blasting through the phone's speaker was the sound of Aunt Bee, Sonny's wife, like a high-school cheerleader, praising the Lord with all her might.

"Yes, Lawd Jesus!" she cried. "Hallelujah! Hallelujah!"

Marcel frowned.

"Thank you, Jesus! Oh, thank you, Lord!"

Lena heard her voice and winced. She held the covers closer to her body, afraid to say or even admit to herself that she recognized the emotion though she had not yet experienced its high.

Jubilation. Shouting much like Lena had seen at the Pentecostal church when she was a girl. When she had no understanding of the Holy Spirit. No way of pretending to grasp the sight of big-bodied Black women and skinny Black men in ill-fitting suits, stomping flailing, then running about the church house, first around the pulpit circling the minister as a vulture does a corpse, soaring, praising, hollering with shouts that mesmerized small children who didn't understand what they saw. Did not recognize glory. Glory.

Glory!

They'd remove their shoes, thick bodies gyrating to their own inner rhythms, to drums, to the sound of the organ's heavy tones. To some mystical beat inside themselves that caused them to run, run, run laps around the church house pews as if on a field track. And they wouldn't quit. Wouldn't stop until they'd spread their lips and spoke in tongues. That twisted dance in their mouths, that ancient language only some were blessed to know. When they spoke that speech, arms raised to the heavens, pointed to the cross posted on the walls before them, flailing.

When they fell to their knees, eyes twisted, mouths foamed with words, words—magical gibberish—it was only then they'd calm. Bodies exalted on high and delivered back to themselves. They'd lie on the raw red carpet of the church until the music simmered like the Sunday soup that awaited them at home. And then, very low. Very soft and without shame they'd cry. Humbled. As though children themselves, their sniffling matching that of the babies who within they'd aroused fear.

Real fear.

Lena held herself under the sheets, the cool sweat and K-Y jelly between her legs moist and slick, out of place inside the moment.

"What do you expect me to do?" Marcel's voice was mean though he tried to hide his agitation. "And whas wrong with her? Why she screaming and carryin on like that?"

"Whatchu mean whas wrong with her? She ninety-seven years old and just lost her husband. Thas whas wrong!"

Rodney sound scared to Lena's ears, his voice low under the calls and shouts of Aunt Bee. And it was as if he were both trying to hide her strange calls and conceal his own fear, but he was failing.

Lena felt it. Marcel felt it.

Aunt Bee shouted again, "Thank you, Jesus!" and the unspoken was confirmed: Jubilation punctuated with another hallelujah.

"Look here, man," Rodney said. "Don't you think the family oughta see bout her?"

"Who is that?" Lena hissed at Marcel. He cupped the phone receiver with one big hand and hissed back, "Shhh . . . it's Uncle Sonny neighbor Rodney!"

He frowned under the lamp's light and pulled his body further erect towards the bed's mahogany headboard, folding his legs on the bed now.

"Whas she sayin?" he asked even though he knew, could hear her as well as Lena could some ten inches away, where she sat huddled in the pale of the moonlight spit harshly from an adjacent window.

"Who her?" Rodney asked, then cleared his throat. "Man, don't pay her no mind. She ain't been right in the head in a long time, man. Her brain like a spider web. Silky but weak. Thas why you gotta come see bout her."

And at that moment the pink plastic dildo, still moist and warm with the heat of Lena's insides, slid from the bed's silk sheets and hit the floor with a loud and abrupt thud. Lena jumped, pulling the covers closer to her nakedness, moving ever so slightly closer to Marcel. He glanced at her with eyes that said *Pick it up!* And so she hurried out of the bed to do so.

"Look man," Marcel said. "I work. I can't just drop everything and fly out to California."

"Marcel man, this your uncle wife! Somebody got to see bout her. Somebody got to tend to business. Now I would but I ain't blood. My hands tied."

In the background Aunt Bee cried, "Oh thank you, Lord! You heard my prayer." Her shriek still strong but shorter.

Marcel sat still as a rock. Lena watched him from the bathroom where she stood washing the dildo. She couldn't help but notice the sturdiness of his back, the ways his ears appeared bigger in the dim light, his face twisted with confusion and fear. Aunt Bee's cries sent shivers across his arms and chest, where the coarse black hairs stood firm—goose bumps illuminated by the moon's glow.

And with that same confusion traveling through his voice, eyes, in the way he cradled the phone's receiver like it might get away from him if he relaxed, he spoke calmly; every decibel in his voice betraying the sight she saw.

"OK, OK," he said. "We'll figure something out," he said.

When he hung up the phone he reached for Lena who stood beside the bed replacing the dildo in its proper place inside the nightstand, underneath an old white handkerchief that had once belonged to Marcel's father. It twirled around its edges in small elaborate circles.

He pulled her very gently to him, and she melted naturally into his arms.

"Aunt Bee?" she whispered.

But he was quiet. So very quiet. Until finally he said, "Nah, she alright. Uncle Sonny is gone."

She didn't bother to say she realized the difference, but instead crawled back into bed and gathered him in her arms, wrapping those wiry yellow legs around his lean body once again until he slept. Breathing slowed. Light snores bubbling from his mouth. Nose.

And she looked at the teal walls. Watched the light of the moon throw itself against the corners of the room, against her skin and thought to herself, just before falling into a fitful sleep,

Lord had mercy on her. Lord had mercy.

But the Lord did not yet have mercy on Lena.

Who took care of Aunt Bee? I say, who took care of Aunt Bee after she arrived at the door a crumpled pile of brown skin and bones? Dentures hanging from the top of her mouth, hair the most beautiful shade of white, eyes bloodshot but bright. Bright as the morning sun.

I say, who took care of her when she stumbled through the door in her polyester clothes smelling like cheap perfume, liquor and mothballs?

Who took care of Aunt Bee, bathing her some days when she found her own weight too heavy to hold in the shower, or she was too drunk to stand? When she was too disoriented to wash her breasts, her behind and most private place? Who washed her sheets and changed them after she soiled them in the middle of night, using the special detergent necessary so her fragile, loose skin wouldn't break out in hives or rash? Who did this faithfully after feeding and cooking her breakfast? Lunch? Dinner? And when she had bad dreams and cried out in the middle of the night, or the afternoon hours, for her mother who'd long ago departed from the Earth, who rushed to comfort her? And when she needed her morning cocktail, her midday mixer, her nighttime toddy, who made sure the liquor remained plentiful and always stashed away?

Brown stuff at night. Clear during the day.

And who prepared the drinks in Aunt Bee's favorite glass, and washed it with her other dirty and sodden dishes?

Who?

Well, who do you think?

. . .

You see, once Marcel declined to fly across skies and see about Uncle Sonny's business and Aunt Bee's well-being, no one was left but his two sisters who begrudgingly climbed their asses on a cheap flight and made the trip. And to their own satisfaction, and pleasant surprise, it was not in vain.

For within Sonny and Bee's ramshackle Tudor-style home was plenty of dust, to be sure, but also plenty of money. Trash bags, to be clear. Tucked away in mysterious corners, underneath floors where aged hardwood had long ago started to crack and give. Up in closets so deep, so dark only shadows lived there. There were bags of $20,000 hidden like Easter eggs—discreet yet haphazardly stored. Because after all these were huge Hefty black trash bags.

But such was the fortune of old age. When no one cared to look anymore at the strange and unusual creatures placed around a home that smelled of impending death. Not to the visible. Not to the hidden. Not even to them.

When Yvette and her younger sister Bonnie walked in they frowned first at Aunt Bee's drunkenness before helping themselves to some of her gin. It was 1:00 p.m. Aunt Bee was sipping her clear, midday tonic of gin like it was water and so fuck it, they did too.

When Bonnie lifted the musty Moroccan rug creeping towards the bathroom door, it was first because it caught her fancy. *My my,* she thought. *This would look awfully nice in my dining room.* And when Yvette said, "Now wait a minute, Bonnie, you can't go taking everything you see just cause you like it," only because she hadn't seen the rug first, they'd began to quarrel. Pushing and tugging at the ends of the rug while Aunt Bee giggled like a girl, watching with red eyes half closed. When Yvette yanked one more good time, and because her weight bested Bonnie's by ten extra pounds she sent Bonnie flying, damn near busting her ass only to reveal a hard lump in the brown floors where the wood jumped from smooth and worn to tilted and humped.

And there it was. They dug out the bag, coughing and struggling with its heft, careful for any spiders or rodents, and looked inside, their plump sweaty faces glistening in the afternoon light.

"Uh-ohhhh . . . ," Aunt Bee called. "Y'all done done it now!" And she cackled, her giggle turning grown, voice low and deep with intoxication.

Bonnie ripped the bag's mouth open further and Yvette grunted, "Easy Bon-Bon, easy." Then, "Hot damn! Hot damn!"

The bundles of green bills were as rank as the rug, dense and dusty as the rest of the home's shabby interior. But they smiled, then grinned like two Cheshire cats. "Hot damn!" Bonnie yelled.

"Cheers!" Aunt Bee slurred from the hallway.

Soon after they called Marcel and said with sly smiles, "Don't worry, brother, we got this! Don't worry bout a thing!" And Marcel had breathed a sigh of relief, the burden successfully removed from his hands, and gone back to poking at Lena's bruised and sullen vagina.

Yvette and Bonnie stayed in California almost a month, each without a job to report to and both with passive husbands who paid the bills. They put Uncle Sonny in the ground while dragging dry tissue across their faces. They kept Bee tipsy, inebriated to the point of compliance so that her weird shouts of joy almost looked like grief. They opened a new bank account and began quietly making deposits, all the while asking family members for financial help with burial expenses. Pouring on guilt trips as thick as syrup. Dabbing at their crumpled faces that looked on the verge of tears, breaking their voices at just the precise moments.

And just when it seemed the gods wouldn't, couldn't do them any better. When it seemed every bottled and pent-up genie existing in the world had not a wish left to grant, they happened upon another great fortune.

You see, because Sonny and Bee lived on the West Coast, no more than a twenty-minute drive to the beach. Because they lived in an old Black neighborhood that had been Black since the late '40s, when they'd finally saved enough money for the blue-trimmed house on the corner with the sole palm tree out front that made them think of dai-quiris. And because that same neighborhood had begun to change in the last five years of Sonny's life, and the old soul food joint had turned into a coffee house. And the Latin market had become a Whole Foods. And the public schools were now chartered institutions with "magnet" in their names. No longer Paul Robeson Academy. No longer Fred-erick Douglass High. And because in the mornings, before the sun even opened its eyes and yawned good morning, white people could be found jogging and walking miniature-sized dogs that looked like they barely had enough leg to walk with much less needed the walk-ing. And too, and most importantly, because though half an hour on the expressway without traffic from the Pacific Ocean, the distance did little to discourage eager buyers hoping to move closer to the water. That one substance that Black folks had a healthy respect for, perhaps their own genetic memories holding different ways of looking at the shores, even if it weren't the Atlantic. Because after all, weren't it all the same body?

But, not so for white folks who kayaked, surfed, swam, drank and sun-bathed at the ocean's lips. Whose only watery memories took them back to birth, to the warm cocoon of the womb.

And these differences meant a lot for the pockets of Yvette and Bonnie who were able to sell the tiny house in a place still referred to as "the hood" to a young white couple for so much more money than they ever figured it was worth that they couldn't help but laugh at what they assumed was the white couple's ignorance.

"For shame," they snickered. "Put a little water and salt in the air and white folks take like kittens to catnip!"

No one in the family asked a question nor said a word, content with their own summation of the truth which was: Aunt Bee was crazy as a Betsy bug. Uncle Sonny, God bless his old cheating scandalous ass soul, was gone. And nothing they ever had could be worth much. Both Sonny and Bee known drunkards prone to fighting at the full moon. Both Sonny and Bee older than the four scores and ten God promised. Both never having made a living doing little more than what equaled domestic work. He was a shoeshine man down at the county courthouse who took to fixing shoes later in life. She was a teacher's aide to the so-called at-risk kids at Frederick Douglass, never having attained the necessary degree to run the classroom though she'd basically done as much for thirty-five years. He never attaining no papered degree at all though he could tell you more about a man's soul just by looking at the condition of the soles of his shoes.

Nah. Nobody expected much from them two. And Bonnie and Yvette didn't hip nobody to the wiser. Didn't say a word until the lawyer made the mistake of calling Marcel one day asking for his signature on an affidavit. Till he told a stunned Marcel that Aunt Bee was worth close to a million dollars. "Didn't you know," he asked innocently, "the house alone brought in almost $600,000?"

Nah. Marcel didn't know. But he called Yvette, who feigned ignorance and sweetly said, "Whatchu talmbout brother?" Then angrily said, "Well if you care so much why ain't you come see bout her?"

To which Marcel said, "You know what? Bring her here to stay here. Our house big enough."

To which Yvette, then Bonnie both excitedly agreed. After all, they shared power of attorney duties now. And they had the trash bag money that no one knew a peep about. And truth was, they had Aunt Bee whom neither wished to have responsibility for. They couldn't stick her in a nursing home. Hell nah, they'd sop up her money like a biscuit do gravy.

Marcel had a big house. Marcel had Lena. She'd do.

"Hmph," Yvette said to Marcel. "OK, she'll stay with y'all but me and Bon gon continue to handle the business."

"Hmph," Marcel said. "Well we gon need a lil somethin to help take care of her every month."

Yvette sat quiet. Yvette thought long.

"Yeah, OK," she answered. "Me and Bon see y'all have a lil somethin every month to tend to her right."

Marcel grinned.

Yvette grinned.

And an agreement was reached.

"You know we wouldn't try and cut you out, lil brother," Yvette cooed.

But Marcel was already too busy making plans to acknowledge her triflingness. Lena would have to do this and do that. Do this and do that. But she'd do it. She always did.

He hung up the phone never bothering to tell Lena a word. So when Aunt Bee arrived, as fragile as an ant bed and as high as a kite, Lena had only looked at Marcel first confused, then understanding. He'd been working on converting the guest bedrooms on the west wing of the house into a small apartment for weeks. Now it made sense.

Resigned. Dejected and too accustomed to the bullshit to be angry, she only sighed and helped Aunt Bee to her room. To her new home.

She'd taken care of her that night, answering her questions like a mother would her child when Aunt Bee sobered and homesick asked, "Where am I? Who are you?"

She'd tucked her in like a baby and sat watching her by the light of a blue candle until she slept. And she had done as much and more ever since. By herself.

She was doing as much on the day we arrived. It was raining. Clouds pregnant with darkness, the air heavy and sad.

When Lena opened the door she looked skinnier than we'd ever seen, the synthetic ringlets of her latest wig glossy and stiff at her shoulders. There was no movement at all when she shook her head, hurried and distracted, and said, "Come on in for y'all get wet!"

"I like listening to the birds at night," she said.

We were sitting on the patio out back. Lena was nursing her third glass of white wine and my mama her second cigarette. They moved gently back and forth on the porch swing, and I sat in front of them in a white plastic chair, head thrown back watching the stars.

"You always liked the birds," my mama said, taking a long pull from her Kool Light.

"Yeah," Lena hummed. "Yeah."

I was high as shit. I listened to the birds chirp, whistle, call. Once the rain slacked, I'd snuck to the side of the house and pulled the marijuana from my pipe twice. Deeply. Taking the smoke inside my lungs like it might give me life. The burn providing clarity. Relief. And now the stars looked like home, and Mama's and Lena's voices sounded just as distant as the stars looked.

I wasn't there.

Truth was, I was heartbroken. Had been so almost three years and so it had become one of those quiet things that everyone knew but learned to ignore. My somberness familiar and no longer interesting or cause for concern. And the stars? My god, the stars were a sanctuary. The sound of the birds like music, and I wondered what they were talking about. And I wondered why I couldn't talk to them, certain they might understand what no other human had thus far shown a capacity for comprehending which was how very deeply I was hurting. Disappearing each day to a foreign place inside myself that I was convinced was like the moon, or some galaxy unlike where the Earth resided.

So many nights spent at home mourning and writing shitty poetry.

I feel you birds, I do. I thought. But I was high. High as fuck, and who knows what they thought of my pitiful energy.

"How long she been here?" my mama asked.

"Bout three months."

"Three months?!" Mama jumped a lil, her weight momentarily ceasing the swing's rock. "How come you ain't told nobody?"

"Tell anybody what? That we keeping Beatrice?" Lena took another sip, her long acrylic nails briefly tapping her wine glass and creating a shallow ring that to my elevated mind sounded like chimes. Bells, light and sweet, that coupled with the birds' chirps created a magic in the air.

"What for?" she continued. "What's there to tell?"

"Well, maybe some of the family could of helped you and Marcel."

My mama's voice was higher than usual and I looked up, searching for her silhouette in the darkness of the patio and saw only a stream of smoke where she sat.

"Hmph," Lena said bitterly. "When Marcel ever helped with shit but himself? When?"

Lena always had a habit of asking things twice in a way and with a finality that meant there was no answer at all.

We sat quietly. There was no moon and the birds went silent. A wind blew across our bodies and the rain commenced again, cold drops falling as rain had a tendency to do. Slow. Full. Teeming with possibility, mysterious in its intention. Would it be a gentle thing or become a storm? We did not know.

I leaned back and felt the water fall against my face and imagined a baptism. Tilting my face further back, I was willing. Ready to be saved from everything.

Mama and Lena picked up their conversation, tucked safely away from precipitation, the swing placed solidly under a canopied covering. Their voices, murmurs, distorted songs with simple lyrics like "Hell nah," and "Fuck that," and "Girl, he ain't shit."

I popped my earphones in and set my player to a Minnie Riperton song and began to move towards the clouds beyond the rain, and thunder—where I suppose the birds had retreated to a place warm and dry, free of sentiment. But not before hearing "You know they say Aunt Bee did somethin to him."

"Did somethin like wha?" Mama asked, her voice thick with mucus and smoke.

"I dunno," Lena said, drinking. "Put somethin on him."

"Somethin like wha?"

Lena drank, and drank again letting her pause grow the suspense, allowing the rain to fill the blank spots with intrigue.

"Roots."

When she finally spoke it was without emotion or thought. Voice plain save for the wine, her piss-colored beverage almost depleted, glass going as empty as her voice sound.

"Marcel say folks whispering she the one who did it. Planted a seed. Stopped his heart."

"But why?" Mama cried and I could hear the horror in her voice. She preferred not to acknowledge the supernatural. Hoodoo was something we prayed against, refusing to absolutely believe in but we crossed our hearts and burnt candles just in case a nigga would. And it sounded like Aunt Bee had.

Lena shrugged. My eyes made out the slim rounds of her shoulders travel up, then down as if in slow motion. She took another drink, the last bit of her wine. Beside the house I heard the gurgle of the drainage pipe swallow and deliver a stream of rain into the grass, creating a muddy slush.

"They say he wasn't nice."

"Well goddamn!" Mama exclaimed. "Who in this world is? If thas all it take we should all be dead!"

Hell yeah, I thought. *Hell yeah.* Then closed my eyes and faded into the rain, now falling harder, heavier, lightning filling the skies above our heads with its disapproval.

Sleep that night didn't come easy.

Lena and Marcel's house was big. Huge. Some say especially so for the east side of San Antonio, where it sat like a Christmas tree most nights—all seven bedrooms, sun room, theater room, formal dining room and den alive with light. Lena kept all the lights on cause most evenings she was there alone. Marcel at work and . . . other places.

If you looked out the east window upstairs during the daylight hours and squinted real hard you could just make out the housing projects where Marcel grew up; ugly brown tops of the buildings clustered together like a brick stain on the neighborhood. Which was an old Black neighborhood, small wood frame homes, liquor stores, hair depots and dollar stores. Poor. Black. Old.

And then there was Lena nem's house. Mansionesque. New money. How did they afford it?—what with Lena, a retired social worker, and Marcel a former UPS man. That's what all the neighbors asked until word finally hit the streets.

It was simple. An easy, unromantic though fateful tale.

They say one day while making a delivery to a bakery on the north side of town Marcel was hit by a FedEx truck while crossing the street. He had the right-of-way, though apparently bad timing, and afterward he also had back problems, neck problems, pain through his shoulders; said he had trouble sleeping at night cause his legs had developed restless syndrome. Related to his trauma, his doctor later testified, and after a year and some change he'd limped outta the courtroom with a fine settlement.

"The Lord blessed you!" his sisters cried, and he wasn't sure if they meant the fact he'd survived the accident or that it happened at all and as consequence brought with it a small fortune. Deep down in that small place where intuition lived, he was sure they were referring to both. And he agreed. Wholeheartedly. He got blessed!

So their home sat upon a flat two-acre lot smack in the middle of the hood, an unchanging, unyielding area where residents were still too tough and gang activity too high for gentrifiers to bravely bulldoze their way in.

When asked why they chose to build in a place where winos and Black kids routinely paced the streets, some even spitting at the gaudy red brick house with the huge Civil War cannon on the front lawn, Lena would say it was because Marcel didn't intend to forget where he came from. My mama spit her food into her napkin the first time she heard this reasoning and said, "Well damn you ain't gotta forget to remember!"

It didn't make sense to nobody but Marcel. All of his sisters had married good and hightailed it to the north side, always careful when crossing the streets because as Yvette told me the first time we met, "You know white folks can run over a nigga and not get nothin but probation." She sucked on a chicken wing bone, and wiped her greasy fingers against her jeans.

"Yes baby," she went on. "Keep a sharp eye when you out there in dem streets, especially for white women in minivans and SUVs with children in the back." She bit into another chicken wing, pulling down her blouse that was beginning to creep over the first, then second soft rolls of her belly. "Dem the worst ones!"

But all I could think, though I said nothing, was *Hell, we in Texas! Who the fuck walking around here?*

I couldn't sleep.

I sat looking out the window down on the street where even in the rain, two old Black men stood under the streetlight, black hoodies pulled tight around their faces. They were sharing a cigarette. I could tell the difference by how the smoke rose in the air like a white sheet that blanketed their brown faces before crawling out into the night in search of better things.

I was wondering what they were discussing, trying to decipher their body movements, mostly subtle steps side to side as if anxious; determined to ignore the fact they were soaked with rain. And because I was still faintly high, I wished them too a baptism that would keep them safe.

I was thinking this as my mama lay snoring, straddled across the bed, the sheets twisted about her round middle parts—Lena's house was big and I'd never felt comfortable sleeping there alone.

I was thinking this when I heard a piercing scream. Like something primal and from the gut of a person, and nothing I'd ever heard outside of movies.

My mother shot straight up in the dark and reached for me—motherly instincts a driving force.

"Ketinah!" she called.

"Shhh . . . ," I whispered. "I'm right here."

Screams rang out again, followed by the rush of footsteps. The sound of a door flung open hitting the wall with a boom. Then more screaming.

And because I was faintly high, I was calm and unafraid. I moved gingerly, eyes having adjusted to the black of the room, towards the door. My mom reached for the bedside lamp and I stopped her with a quick hissing of my teeth.

"Stay here," I said.

· · ·

I followed the rise and fall of voices downstairs and around corners, down a long hallway. There was little light save for the sliver of yellow that shone from the crack of the door. More screams. I flinched. Felt goose bumps spread down my arms, tickling the back of my neck. I kept walking till I found the door's handle and twisted slow then pushed slow until I made a view for myself.

There on the floor, in the corner of the room, was Aunt Bee. Hair like a white mushroom, wild upon her head. Brown body like a small package discarded and unopened. She had her legs pulled to her chest, nightgown around her knees. She was bare between her legs, delicate flesh smooth as a baby's skin. She lashed her arms about, hitting Lena hard against the side of her face, causing blood to gather beneath the skin turning her cheek a rosy pink.

"Get away! Get the fuck away from me!" Aunt Bee yelled, and my eyes moved from Lena's blood-flushed face to Bee's red gums. No teeth. Lips puckered, face swallowing itself. Words an ugly lisp, tongue thick, and still she yelled.

"Sonny, I told you thas the last time you lay a hand on me!" Tears streamed down her face.

"Aunt Bee," Lena said, struggling to contain her. "It's OK, baby."

She grabbed one arm then another, each time Aunt Bee's swings stopping her from reaching in and maintaining a hold.

I ran to her side and without a word, reached for Aunt Bee's right arm, suggesting with eyes and a nod of my head that Lena grab her left.

If Lena was surprised to see me there was no time to show it. Aunt Bee's eyes, as round and buck and wild as her hair, took me in, frantically searching my face for answers and recognition.

"Get him off me!" she cried.

"I will!" I said, grasping her hand, then shoulder. "I will!"

Lena secured her other side and we sat there on the floor acting as a human straitjacket.

Bee began to rock, crying, legs lowered and bent. Her flannel gown idled at the top of her slim thighs and I reached and pulled it down with one quick jerk.

"Look what he done to me?" She raised her leg again, revealing a purple bruise, deformed but large in a shape that wove its way around her thigh.

"He won't stop," she cried softly, whimpering, her chest heaving, body still rocking. "He ain't ever gon stop is he?"

She looked at me with the saddest eyes I'd ever seen. So sad. So deep. An endless brown pool of hurt and anger. Goose bumps returned. And it was as if she were genuinely awaiting my answer, some resolution, comfort, and I found my words gone down into my feet which felt deathly cold. I found my breath gone and eyes burning till her little brown toothless face became a blur. A haze. A blue. A red. A fragment of light.

"Shhh . . . he gone, Aunt Bee. He gone now, baby." Lena rocked their bodies in sync as though rowing across waters.

"He gone," she repeated.

I was too busy crying to speak or rock or console anyone but myself. The emotion, the depth of it having seized me in a way I was unprepared for and I became afraid.

"You think so?" she whispered. "You really think he gone?"

And I knew she was asking me still only because I felt the sweet amber of her breath against my face. But, I couldn't answer. I couldn't lie nor tell her the truth so I kept my eyes closed tight, wishing my tears to wash away the sight of the man standing on the other side of the room wearing a sad face and clenched, angry fists.

Nah. I let Lena handle it.

"Shhh . . . ," she said. "Shh . . ."

—#—

Lena

Lena spent the bulk of her childhood living in a fantasy, as most children do but especially the poor, abused and neglected. At various points she had been all three, so she retreated into the safety of her mind.

She was romantic in the worst and best of ways. Outside, beneath the hot glare of a yellow sun she'd tiptoe to the smokehouse behind her family's old shack, carefully dodging each wildflower that blossomed from the cool brown dirt. The Earth's surface something she intuitively respected long before she was given a logical reason.

She loved. She loved. She loved. And that's all it was.

Dainty. Quiet. Petite.

She kept her body firm and lean as the white fashion models, for weight represented something she didn't understand thus did not trust nor desire. And besides the fact there was little food shared amongst herself and seven siblings—each who were somehow still much fuller, bigger and rounder than her—she considered it a sin of sorts to indulge in food to the point of ruining your shape. Of the silhouette becoming a distorted thing, unrecognizable; especially when caught cast against a brick wall in the middle of the day while the sun was at its highest point, and shadows came out to play. And one saw, one experienced very briefly the darker parts of themselves.

So she was a skinny girl, stepping softly so as not to disturb the Earth's multi lives that bloomed in the spring, quietly going to sleep in the winter.

On cool days, after a fresh rain, she climbed to the top of the metal roof of that smokehouse and lay for hours daydreaming. Running through her mind the many clothes she'd one day have, the size of the house in which she'd one day live, and the man, the sweet beautiful man who would rescue her from her life and provide a new one. She would in fact be reborn by his hands, the natural goodness of her savior. And on the roof she'd wait for him, her imagination building his every feature. She determined he'd be rich, handsomely dressed, a pleasure to look at, and possess a big dick.

She was a simple country girl and these were to her mind simple wants.

At night before bed, she pulled out the fashion magazines from beneath her bed that she'd stolen from the dime store and fingered each page of smiling white women as if she could feel the silk of their dresses. She'd come to equate love with silk and lace, soft and exotic features that she believed wearing against her body would be the same as feeling her lover's touch all day. And so as a woman, this version of love and romance translated to her bedroom with its silk sheets, lace curtains, lace panties.

L-O-V-E.

Love. There was not a time when Lena had not thought of fantasy and romance. Her mama was sure it would ruin her. It wasn't right, she'd say, for a woman to be so soft. Soft till it appeared she might fade away into the farthest and darkest, most mysterious parts of the universe. So soft the rain, even when gentle on those rare cool summer days, seemed enough to harm her most delicate parts.

But Lena. Poor Lena didn't have to wait for pain to find her. She invited it in. You see, she attracted men who loved her very hard and hit her even harder. Love.

L-O-V-E.

Her mama told her once that the Latin root of passion meant to suffer and endure, and in spiritual terms specifically referred to the suffering of Christ.

"Thas what it is," Lena said. "Thas it."

"Nah," her mama replied. "Ain't none of this shit you lettin men do to you love. Damn sure ain't Christ-like."

"How you know?" Lena asked. "How you know? Look how they did Jesus—whooped his ass somethin awful and he loved them. He loved and forgave."

"So you tellin me you ready to die behind a man?" her mama asked.

But Lena never had a chance to answer that question. When she was shot once in the head and twice in the shoulder by a jealous lover of five years. When she lay hanging on to life by a single thread in intensive care, her first words out of coma were as soft as her drawers and as firm as every erect dick she'd once worshipped.

"Love ain't shit."

To which her mother had only taken a cool towel to her face, hoping to drive the fever down, and said, "We all got to learn sometime."

Truth was we all thought Lena's romance and tragedy had ruined her. And sometimes I still thought it did, you know? Because when I looked at her now, rather than seeing romance, I saw weakness. Weakness held within the warm cracks of her yellow skin where worry and disappointment had left their marks. Weakness in the way she spoke, low and fast or not at all when Marcel talked.

And then there was the hole in her head. The goddamn hole.

The black hole. A black hole.

When I was a little girl, no more than ten, maybe eleven. (The mind forgets what time creates of life.) I was in what they called "gifted & talented" because my standardized test scores were higher than expected—those trickster, bullshit tests my child mind somehow outwitted. And so I was called gifted, and I suppose it was a gift. My imagination strong long before I realized what it was and that it had power.

I was in Gifted and Talented learning about the black hole. That there were many of them, these pockets within the universe that were said to suck, drain and deplete all of everything. Light. Time. Memory. Name it. If you imagined the body as a straw, then the black hole drank from it and it was thirsty. Thirsty as shit.

I was a fifth grader learning such things existed and what was I supposed to do with this information except absorb the fact?

The lesson:

One day we built a black hole using cardboard walls and painted them black, because of course black holes were black. Opaque. Like the skin of the other little girls who for whatever reason were not deemed gifted and talented. Matter of fact, I was the darkest skin. The brown spot, perhaps a dwarf swallowed within this black hole where every other person around me building this phenomenon was white and was something my ten- or eleven-year-old mind didn't know how to describe.

We painted it in swirls because we figured a mechanism as powerful as this wasn't content enough to just sit still. No. It had to circle and bend and twist about like how our own bodies did on playgrounds. Contorted and deformed. Flipping. Spinning. Jumping. We imagined the black hole was not very much unlike ourselves. And why should it be?

When the teacher told us: *This is a black hole. Not even thought can resist its question. Though it may never know its answer without becoming it.* We had no way of understanding this concept. Something so abstract, and vague to our minds.

But when my grandmother's sister Lena was shot this is what I imagined was left.

In some metaphysical way that I couldn't even begin to articulate, not even now, the hole in her head was and had become as elusive as that universal wonder.

I saw the bullet scar. I saw the flesh dented and curled around her brow, stretching to her forehead where it almost looked as if someone had kissed her too hard. I knew the doctors had removed most of the metal but there remained a hole. So deep. So dark. So unlike anything we could ever understand that it, much like a flower, seemed to have taken root and transformed itself into something unknown.

Like a *Twilight Zone* episode, or some biblical character, she was declared an oddity, a miracle walking. A brain with traces of copper and lead lodged in its membrane but still she talked, walked, shit and cried. As if nothing had happened at all. Thus, I knew in my child's mind and then woman's mind that she was no more of this world. The hole in her head might as well have been another plane or a door to another dimension. A dark, murky and moonless night inside her skin where she drown each day and yet was blessed to live.

A resurrection?

And she was alive.

When I'd watch her in the women's department stores picking her new pair of lace and silk panties, I knew she was alive despite everything.

Because the romance remained.

—#—

"I say, goddamn! Uncle Sonny gon beat both of our asses every night if this shit keeps up."

Lena sat at the kitchen table holding an ice pack to her face. My mother sat across from her smoking her first cigarette of the day, drinking her first cup of coffee. She didn't like to talk during this time, and despite the previous night's drama she held fast to her rule.

I sat at the table next to them, still wearing my pajamas, watching my mama eye Lena's swollen face in silence.

"I been telling Marcel her night meds ain't putting her in deep enough sleep. I called Vette and asked her bout taking Aunt Bee to the doctor."

"What she say?" I asked.

"What it look like she say?"

The water in the teakettle on the stove whistled with heat and Lena jumped up to turn the fire down. Pulling two cups from the cupboard she went on, "They don't say a damn thing! They expect me to take care of it."

She poured the water, filling both cups, her lean body propped against the oven as though she couldn't stand without help.

"But I say to them," she continued, "I ain't got the power of attorney to speak for her at the doctor or make decisions. Thas for Bon and Vette nem to do."

"Well, what Aunt Bee say about it?" I asked, dropping a bag of green tea into my cup.

Lena snorted her nose.

"Hmph! Aunt Bee don't say shit 'cept where's my drink. Old woman don't remember nothin either, even lookin at her own bruises."

"She don't be sore?" I asked.

"Hell nah," Lena said, dangling her own bag of tea in ragged circles round her cup. "Marcel say she too pickled with liquor to feel nothin."

"Hmph," I said.

"Hmph," Lena said.

"Hmph," my mama said and took another long noisy sip from her coffee.

"Well I'll say," I said.

"I'll say too," Lena said. She picked up the ice pack and replaced it against her puffy face. In the morning light she looked like a sullen child. I tilted my head again, capturing another angle and yes. A child was what I saw.

There was a long silence that stretched before us. I watched it grow, tossing the warm tea against the insides of my mouth, thinking, thinking. But as usual, not saying much. Choosing to say nothing at all though my head felt as fat with questions as Lena's right cheek appeared.

"What time we gettin Mama from the nursing home today?" my mama asked. She rose from the table, making her way towards the coffee pot. She was coming alive now.

"Imma have to call the nursing home and see," Lena said. "We may need them to bring her out here."

"Why?" my mama replied sharply.

"Cause you know I don't like drivin in rain this hard. You know my nerves too bad for drivin in rain this hard."

"Will they do that?" I asked, sensing my mom's temper rising as it was prone to do when she was anxious or felt out of control of serious matters. And nothing was more important to her, other than me, than seeing her mother. It was the reason for our trip from East Texas all the way to San Antonio.

"Oh yeah, they will," Lena said, oblivious to Mama's mood and tone. "If we give them enough notice."

"Well here!" Mama said, reaching for the phone at the wall and shoving it at Lena's hands. "Call em now."

"In a minute, Peaches! Damn!" Lena slammed her ice pack on the table and took a clumsy sip of her tea, leaving a damp shadow clinging to the tops of her thin upper lip. I watched it linger there, waiting for her to lick it away but she did not. When she spoke again it was with that dew forming a mustache that refused to go away and distressed eyes.

"Eloise ain't goin nowhere!" she said.

"Awright now!" Mama stood beside the coffee pot, holding one hand in front of her, the other on her hip. There was a dramatic pause and when she spoke again the pink foam rollers in her head went to shaking. "I'm ready to see my mama!"

I could see the fire in her eyes. I could feel the tension in her stance. Even if Lena chose not to acknowledge what it meant, the child in me couldn't help but to respond to the seriousness of the gesture.

"We gon see her mama," I said standing up, reaching for her arm still held in the air before her body. "It's cool."

"Now wait a minute, Peaches," Lena said, standing up. "You gon make me have to dig off in my purse." She stood, her eyes scanning the cabinet for it.

"I'll find it," I said. "And I'll call too. I don't mind."

"Nah," Lena said. "They ain't gon know you. Imma have to talk to em." And then, "Peaches, just calm down. The rain might slack up and we can go get her this evening."

Mama sat back down, her face showing she was unconvinced but content to be quiet for the moment.

"We'll see," she said finally. "But if by noon it's still raining, I'm callin. And if it's too late for them to bring her then I'll take a taxi."

She sucked her teeth.

"Don't make me no mind. All I know is I'm seeing my mama today!"

But it didn't stop raining. In fact, by noon the clouds had taken on a dark sinister look, and the rain began to hammer the house and the lights blinked twice—on and off. On and off.

Lena was busy tending to Aunt Bee's bruises when at lunchtime my mama called me into our room and whispered, "Here go the number. Call and see what they say bout bringin Mama when this pass over."

You see, much like Lena, my mama's nerves wouldn't allow her to drive in heavy rain, especially in big, foreign cities. And I knew this limitation only further agitated her.

But the rain didn't pass. Not that evening anyway and with the sound of thunder crackling in the background, causing static on the phone line, I called the nursing home.

"They say they don't think it's a good idea," I reported back to my mama. "But they have a driver on call and Mama Eloise is anxious to get here too."

"Is she?" Mama smiled.

"They say she ain't slept all night or ate nothin."

"Did they say what time they gon head this way?"

"No, ma'am," I said. "Just that it'd be sometime this evening."

"Hmph," she said, rising up on her elbows in bed. "Well, thas fair. Thas fair." And then, very quietly and still, looking as much like a child as Lena had at the breakfast table, she said, "Call back and see if they let her talk to me."

I sighed. Took the cordless phone in my hand and dialed.

And they came. A big ole white man and a lil bitty white man both wearing blue bloomer like pants, blue tops and heavy jackets slick with rain. They struggled at first to ease her body out of the white van. Mama Eloise was big, had been big for several years, big enough to the point where her own ankles had long ago said *aww to hell with this shit* and given up carrying her around. Big enough where her knees had long ago said *fuck this!* and buckled under the expectations. Even her oval-sized, though beautiful face, plump with greed and dissatisfaction, had lost hope and kilt over; neck grown weak under the burden of hot water cornbread, ham hocks, mustard greens and peach cobbler.

You see, Mama Eloise living in a nursing home for the past five years meant she accepted her new position in life and her daughters' lack of constitutions with the condition that she be given everything else she wanted in life. Which had become—not orgasms, not money or fancy clothes but as much of whatever food her wide mouth craved.

As the white men lifted her bloated body and placed her in the wheelchair, her jaws hung low, lips bent over, permanently ready to receive something good.

Me and Mama watched them load and lift her then lower her chair onto the wet cement, covering her with a black tarp that they tripped and fumbled over while trying to cover the whole of her. Word at the nursing home was that she could be mean. Cruel words easy about her tongue, and so some of the nurses and aides were quick to accommodate her wishes which were simple though unhealthy enough.

Keep her sedated, washed and fed. Simple.

And her daughters followed suit. I'd once heard my aunt on the phone say, "If you're gonna give her butter pecan ice cream just make sure she has her Metformin soon after. She's diabetic, ya know?"

She said how high and we all jumped.

I stood in the door beside my mother watching them roll Mama Eloise towards the house both bewildered and afraid. Her face, pale as a summer moon, was flushed with blood and her body fat under the red blankets they'd thrown over her before covering her with tarp. Her hands, stretched out front, were twisted and thick with something I didn't understand. She held them frozen in place as if waiting. Not on us, though, not her daughter or kin. But perhaps something else to eat?

As she made her way closer, closer still, my mama smiled and reached towards her, arms ready to take her fullness in.

"Hey baby," Mama Eloise said smiling, teeth barely visible beneath her slim pink lips.

"Mama!"

My mother grabbed her, tears falling and joining the rain; her own thick body growing wet. I watched the raindrops gather in the small of her back where her blouse melted into her skin. I tried to smile at the two white men, who stood like Greek statues only not nearly as fantastic save for what they'd safely (and without error) accomplished all the while wearing plastic smiles.

It was dark. The porch light was yellow and bright against the night. Mama was a translucent haze adorned in red and black and now brown flesh.

"Come on in y'all before you get wet," I said.

"Yes, yes," Mama Eloise said. "Get me out dis rain fore I get sicker than I already am."

And we all rushed in to push and pull her into the dry and quiet of the house.

"Eloise finally made it, huh?" Lena stood at the end of the hallway with her arms on her hips watching us pat Mama E down with a towel I'd grabbed from the bath.

"How you doin, big sis?" Lena walked to her, bending over to her face so she wouldn't have to bother turning her head in either direction to find her baby sister's voice.

"Oh," she said, "I'm lookin like a ding dong with a mouth full of doggon shit! Thas bout how I'm doin!"

And then, her eyes found my face and she said: "Who's the sad-lookin Negro in the dingy pants over there in the corner?"

I looked up and saw a man, Sonny, standing there, his hands falling along his sides, watching curiously. Confused.

Mama and Lena exchanged worried glances.

"Mama, have you had your evening meds?" My mom went about digging in her bags, searching for her medicine.

"Hell yeah I done had it—" Mama E started before I quieted her with the shaking of my head.

I placed a finger to my lips. *Shhhh.*

"We'll talk about it later," I mouthed. Silently.

—#—

Eloise

When Mama E was a lil girl they say she was so pretty she made other girls sad just at the sight of her. And just as it was with any grieving process, they soon transitioned from sad to angry. Then they tried to fight her. But she was too tough. Red rosy lips without the aid of rouge. But tough. High cheekbones and milky smooth skin. But she was mean. Long raven hair that cascaded down her back like she was mulatto even though she wasn't. She was all Black. And she was strong.

As a child, the first time I ever saw Disney's *Snow White* I could have sworn it was my grandmother. If only she were a shade darker and packed a pistol in her bosom. If perhaps she kicked the ass of one of the seven dwarves every so often just to remind them what was what. And the wicked witch? Well, she wouldn't have stood a chance against Mama Eloise, who by the age of seven had cut the first girl who pulled her to the ground at the Negro grade school with one of her Papa's straight-edge razors. Who at eleven jumped up and punched a white man dead in his eye then followed with a swift kick to his nuts after he dared say to her, "Ain't you bout the whitest lil nigger gal I ever seen." Then she ran home fast, faster than any of the boys her age could manage, before the white man could even recollect what happened. And once he did, he'd been too shamefaced to tell anyone a nigger child got the better of him.

Mama Eloise was tough cause she always had to be. Black women despised what they saw as privilege in her skin. Black men lusted after her skin for what they saw as a pedestal waiting to be erected—the closest thing they might ever get to lying down with a white woman who wasn't deemed trash, who wasn't a white woman at all. And the white people, who despite her fair complexion and long curly black hair, at the end of the day still just saw a nigger.

Her life had been poor, tough. So she learned to shoot straight and cut deep very young. She didn't trust no one. Not even her own family and it was a big family. Big, hungry, dysfunctional and looking to the eldest child, Eloise, to make sense of it all. Be it cooking. Be it cleaning. Be it snatching the drink from her father's grip when he was drunk and threatening to hit her mama, in his voice, with his eyes then his fists. Be it tenderly wiping her mother's swollen face with rubbing alcohol when he did.

She held her baby brother when he cried, nightmares a scattered, abstruse thing his small mind couldn't understand and neither could Eloise—in sleep or waking life. But she rubbed his back, said *Shhh . . . everything will be okay* even though she had no way of knowing if this was true. Didn't believe this was true. And she bathed the youngest, dragged the wet dishrag used for washing bodies come nightfall, across her small face and flat chest. Told her it would be okay when Lena, scared and bruised, came home saying the man down the street had hurt her. Raised her dress, pulled her bloomers down. Hurt her.

"It hurt!" Lena cried. And Eloise cried too because this she knew. Pain and defilement she knew. Lena was five years old and Eloise fifteen, newly married and making daily trips to her mama's house while toting her own baby on her hip.

To see about the children. To see about her mama. Restrain her daddy.

Cook. Clean. Fight for those she loved and even those she wasn't so sure about, her feelings wound up tight in a knot she didn't have the energy or time to unravel. But they were blood. She didn't trust all of 'em but they were blood. So she did her best.

She married four times. The first one she didn't speak of. They were young. She got pregnant and they got married. It was enough. She did the best she could with it until she no longer had the energy or time to see about him, with her big family, with his drinking and jealousy. With his midnight accusations of the many white men his adolescent mind was convinced she'd slept with. He was seventeen and his imagination had no place to expand and play but inside the tin shack he shared with the high yellow girl he'd made a child with then made his wife. And his mind was wild with lack of stimulation. One day it was the postman, cause he thought the white man's eyes lingered too long on Eloise's breasts, wound up like balls of yarn, tidy knots, in the only dress she felt secure wearing. The one dress she thought wouldn't bring any more attention than she had the energy to respond to or absorb.

By fifteen she was tired of fighting. So she wore that dingy pink dress all the time, so much that it was no longer pink but an exotic blush color only white people had a name for and wrinkled to the point that no amount of water or heat would straighten its folds. But nah, Henry thought it only accentuated her small curves, where her hips had spread a few centimeters after the birth of their child. He thought the way the thin material dipped and clung to her breast-feeding nipples was suggestive. He saw them as erect points reaching out beyond his slender body for more. He couldn't close the distance because his existence wasn't important enough to reach that far. For the white men he was certain shared more in common with her, had more to offer her, to please her. In the mornings, he woke up erect and fucked her hard imagining all their pale bodies conspiring against him, and he was determined to show them otherwise.

She shot him twice. Once in the right thigh. He was drunk and accusing. So drunk he didn't feel the heat of the bullet nor the blood or stitches when his frail leg was put back together. And again, the last time, in his left shoulder. He'd called her a piss-colored bitch for the last damn time. And he cried. Cried for her and then his mama when Eloise left him.

She took up their baby girl and moved back to her mama's house. She was seventeen, cooking biscuits at the colored people's diner in the mornings for five dollars a week paid out by the white man who owned the place. She decided she'd never marry again.

She sifted the dough between her fingers, squeezed. Pressed and pounded the white sticky stuff with her small fists. Squeezed. Silently entertaining thoughts of killing Lena's violator while walking back to her mama's house at high noon, her pink dress saturated with the smell of smoke and grease, her gun hot and heavy beneath her pillow at home. But she was tired. Didn't think enough of men, to kill them or mate; not as daddies, lovers or abusers. She made peace with the idea of dying alone because marriage was not for her. She laid her head on the pillow at night and held her daughter close, felt the gun's steel anatomy, cold and hard against her head. She said her prayers and slept. Felt secure.

But then she met the black French man from New Orleans at the blues club across the river. She was nineteen and she loved the way his lips curled with his native tongue when they made love. The words, though she never understood them, sounded like music. She moved her hips all night, sometimes till the sun came up, to the sound of his breath in her ear and it felt like dancing. And she realized she'd never danced. Been free to dance. She sat listening to music but rarely moved her body, and everything he gasped during orgasm sounded like *we*—Oui!—rather than the very singular *I* she associated with most men. She'd walk to the diner, the morning sun embracing her body as gently as Maurice had the night before, trying not to skip. Feeling like a girl, the little girl she'd never been, only safe now and optimistic. She had thought he was the one.

Oui!

He left after she shot at him for threatening to hit her kid. And she cried and cried, holding the cold metal tip of the pistol against her tears. Disappointed in a way she hadn't ever allowed herself.

She decided marriage was not for her.

Until she married again. Times were hard and the colored diner had turned into a nighttime establishment more interested in booze than biscuits. Money was tight. Her family was big.

So there she was again saying *I do*, only this time to an older man who'd lost his legs in World War Two. She thought he was safe. Limited in the ways he could reach her.

He was forty. She was twenty-three.

My mama said she heard Mama E once knocked him out his wheelchair for drunkenly calling her a high yellow bitch. And she let him stay on the cold hardwood floor long enough to pee his pants, before snatching him up, bathing, then fixing him some chicken and dumplings with hot water cornbread—his favorites. They had two kids, a girl and then a boy who was born blind and mentally disabled, who both along with their older sister all witnessed Eloise stab him in his fingers and arms when she heard he'd pulled himself out. Set his tiny penis upon his lap and stroked its head while asking her girls, "Know what this is?" Mama said she was going for his dick when his screams forced her back to sanity because for a moment he sounded like her mama when struck. Eloise was sweaty, chest moving up, down, up down when she cried, "No legs and now no hands, nigga! Try pullin that shit out again!"

She married finally, again, to my grandfather, the supposed love of her life, though she'd never admit as much.

He, like her, had pale skin. Sky-blue eyes. Black curly hair. People said they might have passed for kin if Deo didn't have so much Indian in his blood that turned his skin burnt red under the summer sun. He was a farmer. The father of my mother. He drove a raggedy blue pickup truck and never raised his voice. He watched sports on the television only to root for the few colored players allowed on the field. *Go nigga!*

I was a little girl laid out in the middle of the floor, watching the television then Papa Deo rise up from his chair. He spit tobacco juice in the soup can Mama Eloise prepared for him and whispered, "Go nigga!" at the screen. His voice urgent, intense but still soft. I was five years old. I'd watch the Black man hit the ball, run with the ball, shoot the ball. Think, *Go nigga!*

And I'd ride in the back of his truck to the farm. Crying and pulling away from his animals—chickens, cows, horses, dogs, cats—while he murmured, "Stop being so scary, gal." He'd pull me back in, make me touch the object of my fear. Gently. Tenderly.

"They more scared of you than you are of them," he'd say. And I'd feel their pulses; quick hot heartbeats matching my own and believed him. I'd relax and reach out with a gentle, tender touch. Feel the animal relax.

Mama said Papa Deo had that effect on people and animals. He was early to rise, early to bed. Black. Pale. Skinny. Chewed tobacco. At one with nature and Mama Eloise.

Eloise who began chewing tobacco too, riding with him to the farm in the raggedy blue truck. Who enjoyed cooking the greens, cabbage and peas he brought home from the farm. Who raised the lace hem of her skirts and let the breeze touch her in places she'd once been afraid. She watched Deo pile the hay and she felt secure. Like dancing.

She started a garden. Learned how to plant and plow. Watched her flowers grow with pride. And she'd play music in their wood frame house. The blues, only she wasn't sad or angry. Afraid. She made biscuits at home in the mornings, kneaded the dough with soft hands and danced in front of the stove.

She was fifty-two.

They stayed married almost twenty years until cancer ate up his body and dementia his mind. If I asked her, did she love Papa

Deo—did she truly passionately love him? She'd only say, "We understood each other."

When I'd broken up with my love almost three years ago, I called her at the nursing home with a glass of wine in hand, trying to control the slur and sobs in my speech.

"How did you know Papa Deo was the one?" I asked.

She was quiet.

Then she said, "Don't you think you gettin' a lil too old to believe in *that* shit?"

And I knew she saw me as weak. Not quite Lena-weak but inadequate. Still believing in *that* shit. And I didn't want to admit to myself that I saw her too as weak. Unable and unwilling to acknowledge *that* shit. Her love.

L-O-V-E.

But where we did connect, where we undeniably met in this world with mutual understanding was inside the gift.

Our secret.

I was ten years old when her baby brother Alfred died. A drunk. The nightmares, both in sleep and the waking life having taken its toll. So he drank. Whiskey. Wine, both red and white. And Mama Eloise had taken care of him still. Tending to his wounds when drunken falls or fights left him bruised and blue. Bathing his puny body while dodging the stank of alcohol in his breath and pores. When he was found dead, she stayed in bed for days inconsolable while the family consoled his wino friends who all came to Eloise's home knocking with loud fists, high off the liquor and mourning their friend. Alfred. Crying unabashedly for their friend and I was ten years old watching it all, thinking, now *this* is love.

L-O-V-E.

At the funeral, I sat next to my mama who cried, and beside her was Lena whose body trembled with grief. And I was ten years old and watching it all, then watching Alfred standing at the pulpit next to the wino woman who was supposedly his girlfriend when he died. Her body trembled too, but no one was sure if it was the grief or the few minutes spent without her fix: Jamaican rum. Her favorite. Because she talked, words slurred and incoherent, and cried but there were no tears and I saw Alfred standing there beside her, first looking sad then angry. Then he pumped his pelvis at her as though fucking or dancing. Was he dancing? I laughed and quickly reached to cover my mouth but it was done. And my mama pinched my arm so hard I'm not sure the blood circulation there has ever fully recovered. Then I cried for real. Until I saw Mama Eloise looking at Alfred with those sharp eyes that said *Nigga if you don't cut it out!* And he stopped. Smiled. Walked away. The wino woman said hallelujah and the church said amen.

The service was over.

I was ten years old, hiding behind a tree and from my mama, arm still stinging from the grip of her fingers. I watched Mama Eloise behind the church with Alfred.

"Do you know where you supposed to go?" she asked. He shook his head. He cried and smiled; Mama Eloise hugged him tightly.

He said to her, "You was a good big sis, Fish."

She rubbed his back and told him everything would be okay. He looked at her, smiled and said, "I know."

Then he was gone.

Mama Eloise stood there for a moment, watching the place her brother once stood. She cried. Her shoulders trembled, up down, up down. Then she wiped her face. Took a deep breath and walked towards the front of the church. I ducked further behind the tree but it was too late. She saw me. I saw her. She knew we both had seen him.

She walked towards me, her face unreadable, and I was afraid of another pinch; only with Mama E's fingers, the body who created my mama's fingers. I flinched in preparation for the sting. But she only pulled my face into her warm hands.

I opened my eyes and looked into hers.

"Hmph," she said. Cocked her head to the right then left, stroked my face tenderly, gently. "I always knew it was gon' be least one of my children who had the sight. Never figured it'd be yo scary ass, Boop."

Then she let go, walked away, started telling Lena and her other siblings what to do, where to go, how to get there. They shuffled, sniffled and moved at her direction.

And she never looked back at me. Not once. Never spoke of it again.

It would be years later, well into adulthood, that I'd have the courage to ask her: How do I deal with this? What do they want? Why can we see and others can't?

But she only looked at me with gray milky eyes and said, "Thas for you to figure out." She spit into her cup, said, "And the rest between you and God."

But the Mama Eloise in my dreams was different. So different that the idea was enough to take my breath away, so unsure I was that this version of her existed. Because she'd visit me in my dreams and her hair was black as the Snow White of my childhood, and her back was straight. She'd stand tall before me or sometimes kneel down and her body allowed her to do each of these things without trouble.

Sometimes we would sit in silence while she held my hand, and other times I was the raptured student swept up in the wizardry and wisdom of her words where she finally revealed her most intimate lessons.

Mama Eloise thought that our shared gift didn't make us special. Instead, she said that we'd simply been given the vision to see what was always there for anyone to see if they were willing and open-hearted enough.

We were open-hearted, she said, and if we were chosen, it was only because we continued to love, despite our pain and disappointments over many lifetimes.

Thas enough, she said. Thas really all God requires is to keep loving through it all, and she smiled, folding her snuff beneath her tongue before oscillating it as from one jaw to the other.

And I disagreed with this because I couldn't ever recall giving permission to see anything much less continually love all without repercussions, to which Mama E only laughed and told me that I didn't remember my soul's commitment. She said our souls reached an agreement long before we were born and whenever we were born again, our souls dictated the circumstances, determined what was necessary not only for our growth but the collective's evolution.

Humanity is the most exquisite magic, she said, spitting into her cup.

It was written in the stars, she said, a code so deep that no astrological practice could ever be enough to explain what some of us were allowed to see, merely because we chose to.

It was the only time I'd ever heard her use a word like *exquisite*. It was the only place she entertained my questions, which were few because I wasn't sure how to feel or respond. So I was mostly quiet and she decided my silence was a good thing.

Trust everything inside yourself and always trust your heart, she told me. Sometimes it might steer you wrong, or seem to anyway, but most of the time, she said, the heart be workin' with the soul and they both know more than we remember.

Even I forget sometimes, she said, her gray eyes fluttering as if it were the most preposterous thought in the world.

Honor them both. Think last, she said, because we can't always trust our thoughts. Too many influences, too many folks steady talkin' and we consume it all.

The brain is powerful but capable of working against us. So it's important, she said, drawing me closer to her, that we understand the difference. Look at the lost souls, and know what you seein'. Don't be afraid to trust the reason God allowin' you to see 'em. Learn what you supposed to learn and let it shape you into the kinda person who takes what you've learned into the world and do somethin' positive with it.

And I was quiet.

It was the only time she spoke on it. In our shared dreams.

Love. Ghosts. God.

It's all the same, she said.

—#—

"So how long this nigga been hangin round?"

It was late afternoon. The house was dark. Moody. Electric with heat.

Mama Eloise and I sat in the den with Aunt Bee.

I was on the couch, sipping a cheap cabernet held within a red plastic cup. Aunt Bee sat to my left strapped down in her wheelchair, sipping gin, white hair tumbling across her small head. And Mama Eloise was to my right holding a soup can wrapped in tin foil for spitting tobacco. Though it was against doctor's orders, she held the snuff in the corner of her mouth where her cheek swoll in defiance. When she spit a thick hard line into the cup, the paper towel she'd stuffed the can with to catch the stream softened its thud.

Unlike Bee, Lena and Mama had moved Mama Eloise from her wheelchair, straining and puffing the entire time, and propped her up in the chocolate-colored leather chair closest to the television. I offered to help them lift and carry her the few inches required, but they'd both looked at me with the judgmental eyes of church ladies surveying the neighborhood drunk and sighed with equal parts pity and agitation. Now here she was queen of them all, perched on her throne; thick legs standing out front her body like two hickory logs. I watched the broken varicose veins scatter and gather along her calves and took another sip from my cup. The rain saying everything and nothing at the same time.

"I dunno, I just saw him for the first time the other night."

"Hmm," Mama Eloise hummed, then spit again. Brown spittle caught her chin and she rubbed it away with one gnarled hand while never taking her eyes off Sonny. He sat in the far corner of the room with his legs crossed and arms folded as though waiting on the bus, or a wayward child. Determined, if not patient and ready to scold if given the opportunity. He wore brown slacks and a red plaid button-up that complemented the red undertones of his skin. And for a moment, I wondered if these were the same clothes he'd died in. On the toilet.

I cringed.

But then his red undertones made me think of the blue bruises on Aunt Bee's skin and the angry fists he held two nights before, and I couldn't stand to look at him.

I took another swig and picked up the remote control from the glass table arranged in the middle of us and handed it to Bee out of curiosity and amusement.

"Turn it to whatever you want," I said, smacking lips stained with wine. "You know how to work it?"

She looked at me as though dizzy, her mind and eyes spinning with the possibilities. "Can I call home?" she asked and her afternoon booze caused her voice to shake.

I laughed, not meaning nor trying to but the wine had taken hold and we were alone without real supervision. "Who you wanna call?" I slurred and because we sound the same she trusted me.

She tilted her head and caught its movement with the palm of her hand, "Ohhh," she hummed. "I dunno," she said. "Maybe James."

"James who?" I asked.

"James Brown."

"He dead," I said.

"Oh."

Mama Eloise spat and looked at Sonny.

Aunt Bee thought for another second.

"Well, lemme call Marvin then."

"Marvin who?" I asked.

"Ain't but one Marvin!"

I laughed, not having the heart to tell her he too was dead.

"Whatchu gon say to him? You can call but what you gon say?"

She thought again for a moment, small lines around her mouth tightening and releasing. She pursed her lips and sighed.

"Imma tell him ain't shit changed. Same thing goin on as before."

"Mhmm," Mama E hummed. "She got that right." She spit a sharp line of tobacco into her soup can and frowned at Sonny. "Same shit warmed over."

Curious now in a real way and further encouraged by the fruit of the vine, I leaned forward. "Whatchu mean?"

"Niggas ain't changed!" Mama E answered.

Aunt Bee shook her head in approval, fondling the remote with dainty fingers.

"Black people?" I asked, trying with everything I had to sound and look sober. Speech controlled—not too high, low or wobbly.

"Them too," Aunt Bee started.

"But you see, baby," Mama E cut her off. "Everybody a nigga. There's black niggas. White niggas. Messican niggas, *violent* niggas," she said and screwed her face up at Sonny.

"Thas right," Aunt Bee said. "It's a nigga world."

"But see, I love niggas!" Mama E continued. "Even the *violent* ones."

Sonny shifted in his brown paisley chair, crossing his legs and folding his arms and for a moment I could have sworn Aunt Bee acknowledged and met his move.

"Oh, I do too," she said, sitting back against her wheelchair and folding her arms. "Gotta love 'em." Then she turned and looked into my eyes, all earnest and serious. "God would have us to love 'em."

"Is that right?" I said.

"Damn right!" Mama E said and spit in her cup again. "Sides, you a nigga too."

I nodded my head like, *true.*

"Take a nigga to love a nigga." Mama E leaned her big body forward and patted my leg. "Just not nigga shit!" She cut her eyes back to Sonny. "'Specially not *violent* nigga shit."

"Nooo nooo," Aunt Bee sang. "Can't love nigga shit!"

"So that mean *other* folks can say it?" I asked.

"Say wha?" Mama E asked, fluttering those eyes.

"Nigga," I said, rolling my neck like duhhhh.

"Well hell nah," Aunt Bee exclaimed and her voice was so strong and clear it caught me off guard.

Mama Eloise spit in her cup.

"Yeah they can!" she said, "If they wanna get they ass whooped!"

Aunt Bee fell out laughing. I laughed.

Mama Eloise looked at me and said, "Shiiiiittttttt, think I'm lyin'."

"OK y'all need to cut that shit out!" Lena zigzagged through the den, walking fast and talking faster, and it took us each a moment to register her presence, so quickly she was there and then nothing but a high-pitched voice that continued chastising while making her way towards the kitchen. "I don't play the n-word in my house!" she called over her shoulder.

"The n-word?" Aunt Bee looked at me with glossy eyes.

"Nigga," I whispered to her.

"I heard that!" Lena called.

"And you know what else you can hear, oh baby sister of mine?" Mama E called back.

"Don't start with me, Eloise!" Lena called back.

"Oh see, I didn't start shit," Mama E called back. "But I can damn sure finish it." She spit in her cup and readjusted her snuff from one cheek to the other, then spit again. "See, cause we wasn't botherin nobody!"

"I didn't say you was—" Lena started.

"But you had to come hot-steppin through here switchin ya tail talmbout the n-word." She spit again. "Soundin like some Black politician."

I giggled. Low though because I wasn't trying to draw the ire of Lena's anxious attention. Everyone knew Lena took out whatever misdirected, pent-up angry energy she wasn't brave enough to charge at Marcel on the rest of the world. And right now, we were the rest of her world.

I shook my head. *No thanks nigga. Not today.* Aunt Bee giggled like she heard my thoughts. From his chair, Sonny smiled and uncrossed his legs. I cringed, rolled my eyes and took another swig. Mama E looked at him like, *I ain't forgot about you nigga, don't get ahead of ya self!* and he crossed his legs again.

"Now who done told you we can't say the n-word?" Mama E spit in her cup and looked at me like, *Watch this.* "Had to been a nigga. Was it Marcel?" she called.

Lena walked out from the kitchen and stood in full view, holding her hands on bony hips with a wet dishrag dripping down her bony thighs.

"I'll have you know, Eloise," she started. "It wasn't no man. Oprah said we shouldn't be sayin the n-word cause some of our ancestors died hearin that 'fore drawin' they last breath and I happen to agree!" And her synthetic wig shook with the gentle swing of her slender neck as if further emphasizing she was right and we were wrong on this one. And who were we to argue with a cheap wig? With Oprah?

I cringed and took another sip.

"N-word?" Aunt Bee asked again.

"Nigga," I whispered, pointing at Sonny.

"Ohhh," she said, rolling her eyes and took another sip from her glass.

"Oprah?" Mama E whispered.

"The woman on TV," I whispered back.

"Thas what I thought," she whispered. Then: "Well ain't no white person ever called me nigga, but I been a plenty a niggers! Sides, how old Oprah?" she called to Lena.

Lena walked back into the kitchen and out of view, dripping water along her way as though the conversation was over. And because I didn't appreciate what looked like dismissal towards my grandmother, I answered loud enough for all to hear.

"She bout the same age as Mama," I called. "I know they have the same birthday."

From the kitchen we could hear the sound of rushing water in the sink and the clanging of porcelain dishes. Lena was extra loud with it, again making her point. We were no longer worthy, no longer part of her world. A lost cause.

"Awww hell," Mama E called over the commotion. "Oprah young enough to be my baby child?" She spit in her cup. "I was alive to see what her imagination creates." She spit again. "Tell her come see me and we can talk about it if thas how she feel. Tell her come say it to my face!"

The water stopped. Dishes halted.

"But I tell you one thing," Mama E continued.

I crossed my legs and took a sip. Bee took a sip. Sonny smiled again.

"I'm old enough to say whatever the hell I want. I done earned the right and lest you God almighty you should probably shut the—"

"Do y'all remember if I took my insulin?"

I cringed. There she was, my mama stumbling downstairs and into the den with her nightgown hugging the crack of her ass, though it was afternoon, and rollers bouncing off the sides of her cheeks, though it was afternoon.

She looked confused. And Mama E paused, put her spit cup down on the glass table and her voice changed as quickly as the moment.

"Now baby," Mama E said. "You don't remember if you took ya insulin or not?"

In the kitchen the water restarted. Loud. Abrupt.

Mama frowned and plopped down in the chocolate recliner beside Aunt Bee's wheelchair. "I think I did."

Aunt Bee handed her the remote and said, "Here. Wanna call ya doctor?"

Mama looked confused. Frowned again and scratched the soft scalp between her pink foam rollers. "All that hollerin' woke me up," she said and yawned.

I jumped up, scanning the room for her medicine bag.

"I don't think you did," I said and immediately felt guilty for not remembering. I was usually so good. Despite everything I paid attention to the small triangular papers and plastic knobs of the needles she left on the ends of tables denoting to my senses she'd injected herself. She'd done what she was supposed to do. But now I didn't see them, nor her medicine bag.

"Now Peaches, you gon' have to do better than dat," Mama E said.

Mama yawned and scratched her head again.

In the corner, Sonny relaxed.

I looked and looked but couldn't find any evidence that she'd done better and suddenly felt like crying. Was it the cabernet? Sonny? The broken heart?

And as if feeling my thoughts, Aunt Bee began to cry. At first it was a small sniffle. She tossed the remote control to the floor causing my mama to jump. Mama E looked at Sonny as though he were both cause and effect, but he sat still. Watching. Then Bee began to wail. And it was enough to stop me in my meager tracks. She rocked her body, slow then faster till it was as the other night. She was rowing alone on waters, without a life jacket. Without a savior. She wailed louder and the tears streamed as though part of the same body of water she traversed.

Lena rushed out from the kitchen, her pants still damp, wig stiff but flying about her face. My first instinct was to comfort Bee but before I could reach her, my mama was already rubbing her long fingers against Bee's delicate back, cooing something that to my ears sound like something she'd once sang to me as a baby.

"Everything's awright," she said to Bee, patting her back with gentle taps.

"See!" Lena said, falling down to her knees at Bee's lap. "This what I try to tell Marcel. Her meds ain't right and come night this what she do!"

Sonny inched to the edge of his chair and held his arms between his legs as though eager. The unmanageable child had finally arrived. The bus was here. He was ready to go.

Mama E kept her eyes trained on my mama, her child. Aunt Bee wailed louder. Her gin, neat and absolved, sat upon the glass table, the stillest thing in the entire room. Sonny clinched his fists and I wanted to shout, *Nigga! Triflin' ass dead ass nigga!*

"I keep tellin Marcel I need some help with her at night cause she gettin worse," Lena said, meeting Mama's hands and stroking Bee across her back and shoulders. Anywhere her rocking body allowed.

I saw my mama close her eyes and I could tell she didn't feel well. She'd slept most of the day. No insulin. No blood pressure pills. No food. Her head was swimming. Swimming in the same waters Bee traveled.

"You should let Boop stay with her tonight," Mama E said. She leaned towards Sonny then looked at me, then her daughter and spit in her cup. "See how she do at night with someone with her."

I cringed. Red cup with red wine appearing miles away and I couldn't reach it for relief.

Mama rubbed Bee. Lena rubbed Bee. Sonny sat back in his chair.

"Well," Mama said. "If you think it will help."

"I think so," Lena said, her wig shaking in agreement. "I think so."

They rubbed Bee who appeared to calm before belting out another high wail. Her eyes were fixed at the ceiling, then Sonny, then me.

And I cried too, though no one noticed, though there were no tears. And there was a clap of thunder, the rain consistent but harder than before. Lightning lit the den with a sharp arrow that was quick enough to dazzle and disconcert. And then:

"What the fuck is *that*?"

Mama Eloise's eyes were locked on the television and so we all looked. On the screen was a Black woman, blonde wig swinging, face contorted, hips gyrating while wearing a sparkly pink onesie that clung to every lump and bump her thick body possessed. She pumped her pelvic area to one side of the stage and then the other. She dropped to the ground and inched her way back up, still gyrating and sweating, blonde hair stuck to her lips and nose. She wailed, matching Bee's wails, and Mama E shook her head.

"But I can't say nigga, huh?"

She spit in her cup.

Sonny watched the TV, amused. Curious.

"I'm not staying the night in Bee's room."

Mama E rolled her eyes and pulled her gown up the smooth concourse that was her thighs. It caught inside the sweat there before she yanked it, firmly, revealing beige bloomers and her diaper. Incontinence one of the few things she couldn't control despite her will.

My mama lay beside her in the bed. Mama E's bedroom was off the kitchen on the first floor, not far from Bee's. The invalids were kept below, all able-bodied made to take the stairs except Lena and Marcel.

"It's hot!" Mama E said. "You mean with all this house they can't afford to run the damn air conditioner?"

Mama, resting on her side with her back nestled against Mama E's, raised her own gown towards her knees and wiggled her feet atop the sheets as though gasping for cool air.

"Now you know Marcel won't let her run the air conditioner. Not if it mean costing his ass another dime," she said.

"See, *thas* dat nigga shit," Mama E said, slapping the sweat between her legs. And Mama laughed, still wiggling her toes.

"Awright now, don't get in no mo' trouble."

"Shiiiiiiit," Mama E said.

I stood at the foot of the bed, rolling my eyes, a flash of lightning blazed across my face though no one was there to witness our theatrics. There was a clap of thunder and still I stood. Ignored.

"I *said*, I ain't sleeping in Aunt Bee's room!"

My mama opened her eyes and looked up at the ceiling. But the fan attached there continued moving, lazy and disinterested in our lives. It did what it did, and Mama recognizing it was performing as expected closed her eyes again. She'd taken her insulin, ate one of Aunt Bee's oatmeal pies, had another cup of coffee then popped one of Mama Eloise's Metformin and prepared to nap with the rest of the house. I was the only one still behaving as though it were daytime hours and life was still to be lived. Except for Lena who was in the room across the hall anxiously calling Marcel to reassure he was safe wherever he was in the weather while simultaneously treating the bruises writhing along her vagina with Campho-Phenique.

"I hope that Metformin don't give me the shits," Mama said.

"Well now you know white folks' medicine gon fix one problem while causin another," Mama E said.

Mama smiled and inched her gown further up her legs.

There was a clap of thunder.

"I *said* I *ain't* sleepin with Aunt Bee tonight!"

"Aw hell, Boop, stop bein so scary," Mama E said.

I dragged my hand over my forehead and let it settle across my eyes. The lightning shimmered through the haze. I wasn't sure which I despised more, being called scary or Boop, my nickname assigned at birth because Mama Eloise said I came into the world dancing. Arms and legs moving something like jazz. Boop bop diddy doo bop! *Boop!*

So I was Boop.

It was hot. I wasn't ready to climb the stairs and try to nap. Heat rises to the top. Heat rose up my body, my throat and I felt like throwing up. Maybe I should smoke. Alcohol can't be trusted. Men, neither. But marijuana was dependable. Usually.

I started towards the door and stopped. Looked at their bodies. *Mamas.* The way their breathing bodies moved as if in synch; large and sweaty—beautiful.

I wanted to say don't call me Boop. I wanted to say, nah I ain't sleeping with her. I wanted to admit I was afraid but the rain, lightning and then the sound of their soft snores wouldn't allow me to make a sound, much less be heard.

That evening Lena made mustard greens and smothered pork chops, Marcel's favorites, while clanging those same porcelain dishes. But the greens were greasy, the pork chops bland. And we all reached for the salt, pepper and hot sauce. Aunt Bee asked with confused eyes if Lena had a white cook and Lena looked like she wanted to cry. But we weren't sure if it was the insult to her cooking or the fact Marcel still wasn't home.

The rain continued. Smoke wafted up from the stove and Lena scrambled to turn the vent on and catch its exhaust. At the table, we poked at our sad and sullen food. Shook the salt. Shook the pepper. But there was no taste.

Mama Eloise looked at Lena and sighed. Mama leaned over to me and said, "You don't have to stay downstairs tonight if you don't want to." And I looked at Sonny, standing by the stove, inhaling the pork chop smoke as if it were marijuana, and said, "I'll be fine."

My head was a fog and because the house was actually dark, Lena having turned off all lights, even the one over the stove because Marcel still wasn't home come bedtime and she wanted to punish him in some small way, I couldn't see.

Mama was sleep. She took her meds. Medicine bag safely recovered. She kissed and hugged Mama Eloise goodnight with heavy, sedated arms; voice slurring with legal intoxication as she called it. Whenever I smoked weed, whenever I had the nerve to be ornery and when especially feeling the heat of her judgment I'd say, "You stay high every day, except yours prescribed!" To which she'd only shake her head and say, "Thas right, I'm *legal*. Can you say the same?" then tell me to her get a fresh glass of water. The rattle of the pills inside bottles almost like music, a song I knew well. She popped them in her mouth, threw her head back and swallowed.

Well, tonight as every night she was legally high, body rising to the top and ready to lay it down. "Come wake me up if you need some help down there," she told me and turned over in the bed, pulling the covers to her chin.

It was late. The rain brought a cold front that had the house feeling frigid and now Mama wore fuzzy socks on the same feet that wiggled hours before with fever.

And I? I walked down the stairs with light feet, feeling every fiber of dense carpet beneath my toes. And I? I held my nightgown close to my body as though it were a shield. And I? I was sober. Sober as fuck and irritated I'd allowed my body to recover from the day's highs. But the greasy greens and dull pork chops had made me sad. Reminded me of the source of my heartbreak's mama, who couldn't cook for shit. Burnt toast and runny eggs in the morning that I held my breath and threw my head back while swallowing. Took a deep sip of fresh water. Smiled. Tried to be agreeable. Willed my stomach to agree. It had been so exhausting pretending and the memory had dulled any legal or illegal form of intoxication.

Now I tiptoed down the stairs, pretending to be brave and already I was tired. It was still raining and the showers took turns pattering then hammering the roof with their presence. I wished the water would make up its mind. I wished the wine box I'd shoved into the red cup earlier wasn't almost empty and my weed stash already growing low.

Goddamn. Where was the pharmaceutical company of my dreams that wanted to heal and assuage the body rather than numb and lessen something while making the rest of it sicker than it already was? Cause I was ready to pop a pill.

I took the final step at the bottom of the stairs and found myself willing to open my mouth and throw my head back for a small something that would still the nerves in my chest, stop my heart from beating a rhythm I couldn't meet.

I waited a moment for my eyes to adjust to the dark and found solace in the small light emanating from Mama E's bedroom. I made my way there and stood listening before tapping on her door. When she didn't bother answering, I pushed the door open and saw her one leg under the covers and the other reaching towards her wheelchair that sat beside the bed. When she saw me, her pale hickory leg paused before tumbling to the floor with a clunk. She stopped and looked up at me, neck stiff and unyielding so I rushed to meet her gaze, only for her to say, "Well hurry up gal! Help me to my chair. I wasn't gon let yo scary ass stay the night with Bee alone."

And I huffed a lil bit, pushing and pulling her body into the chair. Smiling. Thanking something high above she hadn't ignored me after all.

I pushed her into the darkness of the hallway and she sucked her tongue, making a hissing sound. Not quite snake, not quite human. But it was enough to make me stop, jerking her chair to a halt that I instantly feared hurt her soft neck.

"Damn Boop," she said, shifting in her chair. I felt her weight maneuver from one side to the other much like her tobacco sloshed in her mouth. "Just turn a light on. We ain't gotta live this way just cause Lena mad!"

She had a point. I stumbled through the hall, feeling and pawing in the dark with clumsy hands for a light until I found it. I switched it on and suddenly we were lit up.

"Damn," she seethed, fluttering her gray eyes. "Bright ass light ain't shit but Lena wantin folks to see inside her house." She hissed again, and this time it sound human. Kinda snake. But definitely human. I needed some legal and illegal intoxication to be sure.

I pushed her towards Bee's room while she told me she was convinced Bee was faking dementia. She told me she knew Sonny ass was
triflin and probably hittin on her. She told me we were about to find
out—either way.

I tried to make her hissing sound, not quite with disagreement but
discomfort, and found my mouth unwilling to cooperate. It came out
a pissing sound. Like a man's urine hitting a hot street at night when a
bathroom couldn't be found or waited on, I thought. And then I was
bothered by the analogy and shook my head, pushing Mama Eloise
onward, convinced something was wrong with me.

Aunt Bee was surrounded and propped up on millions of pillows, so
many we wouldn't have been able to find her if not for all her brown
against all the white. Lena said she worried Bee, drunk and blunder-
ing, might fall from the bed one night but as far as I knew it'd yet to
happen. She was certainly fortified.

The lamp beside her bed was on, its yellowish orange glow gave
the room a surreal feeling against the light of the TV where Martin
said *Daaaamn Gina!* And Gina pouted in response.

I watched for a moment like, *Oh yeah I remember this episode* but there
was no time to give in to teenaged nostalgia because Mama Eloise
was hissing again. I ignored her—briefly. Or so it felt. I was drawn to
Bee's nightstand, the glow and petite glass holding whatever liquor I
assumed was her nighttime medicine. *Legal intoxication.* I picked up the
glass. Sniffed. Inhaled the fumes. Asked Bee, "Whas this?"

She looked at me with vacant eyes and said, "Water."

I shook my head like, *True.*

"Hmph," Mama Eloise said, pulling tobacco from within the soft
folds of her thighs. "Thas a damn shame." She pulled her tin foil soup
can from between her thighs and I stood for a moment in admiration
cause when had she managed that? "Boop, I'm beginnin to think you
just like yo no good ass alcoholic daddy."

And because I was sober, I felt like crying. Very briefly.

Then I shook my head like, *True.*

I looked at Bee's glass and pointed, said. "Where it's at?"

She pointed toward her makeshift kitchen and I followed the direction of her long, crooked E.T. phone-home finger, thinking Mama E might be on to something. *Dementia my ass.* Because the alcohol was sitting right there under the high beams of the kitchen light, for everyone to see in the house. Just where Bee had pointed. And I reached inside the cupboard and took down a tiny glass. Poured it. Inhaled the fumes and saw Sonny sitting in the one place the light failed to illuminate. I took a swallow and refilled. Took another drink, refilled. Threw it back. Made me another. Then walked as soberly as possible back to Bee. Back to Mama Eloise. I looked back at Sonny, his sad expression and dingy clothes. The red was gone, in both his skin and button-up. He was only a brown, briefly lit and diminished by whatever slivers of light spilled upon him. And I didn't care.

It's gon be a long night.

I hissed like a snake and lay down on the bed beside Bee, now smelling like her and not caring that the liquor splashed over into the bed as my body bounced against her pillows, soiling the white sheets. Martin was saying *Daaaamn Gina* again and I tried not to take it personal. I frowned at the television and took a sip. Tried to dredge up bad feelings about my childhood show but found myself unable. I smiled.

Yeah, I remember this episode.

"Now Imma tell you right now, Bee," Mama Eloise started. She paused to stuff her mouth with tobacco then neatly folded the top of the Red Man pack and slid it back between those endless thighs. "We might have a problem."

Bee drank from her glass and continued watching TV as if we weren't there. On the screen, Martin kicked everybody out of his house. *Get ta steppin'!* If the humor translated, Aunt Bee didn't show it. But I smiled. Feeling warm and more comfortable within her fortress.

"Matter of fact we might have a couple of problems," Mama E went on. "See this my grandbaby here." She pointed a gnarled finger at me and I sunk deeper into the fortress, hiding from her attention. "This my Boop, and she scary. And she mourning. And we both know ain't no worse combination."

Aunt Bee cocked her small head to the side and took a sip of her drink. It was all the acknowledgment Mama E needed to go on.

"See, she kinda like you. Running from ghosts. Only her ghost still alive. Least I think he livin." She looked at me for confirmation and I nodded my head with irritation.

Duh. He alive. Whatever that means. Least I think?

It was all the acknowledgment she needed to go on.

Aunt Bee took a sip and looked at me, and whatever pain I hoped the drink suppressed was evident. On my lips. On my nose, where the grief got stuck. In my eyes. In my hair, the nappy Afro my family didn't understand. He was there. When I went to take another sip of the drink, I found him there too, inside my tongue and the folds of my mouth. There was nowhere to hide and when he made his way down my throat I almost choked.

Aunt Bee moved her frail hip against mine. If it was an act of comfort, it was enough.

"Then we have the ghost." Mama E spit and looked at Aunt Bee. Her wheelchair was positioned in front of the bed, much in the way I had stood earlier begging to be heard. "The dingy nigga in the red button-up."

I felt Aunt Bee's body stiffen. She took another sip and stared ahead at the television. But the credits rolled. The show was over.

"Then," Mama E said. "We have you."

"Aunt Bee, you need some mo'?" I raised up from our pillow castle, pointed at her glass, almost empty now, while thinking of my own, almost empty now. I thought we might both need the help. She looked at me with glassy eyes and it was all the confirmation I needed. I got up and headed toward the makeshift kitchen with clumsy, sad feet.

Mama E always did this. Always knew the unspoken. Like me. Only while I never knew what to do with it, she always seemed to have a plan.

"Well hell," she yelled at me. "You might as well go head and gimme some of dat potion y'all drankin."

And I paused in the hallway. Tilted my head before continuing.

This was different. New. I'd never known Mama E to drink, save for when she was on the toilet. Then she required a cigarette, some budget domestic beer I'd never touch, and privacy. Always privacy. She didn't play about anyone bothering her while on the commode. It was a sacred time and deep down, I thought she fancied herself too pretty for anyone to know or accept the fact she shitted like the rest of us. Only with a cigarette and bad American brew.

"Ma'am?!" I hollered, pouring my drink and Aunt Bee's. Her potion a bit denser. Her glass, cloudy with the blots of her measly grip; finger imprints wrapped around the tumbler, appearing a series of warped stains on its surface. My own looking fresh and prepared to receive more.

"Pour me some!" Mama E yelled.

I frowned. I looked around, Sonny was nowhere to be seen, and I assumed he'd returned to the land of the dead. The living dead.

I opened the cabinet and pulled a fresh glass. Poured just a little. Frowned, considering for a moment how the alcohol might interact with whatever medications Mama E might be on.

"You hear me?" she yelled, and did so with the voice I often saw my mama and aunts respond to. It wasn't a request.

So I poured a little from my glass then from Aunt Bee's glass into her glass. Figured we could all do with some less is more type faith. Took it to her. Frowned with discomfort and returned to the bed. Bounced, while handing Bee another nightcap.

Mama E spit into her soup can and frowned. Sniffed her glass.

"What the fuck is this?" she asked.

I shrugged because I really didn't know. Hadn't paid that much attention to the writing on the bottle and didn't care as I poured. Aunt Bee looked straight ahead at the television now full and leaping with commercials hoping to persuade about stuff we needed but didn't yet realize, and I was reminded of the obvious. Mama E wasn't a drinker. *A dranka*. Otherwise she'd realize the foolishness of her question.

I sighed. Took a sip, and Bee took a sip as though in agreement. Her hip touched mine and I understood it as a means of communication. A bodily Morse code.

Mama E took a sip. "Damn Boop! You ain't even bother mixin with nothin?"

My foggy head thought, *Mixer?* Aunt Bee laughed and pressed her bony hip gently against mine, and I tried not to laugh. Struggled, tried to rein it in like a wild force only I was capable of taming. But it came, bursting out like sunshine, through all parts of me. I giggled and it matured. Then Bee laughed too. Deep down from the middle of her chest, it came out first a hiccup and then full-grown laughter. Like flowers we bloomed.

Mama E wasn't amused. She looked at her cup as though disgusted and it was difficult not to take it personal.

"Try it!" Aunt Bee yelled and I twisted my head towards her in surprise. Nudged her with my broad hip and took a sip. She took another sip as well. Nodded her head.

Mama E sipped. Looked up at us with her beautiful face and gangsta leaned neck, said, "This taste like the devil took a piss and told the world, come get some!"

I shrugged. She had a point.

I took another sip. Imagined the devil as a man pissing against a dark city street and sounding like my mouth when trying to imitate Mama E. And maybe that's what the devil was. Imitation in the form of flattery and we were supposed to be glad to be acknowledged at all—take it. Aunt Bee poked me with her hip, like, *Cool it.* And she was right, so I did.

The television said, *Feeling lonely?* Call 1-800-somethin'-somethin' and a white girl licked her lips and twisted her slim hips towards the screen with a desperation meant as sexiness and I felt sad.

Why did Mama E have to mention the boy? I looked at my glass. *What were we drinking?* My mind said legal intoxication, my heart said the boy. Mama E said, "OK! Back to the subject matter at hand." She threw up a gnarled hand and dropped it into her lap, and I was worried for a second before realizing—cocking my head to the side, feeling Bee nudge her non-hip—Mama E was drunk.

So soon? I shook my head. She wasn't a *dranka.* This was the second weakness I was old enough to witness and understand. And I took her in for a second, appreciating what it looked like to see her out of control. Her neck all of a sudden sittin straight and legs subtly swingin as though a child on a swing set. And she was moving higher with each sip.

Damn shame, I thought. The effects of the devil's piss.

"Now Bee," Mama E started back up. "Imma tell you right now, we see that man. And we know what he doin. But we need you to tell us *why* he doin it."

I didn't move and neither did Bee, but I wanted the answer as much as Mama Eloise.

"Now sometimes the dead hang around cause they want to." She spit in her cup and took a sip. "Lotta folks don't realize free will extend to the dead as well as the living." She held a gnarled hand up and said, "You can choose to move on to the next place or stay here." She dropped her hand. "It's all about choices." She took another sip, screwed her face up and said, "But here's the kicker, if he's touching you. Never mind beatin ya ass, but can actually lay hands on you? It's cause he's been given authority to—which tells me you did somethin that gave him that power."

This was getting deep. I raised up out of the fortress and away from Bee.

Roots.

Mama Eloise heard and saw me. Nodded her head.

"Now if you put somethin on the nigga that sent him to the sweet by and by, you ain't the first and won't be the last. But now you gotta figure out how to live with him showin out or figure how to make him move on." She took another sip and coughed. "To the next destination."

I nodded my head like, *True.*

Aunt Bee's hip reached for mine and I sighed. Not wanting to give her the comfort if it meant forcing her to acknowledge Mama Eloise. But because I'm sensitive. Because I'm a sucka, I went ahead and scooted over some. Nudged her small side.

"Now me see." Mama E spit. "I ain't ever let a nigga hit on me." She sipped. "Shiiiiit I'd kill a nigga dead just for tryin."

I shook my head cause it was also true. Growing up, I'd seen the strewn bullet holes throughout her home as evidence, stuck my small fingers in the cracks of the walls.

"Did the nigga you mourning ever lay hands on you, Boop?"

Startled by her attention again, my body tensed at her question. I reached towards Bee for a helping hip but she was not there.

"Not with his hands, but his words." I said it quick and quiet, so quiet I wasn't sure they'd heard me at all. Then very quickly buried my face in the tiny glass and downed the remainder of my drink.

"That counts," Aunt Bee said.

It was all the confirmation Mama Eloise needed.

She smiled, looked at me like, *Didn't I tell you her ass was fakin?* and asked me for a refill, as though granting me and Bee reprieve from further questions. As though granting me permission to keep on rising high, so long as she was along for the ride. And I did. I filled our glasses.

Sonny was still missing in action and I considered it a victory of sorts.

When I returned to the room, I turned the television off and Aunt Bee still stared ahead as though it were on. Mama E asked if I had any music. She was feelin it. I was sure she was feelin it and I was happy to share this side of myself with her, to meet where my heart beat.

So I pulled out my music player and plugged it into the TV, then turned it back on. Bee looked like I'd committed an act of magic when the sound came blasting out. It was Luther. He dead too, I thought but said nothing. Let Luther speak for himself. *Bad boy,* he sang. *Last time we had a party it ended when the sun came up.*

Mama Eloise snapped her fingers then said, "This ain't the blues but it's awright!" And her gray eyes fluttered wide before closing. She moved her big hips and thighs in her chair and it rocked. I stood beside her shaking my hips. Pointed my fingers at Bee like, *Girl get with it!* And she smiled. Moved her lil hips though I wasn't there to feel 'em. I closed my eyes (*ah yeah!*), raised my arms (*well awright!*).

Everybody swingin, dancing to the music, on the radio, havin' a party!

And I wasn't sure if we were celebrating having survived both being violent and having it committed against us. Wasn't sure of anything other than my melancholy was lifted for the moment, I wasn't alone and within this space I could be myself. A young woman who saw the dead, who knew the mystical was as valid as the scientific and who was grateful to be with others who shared in that knowledge, whether Bee acknowledged it or not. Didn't stop me from shaking my hips down to the floor and Mama E shouting, "Is you got fever wit it Boop? She need a man, don't she Bee?" And Bee took a sip and laughed in agreement. And at some point, while deeply legally intoxicated, I shouted over the music, "I need a wheelchair to hang with y'all. We gon' give new meaning to rollin up on a nigga!"

"The n-word!" Aunt Bee called back and laughed and laughed. We laughed.

By the end of the night, the morning glow was dim but there. I was still dancing, all serious, flinging my thin arms around, all serious, and singing to Joni Mitchell's "Don't Interrupt This Sorrow" on repeat.

Aunt Bee, having swayed in the bed, raising her arms and shaking those fragile hips, drunkenly dozed off mid-party. And Mama Eloise had started reminiscing about the French husband. Tried speaking the few French words she remembered. Then her fragile neck had given out, dipped into gangsta lean permanency and I knew it was time to shut it down. I pushed her across the hall to her room. Huffed and stumbled with drunkenness, put her in the bed while she cooed, "You shoulda played some Lightnin' Hopkins." Then something incoherent in French and I kept sayin *s'il vous plaît*, the only word I knew other than *moi* while pushing her big body far enough under the covers until I felt secure she was safe. Not all the pillows. But she wouldn't come tumbling down.

I started out the door then feeling my own bladder complaining stopped, went back to the bed and said, "You don't have to use the bathroom, do you?" But she patted her ass and I saw the diaper. I nodded my head and turned to leave.

"Boop," she said low, the covers and pillows smothering her voice. I heard her and stopped. "You gotta learn how to love. He wasn't no worse than you with his mouth. Y'all just ain't know how to love."

I stared ahead at how the morning light dimpled across the hallway, creating small shadows and waves. Outside the trees bent and twisted under the weight of falling rain, their silhouette a moving abstract painting against the walls.

"I want you to have the love you deserve, but you can't be so *scary*."

And I strained to hear if other words of wisdom would come forth but when all I heard were her snores, light then loud, I blinked away the tears and left.

I only stopped again when I heard the sound of voices. Authoritative, faux friendly and formal. And in my fog, I wasn't sure if it was the television or Sonny's return. So I moved in their direction until I found the source. The morning news anchor was too bubbly and serious for my senses. The TV was on in the theater room, a small nook housing several leather chairs and couches before a big screen that showed images projected from a digital box tucked away in a closet where the door remained perpetually open, otherwise the remote wouldn't work.

Marcel's round head was barely visible over the top of his recliner. I walked in closer, assuming he was asleep. I intended to turn the television off and let his unconscious mind rest, grant a reprieve from the bad news delivered in confusingly somber but upbeat tones. *Fucking morning news.* I picked up the remote, heard the blonde woman say something about bombings and dead children on the other side of the planet then segue into the best ways to protect your home from cleaning products that might be secretly killing your family. *Fucking morning news.* A white man with perfectly coiffed brown hair stood holding a mop, and beside him were various brands of bleach, liquid dishwasher, laundry detergent. He smiled. And they went to commercial.

"Ketinah? What you doin up this early?"

I was startled by Marcel's voice. He turned in his chair and pushed the purple blanket from his chin.

"I heard the TV," I said. It was true. It was an answer. It was a way to avoid reacting to the obvious which was Marcel was shockingly thin. He wasn't thin, he was skin and bones. His face was a papier-mâché mask with skin stretched taut and if I looked too long I could see his blood, his blood vessels, capillaries. His lips dry and cracked. Eyes cloudy in the ways dogs and old people become in the last years of their lives.

"Oh." It was all he said and looked back towards the screen.

I put the remote down.

We were silent for a moment save for the voice of a white woman telling us what kinda matte lipstick we needed to be desirable and smudge-free.

"Why you not in bed?"

I blurted it out. It just came out, like my words were sometimes known for behaving—unpredictable, with no real direction but the truth.

"I didn't wanna wake Lena," he mumbled, eyes fixed on the television.

"Why?" I blurted out. "You just get here?" And I could taste the liquor on my breath so I was sure he could smell it. Taste and smell synonymous, so said science.

He shuffled in the chair, his bones from beneath the blanket poking out in sharp and obtuse angles; a geometrical haze. "I just didn't wanna disturb Lena."

I said nothing. Looked at the TV and a commercial asked if anyone I knew or loved had taken a drug and suffered multiple debilitating side effects including death. My mind ran with the many medications my mama took. Mama E took. I frowned and my head hurt. I needed some water and the thought reminded me I had to pee.

I turned to leave and Marcel asked, "How's Aunt Bee?"

I didn't know how to answer so I was quiet, my mouth sworn allegiance to truth. *Check on her sometime and yo ass would know.*

"And how your auntie?" he asked.

"Lena?" I answered. "Worried bout you as always."

"Lena," he mumbled and smiled. "My beautiful Lena."

He closed his eyes. Pulled the blanket to his chin.

"Why don't you go get in the bed?"

"In a minute," he answered, eyes closed.

I went to hand him the remote, place it in his hands so he wouldn't have to move far to find it when he chose to turn the television off, and I was struck by his truth.

"Thank you," he mumbled. "You know my body won't allow me to do what it used to do."

He needn't say a word. One touch of his skin and I felt it all. Marcel was sick. Sicker than anybody knew. Even Lena, his beautiful Lena. The cancer had spread and my body jumped where I felt its presence. His prostate. His colon. His bone. Those tiny, birdlike bones. I saw him at the hospital the day before receiving treatment. Saw him paying at the cashier's desk, pulling out his debit card when the nurse told him how much the insurance covered and what remained.

What remained.

What remained?

After treatment he'd gone to a hole in the wall Mexican restaurant not far from the Alamo. Ordered enchiladas with refried beans. His favorites. But he couldn't hold it down. He ran to the bathroom where he remained, sweating and retching up what little he'd swallowed. He went back to his table and the waitress, whose English was poor, smiled then asked if he was ready for the check. She scanned the table, where his plate sat sullen and sad. Untouched. And he tried to smile but felt nauseous. So he nodded his head. Placed the red piece of cloth he'd been given with his utensils against his mouth, then his face where the sweat and strain of trying to hold his insides threatened to break down. And the young waitress, pretty, big breasts and unaccustomed to seeing Blacks inside the joint, looked confused. But she wanted a tip all the same.

Still Marcel sat there for hours. The check idled inside the black folder but he wasn't prepared to go home yet so he asked for a beer, hoping it might relieve some of the nausea before he gave up. But his fourth trip to the bathroom confirmed there was no cure and his throat was raw, sore from trying. His stomach a puddle not too unlike the potholes he'd circumvented while pulling his Mercedes into the tiny parking lot, where the rain collected as though fresh water poured into jagged bowls. He'd watched the rain from a faraway window, or rather the steam of the rain. The glass was wet and hot, the steam gathered like breath then dissipated and he thought it was probably just like death.

There was music, mariachi music blaring like sharp daggers against his body when Marcel finally pulled out his debit card, placed it in the folder and handed it to the waitress with shaky hands. He looked at his food, untouched, and he wanted to ask for a to-go box but feared Lena might assume worse than she already thought.

Better her think that than know the truth. The dildo. The strap-on was enough. He hated it. Resented its pink plastic, the only one he could find that fit his slim shape and did what he wanted. What he could no longer do. Better she be bruised than disappointed.

Lena, his beautiful Lena. So romantic. So reliable. The only woman he'd ever known—sisters and mother alike—who did what she said she was gonna do. Even what she hadn't agreed to do.

He loved her. Though he wasn't sure how. Didn't know how.

And he was sick. Sicker than anyone knew, and more than he was willing to admit to himself.

I felt it all. Jerked my hand away from the heat of his skin and moved away. He shifted in the chair and snored. Light, airy breaths that were faint enough for me to accept what he could not. What he didn't want anyone else to know.

I went to the bathroom, avoiding my reflection in the mirror. Peed then stumbled through the morning light back to Bee's room and fell into the bed. She was snoring, light airy breaths, undisturbed. I pulled the covers to my chin and placed a few pillows around myself for security. Something to hold on to.

But sleep would not come.

And I lay in bed beside Bee in an agitated fit. First throwing the covers off my body then just as quickly pulling them back up. The dry south Texas air both cool and hot; the falling rain creating a jungle-like humidity, the bedroom still dark as though the world couldn't decide if it was ready to be day or not, save for the glow, that morning glow—and the house now felt both cool and hot. And it must have been, because all morning I traveled through states of chills and fever, struggling under liquor-stained sheets for relief. When Aunt Bee turned her head over her shoulder and said with a heavy voice, "You need to be still!" it was enough to both frighten then send me up and moving back to the bathroom where I stood in the glow of a shell-shaped night light examining my face.

I looked at myself.

Finally.

Frowned.

Looked closer and leaned in, squeezing a pimple on my chin until it gave in and oozed with pus. I watched the blood rush to its surface something like a volcano releasing itself, before cresting over and burning red. I looked in the medicine cabinet for Campho-Phenique, the end-all, be-all, fix-it-all and found nothing but a small container of K-Y jelly.

Ugh.

I sighed and closed the door, rushing to push any visual of Lena's body meeting the jelly out of my head.

But it was too late. There they were in my mind's eye awkwardly fumbling over each other's bodies, his cancer and her romance bumping into the other, private parts slick with gel. I frowned again, pushed my face closer to the mirror and began counting the small eruptions across the canvas of my skin. Anything to distract. At five, I stopped, having returned to the moment; sighed and piddle-paddled back to Aunt Bee's room. Softly, I eased inside the dark room. Gently, I closed the door and slid back into bed where I fell asleep without much effort.

Aunt Bee never stirred. There was no Sonny. It was morning and there was no sun.

And I dreamt.

Inside my dream was Mama Eloise, rocking in the chair on her porch back home. Her hair, thick and gray, slung across her shoulders in two long braids. She smiled when she saw me approaching and without ceasing her rock, leaned over the chair's wood handles where her arms rested and spit a wad of tobacco juice onto the Earth's floor.

"Come on," she beckoned. "Sit yo narrow ass down on Mama's porch."

I obeyed, feeling calm, feeling the midday sun on my neck. I stooped down and sat, glad for the cool cement pavement against my thighs. I wore a sundress not very unlike her own. Instinctively I reached for her laced hem, just as I would as a child, fondling its stiff cotton ends, smelling the fresh starch holding the material at attention.

"You think I don't know nothin bout love and romance, don't you?" She laughed, and her right cheek was fat with snuff.

"Soul mates," she continued. "What you might call true love, huh?"

I said nothing, instead focused on the faded strawberries running down her legs. Bruises and broken veins that had settled over time into sweet patches of pink, red and blue.

"I do though. I know all bout dat dere. But even that ain't so easy. Ain't so fast. Cause even if you lucky nuff to cross paths in this ol' world—" She leaned over, spitting again and wiping a brown trail of spit from her chin. "And even if you say you knew him time you locked eyes, from that day forward it's a slow burn. Knowing it's love ain't enuff. Not until you start the loving. Just like being alive ain't enuff until you start living."

She spit again, this time a long fluid stream that briefly shook in the breeze before falling.

"Look at Mama's azaleas over there," she said.

I let go of her dress and glanced over at the purple and pink buds shooting from the garden that wrapped around her wood-frame house.

"Don't just glimpse at 'em!" she said and slapped my arm hard enough to leave my flesh stinging. "Look at 'em!"

I turned my body around, fully taking in the black soil, the green stems, how the leaves reached for the rays of the sun.

"See, I knew before I bought my seeds what I wanted. Knew exactly how I wanted 'em placed just so, few inches apart and I knew the seasons when they'd grow and the times they might die. But I had to learn all of this over time before I got it right. Hear me?"

I strained my eyes from the intensity of the sun and cupped my hands over them like a visor. "I guess so," I said.

"Aw hell girl, you just like your daddy. All intellect and no more sense than a betsy bug."

"Look," she said, standing up, her plump body shielding me from the sun and blackening her features till all that appeared to my watery eyes was a thick silhouette towering over me as if a giant.

"It don't matter what I know. It don't even matter what I want. So long as I don't tend to them 'zaleas ain't nothin gon grow. You hear me? But if I don't know how to tend to 'em they may as well be dead. Matter of fact, they might as well never been born. Let 'em stay seeds till I'm learned and ready to help them thrive."

She kneeled down in front of me, her back popping, her dress rising enough to reveal scabbed knees and blue broken varicose veins running like a map across her pale skin. She jerked my face up to meet hers and held it inside her gnarled hands. When she spoke again the tobacco was held tight to the inside of her jaw.

"But this is the key, baby, and you remember Mama told you this. For anything to grow in God's world you got to first believe it can."

"Believe?" I stared intently at the black lines of her pupils retracting into the cloudy gray mass surrounding them.

"Believe. That's what it's all about. That's everything right there. Faith."

When I woke up, Aunt Bee was gone. There were only the pillows and a sea of white. The room was dark and I was confused as to where I was. Then I smelled the liquor, on the sheets and in my throat, heard the thunder and remembered. And I sat up and looked for Mama Eloise because I was sure she was there. I looked for Sonny because I was sure he might be there. But I was alone.

My head hurt. I had to pee. The pimple on my chin throbbed with heat and I pulled the covers to my face. Cold. I needed some water, but instead of seeking relief, I lay there, listening to the rain fall and stop. Fall and stop.

Fall.

. . .

I was awake.

My mama stood over me, eyes wide and her mouth twisted. She was yelling and my head hurt. I needed some water.

The room was still dark. Aunt Bee was gone to get her bath.

"She stank like liquor, you stank like liquor and Mama stank like liquor!"

My mama was shouting and I wanted to say *Shhh. Shhh.* But who was I to hush my mama? Her pink foam rollers were shaking in her head and I had no way of knowing the time of day. I tilted my head and watched her big body move, pointing at me then elsewhere, arms flailing.

And I wondered if she'd had her insulin.

I frowned, then the heat of her anger warmed me some and I stretched under the sheets. My limbs felt like forever and it was good until I smelled the liquor. Felt nauseous. Gathered myself and understood her point.

"Now I already let you have your medicine in my house!"

My "medicine" was her code word for the marijuana I smoked. Sometimes all day—on the good days—laid up on the couch watching her watch her soap operas and the soap operas watch me. *Young and the Restless.* Listened to her talk to her best friend Jeanette about her soap operas. Bout Victor. Listened to her say to me, "Jeanette at the game room and lyin' bout it, like I care."

But she did. My mama cared. She tried not to judge but it was always there. Ripe. The harvest was every day, and she picked and plowed until her own medicine was a distant memory and she lived in a strange place where everyone around her had issues she was forced to ignore. For their sake. Never mind her own.

"But the drinking? You know I can't stand that!"

It was true. She equated drinking with my father. My father, still a distant idea in her mind, infinitely separated from the fact he was after all the man she'd chosen to marry, procreated with though he was a drunk and violent.

My father.

She didn't want to believe I was like him. Wanted to deny the idea and fact of him. The idea and fact of me. That the alcohol might very well be in the blood. That the addiction might very well be from both sides.

My father.

Mama.

I listened to her.

"You know *my mama* is sick!"

Uh-oh. She was laying it on extra thick now. The emphasis on *my mama* told me everything I needed to know. I was no longer part of the family, not in this equation. For now, I was a thing in the way, an unhealthy intrusion between her and *her mama's* well-being.

I shifted under the covers and felt nauseous.

"Why you would think it was awright to give her alcohol escapes the fuck outta me!" Her eyes bulged. The pink foam rollers expanded inside her anger, the heat, and all of a sudden her head appeared huge. Like some hot air balloon or kite that was floating away from itself. I wanted to laugh to keep from crying or being sick in Aunt Bee's bed. I tried not to imagine her words sounding like some warped Shakespearean play where I was the villain and it both appalled and "escaped her" that the villain had come from her own body.

Then I thought to myself, shit! If this was a Shakespearean play I was prolly bout to die. I shifted under the covers, smelled a liquor stain, hard and rank beside my face. Thought *Out out damned spot!*

I frowned, and scanned the room for Sonny and he was nowhere. I sighed in relief. Nobody needed him to be the escort to the afterlife cause it couldn't mean good things.

Mama continued yelling.

I looked down at my attire and realized I didn't wanna die in a dingy white gown stained with an unknown alcohol whose fumes permeated the entire room.

"Get yo ass up!" Mama yelled, snatching the covers from my body. "Do you even know what time it is?"

"What time is it?" I asked, feeling weak and exposed. Yet also surprisingly cool, refreshed, and I realized my body had needed the air.

"Hell if I know," she yelled. "But I know it's too late for you still be in bed reeking of alcohol!"

Trick questions. My head hurt. I had to pee.

"Is Mama Eloise awright?"

"Whatchu think?!" she yelled.

And then I was worried. Afraid. Until I heard Mama E's voice in the distance yelling, "Now don't burn my biscuits, Lena, damn!"

"Eloise, don't start with me!" Lena said quick, hurried.

I heard the oven door open and slam, then smelled bacon and immediately felt nauseous. Then the room was filled with beeping. A beeping so loud and pervasive that for a moment I was convinced it meant I was dying. Time was up and I wore a dingy, alcohol-stained nightgown. I held my face in my hands preparing for an afterlife of drunkards and heartbroken potheads until I heard Mama Eloise again.

"Goddamn, Lena!"

"Hush, Eloise! Hand me that towel!"

"Now how Imma do that from way over here in this chair?"

Mama looked towards the door and yelled, "Lena whas goin' on in there?!"

"Goddamn fire 'larm!" she called back. "Shit too sensitive!"

"Maybe yo food too mistreated!" Mama Eloise yelled.

"Hush!" Lena called, jumping and fanning the smoke alarm with her hands.

"My biscuits!" Mama E yelled.

And I laughed. Though my head and heart ached. Though there was still the aching bladder and my mama's venom. I laughed so hard I was afraid again, only that I'd piss the sheets and then what would they say of me? What would my mama think of me that she already didn't? Her drunkard daughter debased to getting senior citizens inebriated for the company. Peed in the goddamn bed. Then died amidst a sea of white pillows and biscuit smoke.

My father's child.

And my mama stood with her hands on her hips, pink foam rollers tired upon her head. When she spoke again they didn't even bother to move, so indifferent they'd become to the outcome of the situation.

"Clean yaself up and come upstairs when you done. We need to talk."

Her words had the kinda finality only a Black mama was capable of inspiring. Fear. Real fear. And death. The real kinda death; mysterious but certain. Muddy waters, bluesy and smoke-filled rooms where Black mamas conspired to bring their children into the world and take them out if necessary. Only now there was a consensus and they were all in agreement.

Ketinah gotta go!

I sighed and wanted to plead my case, but damn I had to pee and Mama turning on her heels to stomp out the room, hands still on hips, meant I too could move on with life. With nature.

Never mind the fact that Mama Eloise sounded fine, and I was sure Aunt Bee, bathed, newly liquored up and soon to be fed, no matter the quality of the food, was also fine.

Never mind my mama, so eager to get Mama E to the house for a visit, had spent little time with her. Whose own constitution wasn't strong enough to witness her mother's state so she was content knowing her mama was near, was clean and fed though she couldn't stand to look at her, interact with her for too long because her grief and memory of what Mama E once was wouldn't allow it. She was happy to nuzzle her wide back against Mama E's in the bed during sleep, her natural state, because knowing her mama was there was enough.

Never mind I felt like the only one who saw Mama E as she was. Who loved her. Accepted her body's changes. Knew she knew. Saw what she saw. Believed in nothing else but the idea, the fact that she saw me too.

—⌗—

Peaches

"What's in the closet?" Faye asked. And Peaches would shrink beneath the covers, fold herself into the dark of the room. She was five years old and there was only the light from the stove in the kitchen that snaked and wove its way into the small bedroom she shared with her older sisters.

She couldn't breathe.

Their bodies were stacked in the full-size bed like sardines so that if one pissed the bed they all swam in the lake. And if one tossed, turned, rolled in the tight space with the miseries of the day, they all struggled to find peace. Nightmares were shared and felt alike, though never acknowledged come daylight. In the bed they were one shining organism of varying shades, each given by that of their fathers. Henry. Travis. Deo.

"What's in the closet?" Faye asked. "The boogeyman?"

Peaches never answered. Peaches was too afraid of the dark as well as the light that wiggled beneath their door. The light that lifted the veil, and the mystery that was her sisters' pain. She felt their pain. Their dislike and taunting that commenced once the sun went down and they were bathed, fed and alone with their baby sister. *Deo's daughter.* The man who made their mama dance rather than shoot. The daughter who was all the colors of a peach combined, fully formed, ripe and healthy to eat come summer so she was Peaches. She had Eloise and Deo's light eyes. Their full lips and curly hair that smelled like white people when gone too long without washing. Her hair didn't dry or crumble under heat; it became wet. Slick with oil that both sisters said made her smell like a wet dog in the rain, and it was true. She knew it wasn't a lie because she smelled it too and shrunk beneath its odor.

"What's in the closet?" Faye would ask.

Peaches wanted to pull the covers to her face, to cover her entire existence because she figured fuck the closet—dark, tiny and stuffed with the few articles of clothing their bodies shared—nothing was scarier than the sight of her older sister Faye, whose face was so close to her own she could smell her breath. Smell the garlic and onions of the gizzards they had for dinner.

What's in the closet?

As she grew older, she'd think to herself: Me.

Moi.

The word she heard her mama holler at them once in anger and accusation. They hadn't come inside the house before the streetlights burned bright; Peaches from playing stickball in the abandoned cemetery where the grass grew too high and unkept so the faded stone templates had disappeared over time and now kids her age used the open field for fun. Unafraid. They ran to first base. Second. Over the bones of the forgotten.

And Faye hadn't come home from dipping and diving against the stone wall of the Baptist church on the hill where she allowed the fingers of Calvin into her body, and sighed in feigned pleasure though it felt awful. His chubby fingers, dirty with peanut butter and cheese and prone to causing yeast infections that she tried a multitude of home remedies to cure, but seldom worked because there she was, allowing his digits into her thick body. Again. She was too afraid to tell him to wash his hands. *Just wash yo muthafuckin hands, damn!* Instead she just took it. All ten nasty fingers, his nails pinning her to the church wall.

And Cora was at the Negro library studying picture books cause she thought she might draw well. A teacher said she made shapes that came to life, and the idea of life was enough to excite her adolescent mind. She drew the sun. She drew clouds, as though a child and not her teenage self. She drew herself and found the sketch so ugly, so dark, so deformed she was determined to draw better. Be better. Be lighter and not Eloise's darkest child. But better. She wanted to get better at sketching but the lines and curves she drew refused to cooperate.

"Don't ever fuckin disrespect *moi* again!" Eloise yelled while bringing the worn leather strap against their asses, their legs, their feet. Anywhere the belt would hit.

Moi?

And all three girls had lain in the bed like sardines, bodies throbbing, and listened to Deo question Eloise. And Peaches cried even harder because Faye had kicked her hard, her leg stretching across Cora's welts to reach Peaches—and Cora was angered by Faye's movement against her aching body; she felt like just cause they couldn't see the deep purple marks against her skin didn't mean they weren't there. But Cora said nothing and Peaches only cried while Faye kicked again and hissed for her to be quiet so they could hear the answers to Papa Deo's questions.

Why she have to whoop 'em so hard? Why was she still thinkin bout the French man?

But there were no answers. Eloise grew quiet and Deo dropped it. He grew quiet too.

And Peaches grew intrigued over time and with age, with the word that brought both parents to silence, a rare and strange thing in their home. *Moi.*

Me.

She watched her body grow like her mama's garden. Looked up the word *moi* at the Negro library. Determined it was her. And she wanted to bring silence to all. Silence representing respect. There was no answer to her. Nor to her brother, whose hand she held while walking up and down the dirt roads in front of their home. Who she prayed to God to heal; his eyes, his mind, his spirit. He was becoming violent with age, as though he felt ignored, unimportant and angry at the body he'd been provided. He would fight against his skin, his mind, and tongue. When he tried to talk his words slurred, betraying him though he'd never had a drink in his life.

Duane wanted to see but his eyes, distorted prisms of light, were too cloudy and they ignored his desires, too, cause he wanted to see. Be heard. Be seen even if he couldn't. And he would push and pull, through his blindness, at anyone who got in the way of his fight.

Peaches would walk with him and he felt the sun against his skin and heard her light footsteps, felt the pressure of her warm hands. But when she grabbed his face and prayed over him, he'd reach out with strong lumbering arms to push her away, cause who was this God she prayed to who'd made him this way? Who'd shaped him not to live but to be something unheard. Unseen. Unable to see.

He stayed in the back room, in his own special closet, in the dark except for the daily visits, walks and kisses of Peaches and Eloise. It hurt Deo and he looked away. Cora and Faye were too scared of what was in his closet so they didn't try to look at all.

Eloise fed, bathed him. She cried and kissed him more. Peaches whispered to him, their secrets. She played him music unlike the blues that filled their home. She danced before him and took his hands, tried moving them to a beat she hoped he'd find. But Duane was discontent, moving closer to the heat of rage every day. He was growing uncontrollable with age, there was no rhythm to his madness and Eloise feared she could no longer care for him at home. She was eventually told by state government officials that she could no longer care for him at home.

And Peaches walked with Duane. Took his face in her hands, said, *Moi!* No matter what—*Moi!* Block out what they say about you, because *moi!* Block out the fear and anger. Be still. Be silent so you can stay.

Silence them all with *moi*.

What was in the closet?

It wasn't a monster. It was Peaches. Waiting.

It was Duane rejected. Expressing all the emotions she could not. Still her sisters acted afraid so they avoided him. And so Peaches felt they were afraid of her too cause she and Duane were the same. Inside the same fight with God that commenced and refused to slumber no matter the time of the day. Turmoil aching, reaching, grasping and choking their bodies.

What's in the closet?

Us.

The day they took Duane to the state home, Eloise stayed in bed for days. Days that turned into weeks. Weeks that turned into months. Inconsolable.

Deo drove down to Austin, a place seemingly continents away from their little town in East Texas and saw Duane was safely put. Clean. Fed.

Duane slurred, his voice rising high and distorted, asking for his Peach and music. The nurse was confused but she rubbed his back as though he were a baby. And Deo remembered the tape inside his back pocket. Peaches had made and sent it with him, and already he'd forgotten. He reached it to the nurse and said, "I think this what he want." The nurse took it, and looked confused before touching Deo's arm as if he too were a child and said, "He'll be alright."

And Peaches walked the dirt roads all day and into the night by herself, past the streetlights flickering on. Crying. Feeling like a failure, like God was a failure. Alone. Alone.

Moi!

God was a failure and her hair stank. She stank and she was alone. And Mama Eloise let her sit within the funk, so taken she was with her own grief, so afraid she was of her other daughters fearing favoritism towards Peaches. Her child by the man who made her dance. So she continued to play the blues, loud. Washed Peaches's head in the kitchen sink with hard and heavy hands that said *Be strong. Whas the matter with you? Be strong!*

But Peaches wasn't strong. She'd go to Duane's room and sit for hours. Cry for hours and no one questioned where she was. Questioned if she was awright.

She made good grades. She didn't mess with boys. Her body was lean and untouched. She went to church with her mama and Deo, bowed her head in prayer. She cried realizing she still believed. And she grew angry that she still believed in a God who made mistakes.

But Peaches wasn't strong. She was strong. But she wasn't strong. Not in the ways Eloise wanted her to be.

She grew anxious to leave home, to somehow escape Eloise's judgment.

Her sisters left home and for a moment there was some sense of peace. Faye married the boy with the dirty fingers. Cora got pregnant by the first man she met who seemed to appreciate her colors. He was darker than her and she was mesmerized by his black. Never mind everyone said he was in love with Lena, that he tried to coax Lena down from the roof of the smokehouse to talk and Lena had ignored him, her head too far up in the blue of the clouds. She couldn't see him as Cora did. A beautiful picture. The best one she ever visualized, only he was real. He was a dark and starry night she was determined to draw. Better. The right way. And smarting from Lena's rejection and feeling seen, appreciated for the first time, he entered Cora. Walked into her sketch. She got pregnant and they soon married too.

Peaches finally had the room to herself. The stove light was off and she preferred it dark. The bed was wide and open. She roamed, explored its spaces, turned over at night alone and feared nothing but God. Herself.

She rode to the farm with her daddy, felt the pull of the engine jerk, the raggedy truck forward and stop before resuming as though all was fine. And it was fine because they kept moving.

At the farm, the animals were kind and gentle. She rubbed them unafraid, and they responded to her touch. They moved closer to her body. They followed her wherever she went whenever she was there. She had that effect on animals, though she wasn't sure about humans. And she wanted to get away, some place far away to figure it all out.

She was Eloise's first child to go to college and Eloise made a big deal of it. She made her cabbage and chicken spaghetti with sweet cornbread. Peaches's favorites. Even made tea cakes for dessert and Peaches ate it all, feeling full and seen.

Her daddy said, "The only thang you can't do is what you believe you can't." He kissed her cheek hard, hugged her and Eloise hugged her. Took her hands, looked in her eyes and said nothing.

And just like that, Peaches left.

First, she went to Houston. To an all-Black college but it felt too close to the things she was running from. It was the '70s and she wasn't always sure when her classmates shouted "I'm Black and I'm proud!" that they were talking about her too.

What's in the closet? Moi?

Who's Black and proud?

Moi.

Peaches thought of Cora's skin and wished she was her. She always had, it was another secret. She knew Cora was Eloise's prettiest daughter. But she also knew Cora never realized her beauty, and when she looked at Peaches's skin she also wished she was her. Neither were satisfied with themselves, neither ever saw themselves as beautiful the way their mother was in their eyes.

By the time she was nineteen, Peaches figured there was no peace to be found, not in the body, not in the many colors of Black women of any shade.

She took the bus to Austin once a month to meet her mama and visit Duane. She sat in class, had daydreams she was too afraid to pursue. Paris, for instance, where *moi* was an everyday occurrence but what was a skinny lightskin girl with white-folks-smellin hair from East Texas supposed to do in *Moi*? She didn't know. She wasn't sure. But Houston wasn't Paris or home, so she transferred, this time to Dallas. She met Jeanette there and they'd bonded over their mutual sadness—Nettie had lost her mother, Peaches had lost her brother. If not to death then to something she couldn't describe.

God had failed them both and still they believed in something good, a greater purpose that designed the unknowables of their lives. That tomorrow might hold something different. Something better.

For a moment Peaches thrived there despite her dreams of another country like France. And she graduated with two degrees, doing so in less than four years because eventually she wasn't comfortable in Dallas with the other young Black women who possessed the confidence she lacked. Though they looked at her: Light skin. Light eyes. Curly hair. In their minds she had every right to stand tall, but her insecurities were too grave.

They didn't understand she was in the closet. Would remain there in the dark, suffocating until she found someone to share the tight space with. Her drunk uncle called her mama "Fish" and she still felt like a sardine inside the can seeking its likeness.

But who liked sardines other than poor folks?

My father.

Drunk. Equally afraid. Poor.

But he was looking for something else. Something the white folks' education might bring and it was the '70s. *Ungawa Black Power!* And his

Afro believed in the heights he was capable of reaching long before his spirit did. Peaches's met him and her fro had the faith too, and in all his broken parts.

My father.

His anger that came out when he drank too much, went to class, and came back to the dorm ready to drink some more. Peaches had faith. Peaches wanted to take him on long walks and pray over him. He was from a small East Texas town too. He grew up in a shack along dirt roads not unlike her own, and she was ready to walk with him. So she did. She took his hand and walked straight to the church. Married. Prepared to heal him. Prayed to God to heal him because in him she saw herself.

When they had me, he was too drunk to be at the birth. But when he finally saw me, overdue with wrinkly skin, he cried.

He was sober.

He cried and held me then said, "She gon have whatever she want." And Peaches cried, shook her head in agreement and said, "Whatever she wants."

And for a spell there was peace.

But it didn't last. Their love was a lost and mistaken reflection visible only on one of those rare days when the sun's rays actually blinded, and mamas like Eloise's and daddies like Deo's warnings couldn't be heard over the pain of a child's heartache. Their baby, Peaches, had a heart that longed for a place to rest, with the freedom to stretch. To be accepted. To believe in God again, truly. For God to redeem Himself, truly. To love, truly.

L-O-V-E.

An imperfect, unconditional love she possessed for everyone but herself.

My mama knew how to love. She loved. She loved. She loved to her own detriment. Then she loved some more. Till she finally said *Fuck it!* My father pushed her into a wall while drunk and threatened to hit her while pushing the vomit back down the corridors of his body. My mama finally said fuck it. She gathered her baby girl and left the small trailer they shared in Waco. She sped down the Texas highways, watching the landscape turn from flat and brown to tall and green.

East Texas.

Divorced with me, and twenty-five years old she moved back home. I was three years old. And she raised me alone. Mama Eloise helped. Deo helped. And no one ever mentioned him.

My father.

Too drunk and too hurt to participate. Too drunk so he'd call on the weekends with slurred speech crying into the phone, asking to speak to his daughter. Ketinah. And he cried. And my mama listened, then allowed me to listen too. Until she hung up the phone. Looked at me and said, "Thas your daddy."

My father.

And Peaches kept moving; she became a teacher. She taught special children, those who couldn't talk or walk, or even see for themselves. Those societies had seemingly given up on. Those in the closet. And she taught them moi! Moi! And they loved her as much as I loved her.

I admired my mama. Loved her deeply. I grew as Mama Eloise's garden, slow to start before stretching towards the sun, hoping to one day bloom, and to me, my mama was as a standard I might never reach. But I was willing to enter her closet and sit. Learn from her all the ways of how to be broken and still give, still blossom. Even if she was judgmental, sometimes. Cause none of us were perfect all the time. Every flower has its flaws and therein lies its perfection.

And Peaches. Well, Peaches was special in only the ways God allowed the chosen to be; to teach and work with *Her* special ones.

Mama Eloise knew it. I knew it.

Peaches was still a child but she was a woman. She loved again, eventually, truly, after the demise of her marriage to my father. She loved a man who saw how special she was and treated her as such. They never married but they were married in my eyes.

And I grew up watching them dance in the kitchen, hold one another close. I grew romantic. I was a flower bending towards the sun, only now to kiss it. Worship it. I believed in love, and I believed in God. Watching my mama be both a woman and child in his arms.

Knowing and accepting it was alright to be both. Ideal, to be both.

I just wanted her to see it too. So maybe she wouldn't be scared anymore of what she saw when she looked at me. Which was Mama Eloise. Which was herself. And my father.

Cause after Duane and Papa Deo died, something in Mama Eloise died too, and her body gave up and caved in on itself. A closet too small for her presence, she was tucked away in her own body's darkness. And Faye, who lived in San Antonio with Lena, and Cora who lived down the street in Austin, all conspired to take Eloise to south Texas. To see about her.

And my mama—whose partner, much older than her, also got sick around the same time—caved in. Left in East Texas alone, she went within the closet and stayed. Didn't come back out unless medicated and prepared to navigate the world sedated. The rest she was content to sleep through.

And I watched it all. Fighting, lashing out against my own fears and anxieties and everyone else. A flower withdrawn into itself. Wondering how my mama could still believe, have faith in a God she likened to the sun. "It rise everyday and so do I, whatever that looks like," she said.

She moved. Kept moving. Slower. Sedated now but in motion, all the same, even though she slept all the time.

And I couldn't help thinking she probably needed the rest. To lie down, escape. So I made no judgments though I missed her, missed her terribly when she slept.

—#—

"You too sensitive, Boop. And it's gon be the end of you if you ain't careful."

Mama Eloise sat at the kitchen table, her wheelchair pulled up to the table's edge, her breakfast plate unmoved though it was long ago ignored. The burnt tops of a biscuit sat there with smudges of grape jelly running along its otherwise pale body where Mama Eloise, feeling sorry for Lena, had tried to make them work. Raised it to her mouth, smelled the smoke of the oven and put it down.

Truth be told, she was a bit nauseous from drinking the night before, this morning. But she'd never show it. And the smoke had tried to pull her down a memory lane she had no interest in traveling down.

I sat at the table, head still throbbing, heart still throbbing. Everyone's words affecting me all at once. Aunt Bee. Marcel. Mama Eloise. *Mama.*

I drank a glass of water poured over crushed ice I'd collected from the refrigerator's stainless steel stomach, the safest thing to consume that Lena's hands hadn't touched, and it felt like a waterfall streaming through parts of my body I didn't even know existed.

"Ya mama is going through a lot," she said.

I drank the water, determined to flush the liquor out. Waited again for the sensation and it was reliably there, lighting up my insides with its sympathy.

"You need to learn how to discern the truth from the moment."

I looked up at her. Held my head in my left hand and continued drinking. I was too exhausted. I needed some rest. The real kind of rest where my body could forget it was a body. Didn't demand anything, expect anything. Was content to just be at rest, allowing the spirit inside it the same.

Peace.

I smiled briefly, thinking of my mama but it only made my head and heart ache more.

Besides, my sensitivity wasn't a new subject, and Mama Eloise's words were not unique. I'd heard it all before. All my life. It made no difference. Saying I was too sensitive was the same as saying I had too much blood, too much bone and oxygen inside myself. I needed them all to live, and it made me who I was. This was a fact—unchanging, unyielding, though no one seemed to accept it but me.

I shrugged. Sipped the water but it didn't perform the same. It slid down my pipes doing what water does, like regular, and I looked at my glass as though a mother at her child. Disappointed. Gravely disappointed.

"She's going through a lot and you have to be patient with her."

Patient?

I made a sound. It was supposed to be a snort but my body, exhausted, wouldn't cooperate, so instead it sounded like a cough. Snot bubbled from my nose and I was confused. Frowned. I put my glass of water down.

"Mhmm," Mama Eloise hummed. "Thas wha yo ornery ass get!"

I reached for a napkin, folded like triangles inside a holder with two monarch butterflies on each side, wings spread wide as if flaunting their beauty. I blew my nose, then spit into the soft tissue, watched it bend under the weight of my fluids and my eyes watered at the sight.

"Bein scary and lackin patience don't have no place in this world," Mama E said. "You won't last long here."

But the notion didn't scare me. Death seeming like the best kind of rest. Light, airy breaths. Except I wasn't sure if rest actually preceded death. Not with the walking dead I watched every day. Both those who'd expired and those of us who spent our days sedated. Zombified. Like me. Like Aunt Bee. Like my mama.

Only that idea frightened me. Caused the kinda fear my mama could inspire and I remembered the sound of the smoke alarm ringing out like it signaled the end of something. The end of me.

I sat up in my chair. Looked at Mama Eloise with tired eyes.

"So what I'm supposed to do?"

We were alone now. Mama was upstairs taking her medicine and Lena having made Aunt Bee's bed, ignoring the smell of liquor, pushed her into the cool radiation of the television. Bee was watching the soul music video channel as we spoke, and on the other side of the wall we could hear the arduous pulse of Johnny Gill's voice oscillating up and down the musical scales like he had something to prove.

I wasn't sure where Marcel was and shivered again thinking of his smallness.

"Be patient," Mama E said. "Learn how to respect what you see, even if you don't understand it. And above all else, love anyway."

She couldn't be hung over. Not as lucid as she sound. I looked at her round face for clues of exhaustion and found none. I felt better that she hadn't suffered too much at the hands of the devil's piss I'd fed her and resentful at the same time.

"Like you do Sonny?" I blurted out and instantly flinched, prepared for whatever verbal blow was coming for getting smart with her.

But Mama E was quiet. And my stomach churned, twisted into knots, so many knots, till she looked up at me with those gray eyes and said, "I don't like that nigga. And before I leave I plan to make sure his ass gone on to where he supposed to be, but Aunt Bee love him."

I snorted and it sound like it was supposed to sound.

"She do," Mama Eloise said. "Same way Lena love Marcel. Same way yo mama love you and me. It don't always make sense in how it look but it don't have to. Not to nobody but the one lovin."

I didn't have a response. I reached for my water and the glass was almost empty. I threw the shallow shot against my throat with no expectations and didn't feel anything as it made its way down except that it was gone. I considered making my way back to the refrigerator for more but wasn't sure my legs, wobbly and jumping with fatigue and nerves, could make the trip without disclosing to Mama E my frazzled state.

"Probably the same way you love that boy," she continued.

I rolled my eyes and Mama Eloise snickered.

"Love is peculiar, baby. And you remember Mama told you this, everybody we love and the ways we choose to love em ain't gon always line up with how we think love supposed to be. How we was taught." She shrugged her hunched shoulders. "But it's love all the same. Same as yo mama got for you. Only a mama's love is special. Ain't nothin quite like it."

She shrugged her hunched shoulders again.

"At the end of the day, we all just doin the best we can, but. . . ." She paused. "I want you to do better."

I looked at her. She looked at me.

"Because I think you can," she said. "You just need some faith."

I shrugged my shoulders and recalled the dream. Paused. Looked at her and she smiled.

"You know what I think we need?" she asked.

I looked at her. Exhausted. Unsure. Kinda afraid.

"Go over there and get us a pot."

I looked towards Lena's cupboards and frowned. I could only imagine how the organization of a woman with Lena's mind and lack of skills in the kitchen translated to her cabinets. And the pantry was dark and messy, as expected. But I reached in with wobbly legs, head throbbing, pulled and pushed skillets and pans until I found a petite pot. Raised it up and asked Mama Eloise would it do. She shook her head and I frowned. Went deep sea diving again into the walls. Wrestled up another pot, this one more full and round. Able to hold enough, more than enough, I thought. And Mama E agreed with a slight nod of her head. She motioned for me to pull her wheelchair into the kitchen and I did so with heavy arms, and felt dizzy, fatigued. Physically. Emotionally. Mentally.

Johnny Gill was still woo-woo-ing as though lovesick and I heard Lena's anxious feet, in the distance, now moving within the theater room. Heard the gentle bass of Marcel's voice.

Mama Eloise grabbed the pot from my hands, then rolled herself to the sink with impressive agility while looking at me like, *Boop, if you don't get yo ass over here!*

But her voice was sweet, which was rare, when she said to me, "Come here."

She reached over the sink with stiff arms, filled the pot with water then turned around and plopped it on the stove with such force that the water jumped before settling down.

"You see that?" she asked, her face all of a sudden appearing small and serious in the dim afternoon light. "Now thas bout how a man is. He got to jump a lil when it comes to love 'fore settling down."

She turned the gas under the pot with a gnarled, pallid hand and I watched the flames burn blue then yellow before peaking, settling down.

"OK," she said. "Now watch this."

I stood beside her, arms folded across my chest, allowing my weight to equally rest against her chair and the stove. I looked into the pot, watched the water simmer.

"Nothing is happening, Mama Eloise."

"Aww see, thas where you wrong." She bent towards the stove and let the steam released from the pot carry and shape around her face. "You wrong, see this is the courting stage. See how dem bubbles beginnin to form at the bottom before risin to the top?"

I looked, watched the bubbles grow, not too unlike the bumps on my face. I frowned but the heat of the water warmed me, erasing all irritation before it could flourish.

"Thas how love is. It's a slow burn, baby."

I leaned forward and watched the water change—the hot, round licks of water starting to crawl along the edges of the pot before making their way to the center, churning now with tiny bubbles before growing fat, spreading themselves out then maturing into a full-fledged boil.

"Mmhmm," she hummed. "See now it's makin' its way to the heart." Her face was turning pink, a brilliant pink. "Don't ever let nobody make you think love supposed to jump hot from the start. Cause you see love is like anything else the good Lord made. Like a plant or a body, it take time to grow."

And with that she yanked the pot from the burner and dulled its flames.

"Now what that mean?" I asked, immersed in her exhibition, face flushed with steam and fire.

"What?" She moved with the pot towards the kitchen table, dragging her feet along the cool marble floor as she pushed her chair. "What *what* mean?"

"What you just did with the water now? Yanking it off the flames. What that mean?" I followed her back to the table. "The good Lord giveth and taketh away?"

"Oh nah. That means it's time for some tea," she said. "We don't waste water."

I smiled and relaxed.

"Reach me some cups," she called, and dragged then pulled herself back to the table.

"But that has to mean something too, otherwise the water just burns out."

I placed two teacups down on the table, purple and blue.

"Leave it on the stove too long and it evaporates, right?"

She pulled a bag of green tea from its container—stacked on the dining room table like bricks with other tea boxes—dropped it inside a cup and then another. With trembling hands she poured the hot water into each cup, not spilling a drop and I watched each tea bag dip under the water's weight before floating buoyantly to the top.

"Well chile, didn't nobody say shit was fair. Everything got to burn out sometime—even us." She handed the pot to me, empty and warm, and I turned and placed it in the sink. Plopped back down at the table and held my head inside my hands.

"That has to be the most depressing thing I've ever heard, Mama Eloise."

She took a noisy sip from her cup and eased her chair closer to me.

"Thas only cause you ain't lived long enough and maybe life's been too easy on you," she said, blowing her tea gently before stirring in a teaspoon of honey.

I looked up at her. Folded my arms across my chest.

"Have faith?"

"Faith," Mama E said and winked one gray eye. "Thas what it's all about."

She drank from her cup and I tried to mimic her move, sipping from my cup too, but the tea was too hot. I burnt my tongue and laughed with pain.

"You move too fast," she said, sipping her tea.

I looked at her like, *Your tongue stronger than mine?* She winked at me again like, *Well hell yeah!*

I laughed again. Head and heart sated. Shook my head like, *You right.*

On the other side of the wall Johnny Gill sang, *And I'm so proud to be with you. So proud to share your love!* And I took another sip. Only now the tea was fine. Its waters having jumped and settled into a warm passion. It traveled my body's pipes. To all those unknown and known places. Settled. And I felt loved. So incredibly loved.

I looked at Mama Eloise. Smiled.

Said, "You right."

. . .

"What you tryin to do with your life, Ketinah?"

I was upstairs, having the talk. *The talk.* Though I wasn't yet clean. My gown and body still stank, I was sure of it. But my insides were placid. A river without waves. No rocks, sticks or stones thrown creating ripples along its surface.

I felt for a moment at peace and determined to protect the feeling.

"You hear me talkin to you?"

I tilted my head to the side and folded my arms across my chest again. My body was the shield, my face the weapon, only this was my mama so neither tools were very sharp. I frowned but not too deeply, because this was my mama and an attitude would only get my existence slapped into the next world where I was now sure nobody was walking—neither the living nor dead.

I was quiet for a second, wondering if it was a trick question which was totally plausible considering her position. In the bed. Sheets and pink flowered bedspread falling across her body like they were both made that way—adjoined since birth. Same pink rollers and flannel gown though it was summertime, late afternoon. I assumed the house's temperature made it a sound decision. It was still cool inside, the rainfall humid and hot one moment then like snow and we mere humans were all trying to adjust to its moods. I looked at the gown curled and bunched between her legs. It was her favorite gown. Mama Eloise's old favorite gown, or at least it used to be. It was a faded version of what it had once been. The yellow flowers stretching along the bodice were now white with too many washes, too much time.

I laughed to myself, thinking it was quite literally whitewashed. White erasing any beautiful thing from what it once was. It was all that was left, when all had been taken.

Damn shame.

I laughed again, and caught my mouth, noticing my mama's glare. That mama glare. I remembered her fingers and my body did too, arm throbbing with pain as though her pinch were fresh. We were at the funeral, only it was my funeral. I was both the dead and the living. Watching it all.

My life?

"Whatchu mean?"

Mama's eyes narrowed and I knew she knew I was high.

Damn shame.

It was true. I drank my tea after it cooled and pushed Mama E into her room for the nap she needed to sleep off the alcohol. I gently pulled her wide body upon the thin mattress. "Marcel so damn cheap," she muttered and I laughed. Kissed her cheek as though the hangover was our secret and her gray eyes fluttered with appreciation before closing. Then I went outside and stood on the patio beneath the canopied cover, watching the rain which showed no signs of letting up. I smoked and felt everything in me go quiet. Thought about the fire. The water. Watched the rain and the places in the sky where it seemed the sun wanted to break out. The yellow was there, obscured, creating a new color. Wanting, I thought, deeply desiring to reemerge. It was a slow burn. But it was coming. Like love. It was coming. Slowly but surely.

But mostly I'd thought about the boy. Mama Eloise's demonstration had left me reeling with unchecked emotions, suppressed beneath the ritualistic use of my vices. And now when I looked at the sun, smothered by the clouds, it was impossible not to consider the ways we loved and failed to love one another.

I used to feel my love obscured me, that he smothered my light while encouraging me to grow despite all the ways he attempted to kill my spirit. He found fault with everything—my clothes, speech, attitude, fears, sex.

Was I loud and enthusiastic enough? No. Was I too loud and thus faking it? Yes.

Everything was all wrong. I was wrong.

My mind was something continually tortured while my body neglected inside the relationship. We seldom touched one another unless it was in anger; sometimes pushing, sometimes slapping, sometimes throwing shit.

But his voice was the first tool of violence.

His screams were unlike any I'd ever heard, primal, ancient yet so new that I was both intrigued and afraid. The men in my family were mostly nonexistent, quiet, save for the ways they privately and discreetly disrespected us—with other women, with their whisper campaigns they spread around town as much as their dicks, the kinda rumors that said the women in my family were crazy. The kinda rumors I heard even now. Because perhaps they knew something we were unwilling to admit? Still there weren't enough of them to matter. They were simply outnumbered. Not many boy cousins or uncles. No fathers.

And men who married into the family seldom stayed long. The younger the women were in my family, the more likely they were to leave, oftentimes before the relationship had an opportunity to lift off the ground. And the older the women grew in my family the more likely they were to remain married; time had that effect.

But the boy despite his imperfections was beautiful to me. The ways he disrespected me were so unique and specific to himself. He was interesting, always so full of words that I had no interest in hearing, but still I loved the sound of his voice until he screamed.

Until we pushed and fought one another as much as we claimed to love another.

L-O-V-E.

I used to think he was lucky that unlike Mama Eloise I was not the type to pull out a gun and shoot, not with the intention to kill but to frighten, to defend my soul's purpose because his lessons were too harsh.

One minute he held my face in his hands, the next minute he grabbed my throat and pressed me against the wall of our apartment, another minute he pushed me to accept my gift with a gentleness I was certain would never be found again, at least not directed towards me. Not with the tenderness, not with the light he held in his eyes when he looked at me.

I was convinced our love was a special passion.

He was a harsh teacher, true enough, but when he took me out into the wilderness and coaxed me not to be afraid of nature, the way the trees bent and stood tall. The way the dirt sometimes fell beneath our feet causing me to stumble while he stood firm against the cold of the ground.

The ways the wind carried our voices and we couldn't hear ourselves.

The wilderness.

It's wild, he said, explaining that its unpredictability was much like us.

Much like the cosmos, he explained when we lay on the beach together watching with wide-eyed stares the night skies, we were a mystery. This was a concept I actually agreed with because for as much as I could see, I felt I understood very little.

What I knew is that when he spoke like this is when I loved him most.

My personal guru. My love.

The thought brought tears to my eyes.

He pushed me. He pulled me. He used to try and teach me how to swim over and over again despite my fear of water, no matter if he let go of my hand, every time the water rose to my chest and I became so scared I couldn't breathe. I trusted him again and again. I hoped to find myself inside him. I searched for myself inside him.

And ignored him all other times, so I understood his anger.

Still we were something too hard to let go of because it was the first love I'd ever known.

We stayed together so many years and yet I was not young enough to let go nor old enough to hold on.

What did you call a woman approaching middle age stuck by her choices to a man she fought at the full moon, who drank with her, cried with her once they'd hurt one another and slept so soundly together they might as well have been as dead as the souls she watched.

I blamed myself for not listening to him, for being weird, perhaps crazy. I blamed him for not loving me past his own insecurities.

The first time I described a ghost to him he'd been high and laughed. And when I frowned, hurt that he was not taking the moment seriously, he'd become sincere.

What do you see? he asked, sitting up in the bed on one elbow.

Everything, I replied. The living, the dead and everything in between.

And what does this mean to you? he asked.

I don't know, I said.

Figure it out, he said, pulling from our joint then exhaling the smoke from his throat. And he lay down as though the conversation was over while my head spun in circles. When I heard the light gurgles of his snores as he slept peacefully, I grew frustrated.

That's all he has to say? That's all? I thought.

Then,

He's right.

I pulled from my pipe and watched the smoke exit my mouth, the most perfect plume.

I bet he couldn't find anything wrong with that conclusion, I thought.

I smiled and wiped my tears away. I took another toke from my pipe, watched the smoke release into the gray of the skies then stood up.

The yellow was still there. Waiting to emerge, like me.

I smiled again, watching for any bits of yellow light, hoping for the sun's release but the rain started again, first one drop then another until it was a barrage of tears.

I knew I was high because everything felt lighter. My steps were even lighter as I went back into the house.

Inside the house was quiet save for the noise of raindrops sputtering about the roof. It was a clumsy, awkward dance the rain did.

I moved gingerly, closing the patio door without sound.

And I knew I was high when I held the banister of the stairs and walked up. Slowly but surely. One step at a time to my mama. Light, so very light.

I only paused before reaching the top when the memory of the first time I'd entered a dream at my own volition struck like lightning through my body, and then the house.

It was with the boy. I'd entered, swinging my fists, cursing him in much of the ways I had when we'd been together, only this time he'd only cried. When I pushed, he didn't push back. When I slapped, he took it. And that's how I knew the dream was real. Because he seemed his true self.

Sweet, weak, vulnerable like me and in ways he was never comfortable being with me in the waking life. I remember crying, screaming at him to hit me! But he wouldn't move. It was how I knew maybe he loved me. It was how I knew I wasn't unlike the women in my family.

It was how I knew I was equally abusive, or at least possessed the potential. If only in my dreams.

I stood for a moment, accepting the idea of my own violence.

Thunder rattled the house.

Then I'd continued, head down, feet heavy, to my mama.

My mama, who looked at me now with the disappointment I imagined Lena held in her face when Marcel didn't come home. Every time he disappeared for any length of time, her heart beat out with the same drums my mama's played now.

"You know what I mean," she said.

My life?

I shrugged.

"I wanna live," I said, and the answer felt more than sufficient.

"Well, the way you goin right now, I'm not so sure," she said.

We were quiet. The silence stretched before us, long and lanky. I thought of Papa Deo. In the garden. At his farm. Watching black bodies run on the television. *Go nigga!*

I thought I might laugh again but the memory got stuck somewhere in my body where the water once was. It idled. It poked around and I found my eyes watering. Again.

"It's been three years. This drinking and smoking," Mama threw her arms around the bed, up in the air, then down, beating the pink flowers on the comforter as though they too were drums but her song had no rhythm. Whitewashed.

My life?

"I've been patient," she said.

I have too.

"But you can't keep on like this," she said.

You think I don't know that?

"What you doin now won't bring you to no good end."

What we doin won't bring us to no good end.

"So you need to come up with a plan."

My life.

"You went out into the world, you did some things and you got hurt. You ain't the first nor the last to fail."

I wanted to cry.

"But it's never too late to start again."

I wanted to cry. My high was coming down, slowly. I watched it outside of my body, lower, cower. Then burn till it was nothing more than ash.

Start again.

"God is good all the time, and God is with you." She turned over some and the bedspread rose against her hip and the flowers there moved as though through valleys, before rising towards the sun.

"Now I know you can do it, Boop," she said. "I have faith in you. I do."

And when I looked in her eyes, it looked as though she wanted to cry. But I wasn't sure because her medications gave her a glassy-eyed stare that refused to budge no matter her emotion.

Faith?

I sighed.

"I'm workin on it, Mama."

She looked at me, glassy eyes full with water. My heart ached.

"I'm trying," I said.

"Well," she said, pulling the covers to her chin. "Thas all we can do." She closed her eyes. "I just want you to try harder."

I closed my eyes. Held the tears and walked towards the door. "Me too," I said.

I went back to the patio and sat there, pulling the smoke but I couldn't get high. Pulled but still didn't rise. Watched the rain, each singular drop a story untold. And I prayed to the place in the sky where the sun sat smothered by the clouds, for the heat to return. I wanted to boil. Fast. I wanted to bubble to the center, to the top and stay there.

Be consumed and understood. Burn. Like true love.

JustwaituntilIshine. JustwaituntilIshine. JustwaituntilIshine.

But the rain wasn't enough. The sky wasn't enough so I walked back inside.

The house was quiet. Everyone was sleeping again, or so it felt. I walked to another room. The indoor pool, just off the formal dining room, was seldom used because nobody in the house could swim. It was merely decorative. A dangerous art exhibit.

A bowl of water.

The house was quiet. I opened the door and walked towards an oval of sparkling blue. It shimmered and screamed at me with tones I didn't recognize and I covered my ears. Covered my face then looked up at the skylight over its surface and saw myself there. Imagined myself falling like the rain. Falling with no cares or worries into the pool. Because it shined like I felt I did beneath the clouds of my sadness, my glory. *Blues.*

It was so *blue.*

I considered my mama and her mama's mama and her mama's mama's mama an endless lineage, the most peculiar trap; some cyclical motion of women having all been related by the mere coincidence of having given birth to one another. It was a strange thought.

It should have been enough to bond us to one another but I'd come to accept with age that wasn't always the case in families. The experience of sharing DNA, of having cosmically traveled from space to the insides of the women we would grow to call auntie, or grandmother, or mother was not always solid enough reason to prove meaningful throughout a person's life.

My life?

The thought brought me closer to the pool's edge. I stepped closer to the pool's edge. Saw my toes, long and brown, curl over the white stone edge that circled the body of the pool. Saw my reflection. My face was a blur. Shining. Saw nothing but blue, the blues.

I miss Maya.

What did it mean to be a mother? Giving birth, bringing a baby forth from a cavity within the body you didn't quite understand yourself. Indeed you relied on the expertise of doctors, many of them men, to provide you with information pertaining to the most intimate and sacred parts of your being.

I missed Maya. I missed my friend.

But where did a baby come from? A void? The black hole? Some deep secret place inside a woman's womb that connected her to the spirit realm? And because the spirit realm was already a contentious topic I felt all the more untrusting, unwilling to surrender my body to its whims.

It's true. I miss her so much.

I looked down into the water and it did not move.

Pleasure, and loving a man was important. I had known both at various times, however briefly with the boy but it was never long, never satisfying enough to answer any mortal questions. How could it be when I knew that the dead still walked? And if they still walked, what did that mean for the newly arrived?

I couldn't bear the idea of my own child someday being a spirit that survived death only to haunt the places they once walked while living. To be confused, and afraid, or angry like Sonny was.

I miss Maya.

Worse than that, I couldn't imagine my own child growing into someone who questioned me, possibly hated me for being the source which brought them forth into this world. Never mind a mythical God, I would be the closest thing, as all women were, to God. A very real, breathing and fucked-up entity, mystical in my own right.

Maya never picks up the phone when I call.

A child would force me to live within their constant judgments and questions when I myself still felt a child though in my thirties.

When would adulthood finally come? It seemed impossible while I was still someone's child.

Maybe I should call again?

I took a toke of the marijuana from my pipe and it was good. I watched my reflection shimmering in the water, my reflection a blur, and it was so apt.

Sometimes I missed Maya; I wanted deeply to pick up the phone and ask her questions that I knew only Maya could answer inside her madness. Her truest form. When nothing was hidden, all laid bare, her most vulnerable state.

Questions like, why did you do it? Were you afraid? Do you trust who your children are, who they will become? Because to do so, to trust them unconditionally means you trusted yourself completely because they came from your body. And how is that ever possible?

I wanted to ask Maya if her own scars were healed enough to worry herself with the wounds of new souls.

But what would it matter? I was sure that Maya would only grow angrier than she already was and if not for herself then on Troy's behalf.

Troy, who lived in a state of perpetual anger and was unwilling to acknowledge the same rage within Maya.

Troy.

The thought of him brought tears that wouldn't stop. I wiped them away, pushed them away as I had Maya's rejection.

I missed her so much.

But I knew she wouldn't pick up should I call. We hadn't talked since the night with Troy and his sister.

Maya was always loyal to Troy.

I'd had dreams of her lately wherein she had gone mad, a mother without a cause other than taking care of her babies at any cost. Inside every dream I'd tried to become lucid but it was as if an invisible wall wouldn't allow me to reach her in real time. Instead I'd watched as she descended into her own black hole. She was being pulled apart. Stretched. Her thoughts, her light, her soul unable to escape the depth of her fears.

Maybe I should text again even if I knew she wouldn't respond.
She never did.

And I couldn't push myself to admit my own fears: I wasn't sure I wanted children. At all. And any time I allowed myself to fully absorb the realization this might be true, was indeed growing more real with time and age so that I might be reaching a point where the decision was no longer in my hands, my body instead responding to my thoughts long before they took physical form, I felt a quiet pain unlike any I'd ever known.

What was life without creation?

I thought of Troy and his sister, whose face was curious and sad. When I'd looked at her I could feel all of her confusion, her mistakes, her pain.

I thought of my father and then finally . . . him.

I looked down into the pool and saw my reflection, shimmering, glowing inside the blue, my silhouette black and soft against the light. It would be so easy to stop the cycle.

Outside the rain was falling.

I stepped closer towards the pool's edge and wanted to fall. I was prepared to fall but there was a clap of thunder so loud that I jumped back. Flinched. Blinked at my reflection but the picture of me was already fading inside the stillness of the water. Then I stepped back, realizing the water didn't care whether I jumped or stood. I remembered I couldn't swim and there were no markers denoting shallow or deep. It was all one thing. Inside the house.

Water so deep. So shallow.

I backed away, slowly. Started to cry again. The rain poured into me and out. It flowed and I let it.

Until I saw Uncle Sonny there in the pool.

I wiped my eyes, rubbed the tears into my skin, away from my vision as I wasn't sure if what I saw was an enigma. Some trick question my mind posed while I wasn't paying attention. Too focused on water and heat. On falling. Drowning.

But he was there. Bathing in the shallow, in the deep end, smiling. All red against the blue.

Telling me, *Come. Come. The water's fine. What you waitin on?*

. . .

I ate my dinner that night. Hot tamales smothered in hot sauce and ranch dressing. Lena ordered out and it was San Antonio so objects you never thought could be delivered, much less to the hood, came right to your door in heavy rain while lightning illuminated the world. The delivery man knocked. Handed a bag over, dug for the right amount of change, gave it back and expected a tip for his efforts because he deserved it. Lena gave him a small tip but still he smiled, said *gracias* before hurriedly running back to his car.

Lena smiled with relief.

Hot tamales.

Marcel had requested it. So we all ate as though they were a gift.

And it was hot, but I was hotter. Nobody knew how hot I was.

I looked around the table.

That motherfucker tried to kill me.

The thought replayed over and over throughout my body like an elaborate drumbeat and all I heard was its percussion.

Inside I was clapping along to its internal rhythm, plotting, preparing to finally become like my ancestors, even if the only one who mattered was Mama Eloise.

I wanted a gun. I wanted to punch. I wanted to cut.

Aunt Bee poked at her food and my mama said it was the best tamale she'd ever had. She said she wanted to find someone in East Texas who could make 'em that good. Lena shook her head in agreement, feeling as though she'd finally done something right. Marcel ate in the theater room. Quietly. We could hear the sound of the news from the theater room, blasting with tall tales and rumors of more bad. More peril than existed inside our home.

I bit into a tamale and felt its heat. I felt like I was hotter. Growing hotter still.

That motherfucker tried to kill me.

And Mama Eloise looked at me. Bit her tamale with timid bites. Tried to make eye contact with me but I refused.

I was nothing but the water and water had no eyes.

It was *the* eye. A singular story waiting to be told.

The water was boiling. It was rising and moving, center to middle. Bubbling. And I didn't wanna be bothered with anyone's advice or desires of who I needed to be.

There was no faith. There was no love. There was only the rain and heat, and I was both.

Finally.

I looked at Sonny standing behind Aunt Bee. I looked at Mama Eloise looking at Sonny. I looked at Bee and questioned if she really loved Sonny.

I knew I didn't care if she did cause it no longer mattered what he was, where he was or why he was doing what he did. I was sure of it.

Mama Eloise took a bigger bite.

"Y'all mighty quiet tonight," Mama said.

Lena looked towards the theater room. Rubbed her inner thighs. Sighed.

Aunt Bee moved a tamale toward her mouth, sniffed it. Sniffed again and put it down.

Lena frowned.

Mama said, "Where did Marcel find this tamale place? I wanna take some back home with me."

Lena tried to smile.

In the theater room, the television was loud.

Lena didn't answer.

Mama Eloise shook more hot sauce on her tamales and took another bite. Her mouth opened wide. I watched the meat and sauce stain her lips and cheeks.

"Now not too much, Mama!" my mama said, arms reaching across the table for her. "I don't want you havin' indigestion tonight."

Mama Eloise snorted, shook more hot sauce and looked at me.

But I stared straight ahead at Sonny. Chewed. The texture of the tamales thick; the beef a stew inside my mouth.

Sonny looked at me. Smiled.

I smiled back.

My mama looked at me, worried. Her eyes darted from my face to the place where she saw my eyes focused. She saw nothing there and she looked like she wanted to cry.

Mama Eloise said, "These tamales awright. They could do with some more seasoning though," and she nudged me.

"It's still good," Mama E said. "I love it just the way it is."

But I didn't see her. Didn't feel her. Didn't hear her.

Outside the rain fell, and I was certain now when the lightning struck, filling the house with its presence, that it too was me.

I looked at Sonny. Thought of the pool. Smiled.

The water is fine. What you waitin on?

Mama looked at me and said, "Sleep with me tonight."

I wasn't high. There was no alcohol or marijuana in my system. No sleep either. And my vision was clear. My intention was made plain.

"Aunt Bee was good last night though, Peach," Lena said, only because she hadn't been disturbed. She took a tiny bite from her plate. Chewed. Listened for the sound of the television and the news. Marcel.

Mama Eloise shook her head and took another bite.

My mama shook her head.

I was a lost cause.

I looked at Sonny and said to my mama, "I'll be fine."

Sonny smiled. I smiled.

Mama frowned. Took another bite of hot tamales and said, "These tamales good!"

Again.

In the theater room, the television said, "Coming up next, a man killed by an unknown assailant on the East Side and police tell us why they may need your help to find the murderer."

It was hot.

The rain fell.

I relieved my bowels and bladder simultaneously. I took a shower. Washed my body. Watched the soap touch my skin wherever I dragged its pink body. It was a rose growing, cleansing my body. Watched the brown and yellow parts of my body, whatever other people saw when they looked at me, covered in white film and small bubbles. I let my face get wet. I let my hair get wet. Shrivel to my face and kiss my cheeks. I let the water in. My tight curls shown the fact.

I was at one with the water. I was the water. I was the garden, the rose and its thorns.

I was ready.

I put some of Lena's scented lotion on. Started from my toes and worked my way to the neck. I lingered there. Looked at myself in the mirror. There were no bumps on my face. The water was good. The water was a baptism and all scars were temporarily removed. Even my heart cooperated. It beat. It beat. And it was a beat and tempo I set. It did no more or less than what I said. And I was satisfied.

That motherfucker tried to kill me.

I walked out of the bathroom. Let the steam fill the hallway and it was dark but I didn't need to see. Finally, I knew that everything I needed was within and I was confident. I made my way to Bee's room without stumbling. Everyone was asleep. When I peeped in on my mother she was fed, snoring and she'd had her medications.

I saw her body as a field of flowers where she was waiting to bloom and join them in peace. She wanted to tremble and wave, rise in the sun. Be free.

Peace.

Mama Eloise had pinched my arm at the table and told me, "Be careful, Boop. I don't like the look in your eyes."

That motherfucker tried to kill me.

I kissed her cheek, then her forehead. I pushed her into her bedroom. Told her to get some rest. The real kind where the body rejuvenates itself. "Don't go beyond that," I said. "Stay here," I said.

She said nothing as I walked towards the door. Left the room with lightning illuminating my darkest parts. I smiled sweetly. Said goodnight.

She said, "I love you, Boop."

I closed the door.

I love you too.

. . .

Now I was clean and ready. My nightgown was a field of daisies. They bloomed along my hips and thighs, at my breasts. Inappropriate places where a man's glance might wander and grow. I smelled like Lena. Felt calm, sedated like my mama.

What's in the closet?

Moi.

I was not afraid. Like Mama Eloise.

I didn't have a gun. I didn't have a knife. But I had me and for the first time I felt it was enough. Anger had a power like that. Death had a power like that.

I was ready.

Aunt Bee was propped up in bed, sipping an invisible substance and watching television. I moved towards her, sober. She looked at me. I looked at her and she sipped. I lay down and felt her thin hips, the warmth of her body a radiator. And I almost sweat, taking in her heat, but I was too focused. The television posed questions that floated to the ceiling and hung there.

That motherfucker wanted me to drown, he wanted me to kill myself, I thought. And the screen blinked with static, white fuzz filled its face before coming back black. Then technicolor.

I rolled over and turned the bedside lamp beside me off. It was the only light in the room. Aunt Bee didn't move. She stared ahead. The TV jumped with colors, all the colors. Relaxed and jumped again. And I wasn't sure if or when I fell asleep, so determined I was. So full. So enough.

But when I opened my eyes there was nothing but black. Just me and my breath. The light snores of Bee. And I lay there waiting because I knew he would come. The digital clock alongside the bed read 3:00 AM.

I smiled and there he was.

Sonny.

Red. All red. And I was there blue. All blue.

I rose from the bed. Felt my gown unfold from my thighs and I could see. I could see clearly Sonny's clenched fists. When I stood he didn't move away to allow me space to bloom. He smothered me with his presence. Tried to intimidate me with death, but I refused to yield. I was a sun ready to emerge. The rain fell hard outside. Lightning lit the room and his dingy clothes no longer looked sad. Soiled. He looked like a man who had seen and done many things. Was ready to do some more. He smiled and I could feel his breath against my face. Knew he was real. Accepted death was real.

And I grabbed him by his throat. Reached out with one swift movement that was so fast it even surprised me. His face lit up with lightning and shock, and I squeezed. Pushed him away from the bed, away from Aunt Bee, towards the length of the hallway to the kitchen.

He moaned and I was shocked to know he was capable of sound other than that beckoning another to death. Beckoning me.

The water is fine. What you waitin on?

I smiled.

I laughed.

I'm scary though, I said. *And you knew it. Could feel it,* I said.

He choked beneath my hands and the slivers of lightning. Slivers of lightning zigzagged across his brown face and his teeth were as pale as Mama Eloise's skin. He clenched his fists, reached for me with hard buds. But my blue overpowered his red and I saw him sinking to his knees. He grew shorter within my embrace. Shrunk to his knees, like Lena did before Aunt Bee's lap. Like my great-grandma did before her husband's drunken tirades. Like Mama Eloise's first husband, he was small and I accused with my hands. I grabbed. I squeezed. I was the hot gun beneath the pillow.

His eyes bulged. He was turning purple.

The moon was nowhere. The sun was smothered.

He gasped for air.

You already dead. You dead.

And I took my other hand and reached for his hands. Unfolded his right hand, unwound the knot there that was a limp fist. I squeezed it. Saw flowers. Yellow bitch. Red bitch. And his tongue was the best kind of pink. Undisturbed pink.

Can you swim? I asked.

His eyes, going black, bulged. He gasped and tried to spit in my face. I leaned closer.

Can you swim?

He choked.

I pulled his body by the throat to the bed, to Aunt Bee, and threw the white comforter off of her body. There was no light besides that in the sky. And when the lightning blossomed above us, Sonny could see clearly the blue bruises on Bee's body. He choked. I squeezed.

I'm tired of men like you.

Aunt Bee, feeling the cool of the uncovering shifted then opened her eyes. Then opened her mouth and the room was full with rum. Coconut rum. She was sweet. Eyes wide. She looked at Sonny dangling between the firm grip of my fingers. My hair was a nappy plant against the room's white walls and it remained. It was a tree. *The* tree and it existed in every part of the world.

I pushed Sonny closer to Aunt Bee's face, let him absorb her breath. Let them exchange breath. Sonny clinched a wimpy fist and Aunt Bee flinched intuitively, and it angered me all over again.

I was new. I was grief and fear combined to its most potent formula.

So I dragged his ass away from the bed, away from Aunt Bee, and he moved as though on a leash. And I hit him. First in the face. The jaw, the lips. Watched his lips evolve from brown to red and brown again. And he swung at me with everything he had. He punched me in my jaw. I was shocked to meet contact with another entity, living or dead. Then my chest, and my weak heart was tired. I lost my grip, so surprised by the blow, and Sonny toppled me. Swung on my face. My neck. My breasts. My stomach. Anywhere his buds bloomed I felt their growth. I grew blue and red. I grew weak. I was on my back and feeling weak. Afraid. Then Aunt Bee jumped on his back and I was startled to see her frail body leap that high, so quickly.

Lightning lit up the room and I saw the places where Aunt Bee's teeth once were. I saw her spit, dangling, then dripping from Sonny's forehead where she tumbled him down with her own fists. One small bud at a time. She blossomed.

The television turned itself on. *Are you tired? Can't sleep? Call 1-800-somethin-somethin. Get the pleasure, get the rest you deserve.*

And it was all the motivation I needed because I was tired. For everyone. For my mama. Mama Eloise. Lena. Aunt Bee.

Marcel.

I wanted the truth to come out. I wanted to never be scared again. So I hit.

I joined Aunt Bee's fists and together we toppled Sonny to the ground where he glowed with pain. With red. We hit. Fucked him up, legs, arms, groin. Aunt Bee raised up as if tired, only to come tumbling down again with a blow to his stomach. I looked at her, mouth bleeding, and lightning lit my face. I could smell the alcohol on her breath. I looked down and saw Sonny, still a tight bud. Refusing to yield and grow. Learn his lesson.

So I raised my right hand. Clinched it into a firm fist. Thought of the water. *Come, come.* Thought of my life and I wanted it. No matter what it looked like, I wanted it. Looked at Sonny and grew hot as lightning that he had tried to take my life from me by persuading me to jump.

My fist was coming down, slowly but surely. His skin was both blue and red as the heat of my clenched fist moved towards contact. Mars. Venus. This was it. This would be the fatal blow, I was sure of it. Enough. Enough to send him back to where he came from, to where he was going. And lightning lit me up, lit Sonny up. My fist was blooming, until Bee rained down on me. Stopped me. Crying. She was crying and there were tears falling.

"Don't do it," she cried.

Sonny cried. Gasped for air, his weak fists knotted up as if he didn't have the energy to unwind them.

I looked at Bee, confused. I yanked her gown up, revealing the blue bruises along her thighs and torso.

"Aren't you tired?" I screamed.

But she only cried, then fell back against the wall of the bed. She moved away from me and Sonny. Raised her frail legs against her chest and hugged them there.

"I'm tired," she said, sniffling. "I'm so tired."

I looked at her. I looked at Sonny. I looked at the garden we were. I thought of Papa Deo. Plowing. Tilling the land with hard strokes. Thought of his words, Mama Eloise's words. The boy's words. I was too weak. I wouldn't make it in this world. I looked back at Sonny. He trembled now, his body a shaking leaf in the wind awaiting its fate. Where would he be blown to next?

I raised up like the wind. Like the water. Like the sun. And my fist was tight, a bud already grown and moving fast, boiling towards the middle, I swung prepared to show his ass the consequences of true love. When unrequited. Unappreciated. Disrespected.

But Aunt Bee cried out and I paused.

Then Mama Eloise's voice yelled, "Boop, don't!"

And I stopped. I looked at her, my face a bloody red and bruised blue. Saliva hung from my thick bottom lip and tears ran. Like the rain they fell into a pool, and Sonny soaked them up as though thirsty. His tongue hung out his small mouth. Thirsty.

"This ain't you," Mama Eloise said.

Aunt Bee sat against the bed, sniffling. Her brown skin, maroon. Swollen with hits and tears. Her gown idled above her legs and I snatched it down with one quick jerk. Covered her private parts up.

I cried.

"He tried to kill me!" I screamed, tears falling.

"But you ain't dead, Boop," Mama E said, easing closer to me. "He is."

I looked up at her. Looked at my hands, swollen and red. Blue. Looked at Aunt Bee, a small brown clump of flesh.

Sonny looked at me. Gasped for breath then spit a clot of red blood into my face. "Bitch!" he hissed.

Mama Eloise rolled towards our bodies with strong pale arms, stretched a thick hickory leg out and kicked Sonny dead in his side. He yelped before going limp. Before disappearing before our eyes, leaving a stain, wide and ugly, on the floor of where he'd been. It radiated heat against our legs, then turned cold. The kinda cold television said only the dead created when near.

I sniffled. Rubbed my face as though rubbing away what had happened.

Mama Eloise looked at the spot and spit.

We were all quiet. Breathing. Chests moving across waters.

Aunt Bee huffed, took shallow breaths and said, "Y'all bout the strongest yella women I ever met."

And I was sure Mama Eloise would dig in her ass. Wasn't sure if I wanted to dig in her ass. My emotions were a knot, bound tight and I didn't have the energy to unravel their mystery. I looked into her milky eyes for understanding.

But when Mama Eloise looked at Aunt Bee and said, "Yeah, and it took some yellow women to help yo ass, didn't it?"

Aunt Bee laughed.

Mama Eloise shook her head and smiled.

"Yeah, y'all pretty tough for some yella heifers," Aunt Bee said again.

"And not sickly either," Mama Eloise said.

I paused.

"Well, not too sick," I said, grabbing my chest, still gasping for air. For life.

"Aw hell Boop, you don't know to stop when the gettin' is good, do ya?" Mama Eloise said.

Aunt Bee laughed and asked us to pull her up off the floor so we did. We grinned at her then each other. Shook our heads.

I stretched and held my jaw where it swelled with fire. Mama Eloise looked at me. I looked at her. And we looked at Bee.

She'd been faking it the whole time.

Damn shame.

Our smoke curled in the air. It drew loops and waves against the walls. It met the lightning and shined. Gave. Gave away and then returned to our bodies. We swallowed it in silence.

The television was still on but it didn't say shit worth acknowledging. It was a multicolor face, shallow and deep in what it revealed.

We smoked, ignoring its movement.

I'd made my way, gently holding the banister, upstairs and pulled three cigarettes from my mama's box. Took them downstairs. We took Mama Eloise's soup can and set it on the nightstand closest to Aunt Bee's side of the bed and it caught our ashes.

We pulled. Blew. Watched the smoke move. The lightning move.

We were Kool. Kool lights.

The rain was a gentle thing now. But it fell and we took it in accustomed to its sound, its mood.

Aunt Bee was in bed resting against its mahogany headboard, Eloise's chair pulled tight to its face. And I sat there on the bed's edge close to Aunt Bee panting—in and out. In. Out. I ashed my cigarette in the soup can and felt the places I'd been hit. Aunt Bee turned to me as if to radiate her warmth in my direction with healing, with a confused thought that my mind unraveled to mean *Get yo shit together, Boop!* And instead of feeling criticized, I felt reminded of my power. My strength.

She was right.

"He ain't gone yet," Aunt Bee said.

Mama Eloise took a deep drag and coughed.

She coughed and I looked at her concerned until she stopped.

The devil's piss was one thing but what was this? I held the long white cigarette between my fingers, searching its body for meaning. *His shit?*

I frowned.

"You OK?" I asked.

"I know," she said, through coughs. Her face puffed out, swole then deflated. She coughed again, a hacking noise that ruined any momentary peace I felt. "I know he ain't gone. It ain't as simple as that."

Aunt Bee pulled from her cigarette and dabbed its ashes in the soup can.

"So long as you know," she said.

The room felt cold. I could sense Sonny was still there. Only tucked away, and invisible like Aunt Bee's right state of mind—healing, regaining his strength, sharpening his strategy. I watched goose bumps form along Aunt Bee's arms.

She shook her head, nodded towards her left arm where the skin recoiled into itself. She took a drag and said, "See?" And smoke drifted from her head's entrance, settled along her hair as a mushroom. A gray, white, black organism deep in contemplation. Rapt in acknowledgment of him.

I pulled from my cigarette until the fire turned its butt red. Drew the fire into myself.

"I feel fine," I said. I shrugged and felt the tenderness in my breasts where he'd hit me.

Mama Eloise coughed then laughed through her drag, and the smoke blossomed from her lips as though a quote inside a cartoon character's mouth. It grew in size above her head, filling the room with its magnitude.

It read *Only roots can send him home.*

And it made sense. At least I thought it did. I wasn't sure. Sore but sober and yet I'd fought a ghost. I wasn't sure anything made sense. Nothing beyond myself.

Aunt Bee smoked. Pulled the smoke deep into her body and blew it out, a cloud that rivaled her hair. It blossomed. It grew. It spoke and commanded attention.

"This is true," she said. She dabbed her ash. Let the lightning fill her dark eyes, make them green, blue and yellow before fading. "I made a mistake."

"You did," Mama Eloise said, nodding her head.

I felt the cold, but was no longer afraid. The night was a testament to that. I pulled from the cigarette and watched its ash grow like a grainy finger. I let it grow and refused to dab it out.

"I took some of his hair and a watch," Aunt Bee said. "My daddy's old watch." She pulled from her cigarette and blew. "You know the old kind men useta stick in they pockets? A pocket watch."

Mama Eloise shook her head, said, "Mmhmm."

"I took some of his hair." She paused, puffed. "I took some dirt from the backyard and I walked all the way to the beach one day after work—it wasn't too far from the house, not for someone like me who grew up having to walk everywhere. I took that dirt and his picture. The one we took the day we married, the only one we had together."

She puffed. The smoke was a stream. It floated to the ceiling, hung there.

"When I got to the beach I took some ocean water and poured it in a cup," she said. "And then I started digging, I dug deep until the sand was no longer brown but black, its most original form, and I placed his picture there and watched the water flow over his features." She smiled. "It was like lava beneath the sun."

Mama Eloise puffed. I puffed. We listened.

Aunt Bee laughed. "And you know what?" she asked, looking at us. "I felt like a volcano." She laughed again. "I was the volcano and the sand turned from black to red, like blood. And when it turned I added his hair. I took his picture and let the sun and water ruin it. I had blacked out my face so I wasn't there as any more than a witness. I was the judge. I was the victim and volcano."

Silence.

Our smoke rose, hit the ceiling. Lingered. Thunder rang out and none of us acknowledged it. At one we were, at peace we were with the truth. Finally.

"I buried my daddy's watch there with his picture in the mud, cause see I felt my daddy watchin it all and knew he was in agreement." She took a pull from her cigarette and her hands shook. She looked at us as though for approval, her eyes searched our bodies and we gave it back to her. At least I gave it back to her.

Mama Eloise was quiet. Her body didn't move or give anything. She smoked. She listened. Her eyes were moist. It was the only sign she was there in the moment.

"And I knew come noon the next day, when the sun was at its zenith it would be enough. Tick tock," Aunt Bee said, thumping her chest. "Tick tock."

Mama E shook her head, looked at me then closed her eyes. "You took from Her," she said.

The Goddess hour. Twelve o'clock. The sun's zenith.

They say ocean water is the strongest. The most potent. It carries all the waters; past and present. Fears. Love. Death.

Aunt Bee said nothing, shaking her head, eyes streaming with quiet tears. She felt understood. Not approved of or otherwise but sometimes understanding was all it took between humans, and especially women. It was all that was needed.

"You were tired," I said.

Aunt Bee cried, shaking her head.

"I didn't expect it to work," she said. "Wasn't sure it would."

But Mama Eloise hissed.

"Stop that shit!" she said. "Now if we gon do one thing we gon be honest with the other now." She took a puff and picked up the soup can and spit the nicotine into it.

I was quiet. I wasn't sure of the time. The television was no reminder other than the sex commercials that revealed nothing beyond it was late. These were the hours of loneliness and vulnerability.

"You knew damn well what you were doing and that it would work," Mama E said.

Aunt Bee was quiet. She dabbed her cigarette out, pressed its weight against the body of the soup can. She watched the fire go out until it was nothing more than soot. Ash. She looked up at us, slowly, a slow burn. Smiled, her lips twisted, eyes scattered and focused.

"OK," she said and shrugged her shoulders.

Mama Eloise finished her cigarette. Pushed its fire out. Listened to the rain.

It fell. It fell. It fell.

"If you wanted his ass gone? Truly gone," Mama E said. "You needed some loose gravel. Keep his ass walking a road to nowhere, least then he wouldn't be able to find his way back to you."

She looked at Aunt Bee in the eyes. Her gray met the black there and merged. "But you know what?" she said. "For some reason, Bee, I don't think you really wanted his ass gone."

Aunt Bee raised up, her small body lifted from the bedframe and it was enough that I felt the bed shift with her weight, as light as she was.

"Nah, I think if you was done," Mama E said. "You knew how to be done."

Mama Eloise sat back in her chair. Her hickory legs tired but satisfied. All parts of her body satisfied cause she knew the truth when it was the truth and nothing gave her greater pleasure.

Aunt Bee was quiet.

She wanted a drink. I knew the look. She wanted a hip.

Aunt Bee leaned back against the bed's headboard and it shook with her weight.

"Hmph," she said.

We were quiet.

For a moment we were quiet.

Mama Eloise looked at me and said, "So what have we learned tonight?"

And I looked at her like, *Is this a trick question?*

She frowned.

"Not only do we have to fight, figure shit out and clean it up," she said.

She paused. Raised her neck and looked me in the eyes.

"How do flowers grow, Boop?" she asked.

Aunt Bee looked angry, confused. She shifted and I felt her weight move from right to left.

I smiled.

"With sun and plenty of water," I said. "And knowing how to help 'em grow."

Mama Eloise rolled away from the bed. She nodded her weak neck and said, "Mhmm . . . good thing it's raining."

Aunt Bee explored my face like a navigator seeking out new land, she watched and looked for an explanation. But seeing her there, a frail mushroom, in love and unwilling to commit to the truth, I knew better than to try to explain.

Nah, I was quiet. Let Mama Eloise handle it. Knew I could handle it.

We would handle it.

I slept that night, confident. Knowing what had to be done. In my dreams Mama Eloise was there and we conspired. In a smoky room, filled with equal parts fire and water we devised a plan. And she said to me, just before waking up, "Don't go gettin scary and fuckin shit up, Boop."

I woke up, first envisioning myself in an endless field of flowers. There was the sun. There were clouds. Black clouds that didn't mean impending doom but simply water. The birth. The Mother of it all and so everyone feared Her. Ran. Scared. Buried their hate inside Her skin and expected Her to resolve it all.

Because She was Mama.

Black. Fire. Water.

I woke up smiling. Knowing what had to be done and ready.

Ready for it all. Or so I hoped. Because I knew though I hadn't seen Sonny yet, he was still there. I could still feel him, his energy, his rage. I dressed that morning accepting that he might be just as determined as we were, and suddenly felt a sense of dread. What his end goal was, I wasn't sure. But I felt him, and the fact I couldn't see him made it all the more frightening in a way I wouldn't admit aloud. Not to Mama E, anyway. When I moved to put on my shoes my body ached and I wasn't sure I had another fight in me. But there was no time to be scary.

I brushed my teeth. Watched myself in the mirror chant, I'm not afraid. I'm not afraid. I'm not afraid anymore. I won't fuck this up.

I repeated it until it felt true.

"We need a seance."

Mama Eloise said it so casually it almost made sense.

But I wasn't sure the Black Mama of All would approve. Seance sounded so white. So unlike anything Black, and then Mama Eloise reminded me that white came from Black and I sighed.

She was right.

"What that supposed to look like?" I asked.

"Look like?" she asked.

My mind went to a childhood favorite of mine: *Beetlejuice*. The white people sat wearing variations of black at the table, holding hands, but not before it rained and lightning struck. Not before they danced, involuntarily. Daylight came and they wanted to go home. And eventually they held a seance. At the movie's end, the star of the show danced freely towards the ceiling. Then the credits rolled. And it was like the ghostly possession had been all that was needed for them to become the black, brown and gold they wore but their skin still lacked. I figured they just wanted to dance, and for the first time and actually have some rhythm to it. At least that was my takeaway. I was ten years old at the time though.

I shrugged.

Mama Eloise frowned.

"What we gotta do?"

"Commune and let go," she said.

I was confused. It sounded easy enough which worried me. Anything in this world that looked or sounded easy was usually the opposite. I lifted an eyebrow as far as it would go up.

"There's more to it but let me handle that," she said.

I was comfortable with that idea. Whatever it was, I knew Mama Eloise could indeed handle it.

"So what you need me to do?" I asked.

"Be open," she said.

I paused. Thought about open. Thought about my body. Open fields. History. Present. Future. Open. The dead and living. My eyes.

I shrugged.

"OK," I said.

We were in the den. It was dark, as usual, though midday. The rain was unrelenting. And though I thought we'd covered everything inside the dream, here in the waking life everything felt new. Unfamiliar.

Mama was sleeping. Lena had heard the night's commotion and told us she was worried. She scolded us for our actions while asking question after question.

What she didn't tell us was that though she'd heard the confusion she'd been too attached to Marcel in the theater room to come see about us if there had indeed been trouble. Make sure we were alright.

Nah. She'd taken the strap-on, tied it to his weak waist and eased down on the pink plastic as though it were a limb. Sprawled across his lap while the television blared that the rain would continue well into the next week. And she'd moved her hips to the side, then up and down, then up, up and away. Faked an orgasm and kissed Marcel's small face, starting first at his temples. Then his forehead. Kissed his nose and lips. Ignoring our sounds. Ignoring his illness. She tried to revive him with the power of her womb and he'd pretended she had. He sweated, not from ecstasy or movement but from trying to hold himself together. He tried to be a rock that was enough to hold Lena's weight, and he was tired, so very glad it was over. He was fulfilled when she'd faked her orgasm, squealed in that high-pitch he was accustomed to and knew well. He had no interest in whether it was born of a natural place, her soul, her body. Her pleasure. This was how they lived. It was enough.

She crawled off him, asked if he wanted to go lie in the bed with her and when he shook his head no, weakly, she'd tried not to cry. So she wiped the gel from between her legs with a face towel, pulled her gown back down and kissed him again. She'd walked to Aunt Bee's room and peeped in, prepared for whatever she saw. Drunkenness. Death. But finding only Bee bruised and sleeping. Finding me before I'd retreated upstairs, still standing before the window watching the rain and smoking another cigarette, bruised and awake, the room lit up with a haze of smoke; she'd simply said, "You can sleep with your mama tonight," and shut the door.

"We have to get Lena and Peach in on it," Mama Eloise said.

I laughed. Rubbed my jaw and right eye that swole, threatening to blur my vision. My mama had seen me briefly, glanced at me that morning—the bit of concealer and my eyeglasses blurring any sight of anything wrong—and she hadn't looked any closer so didn't see anything unusual. Or different.

She went about her day. Popped her meds. Poked her body with insulin. Peeped in on Mama Eloise and returned to her room. The rain was falling as she fell back in the bed. It was another day and we were all here. Together. Thus all was well.

"Convince them?" When I laughed again my face hurt and I remembered Sonny's purple face and red fists. "How we do that?" I asked.

"Leave it to me," she said. "But in order to do this, it requires all the feminine energy in the house."

Not gonna happen, I thought to myself. But who knew? With Mama Eloise anything was possible, or at least seemed so. I thought of my mama. Thought of Lena's romance and Marcel. Shook my head. Thought, nah. Not gonna happen.

Aunt Bee was still sleeping. I peeped in on her after my talk with Mama Eloise and saw Bee's chest moving steadily with even, shallow breaths and her face was relaxed. She didn't look scared so I told myself I wasn't either. Nor worried or pessimistic.

I went upstairs and lay beside my mama; eventually I slept. I rested and let my body heal. There were no dreams. No Sonny. No seance, other than that of my beating heart. It played a song that lulled me, coaxed me to fall and so I did. Deeply. More deeply into a sleep, where Mama Eloise explained everything more fully to my unconscious mind that I needed to understand.

And when I woke up I felt at ease. Trusting. My bruises appeared dimmer than before. The rain was light. My mama snored, and her body rising and falling gently was all the peace I needed.

Seance. I rolled it over my tongue and it felt foreign.

Maybe that's what we needed. A stranger to come in out of the rain. Pull. Push. Awaken.

Something.

Lena wanted me to go to the store with her. I hadn't ventured out into the world in days, and the idea of moving beyond the house's walls stretched my mind in directions that irritated me.

But Lena didn't wanna ride alone. It wouldn't stop raining. Light then heavy.

How could I say no?

It was evening, just before dinner and she was determined to cook. The rain fell and we pulled out of the driveway, car headlights the only coherent thing inside the misty chaos of outside.

I didn't wanna go. My body hurt. Away from the warmth of my mother's body, my mind struggled to understand everything. Living it was one thing, making sense of it another. *Seance* rang like bells throughout my head and it hurt, signaling something I was still unsure of. I trusted Mama Eloise but my mind worked against my heart, desiring some explanation. Some way of working its way through the maze that we were stuck within.

Was this a game? The dead and living. The loved and unloved. Fighting it out?

I wasn't sure.

But my mama didn't look at me as I pulled on my jeans and T-shirt. As I pulled my hair back and wrapped it up in the stiff folds of black cloth. Spun it round and round my head, then my face until I figured it covered everything. Bruises and personal truths. When I put my glasses on, I was sure I was unseen. A ghost. The invisible.

Now we moved down the road, Lena gripping the wheel as though our lives depended on every inch it turned. The radio played old soul songs. Dionne Warwick sang "Walk on by . . ." and I looked at Lena. I looked towards the road, out the windows and saw nothing but the pounding of water. It fell as though we were moving through a car wash, only without the huge brushes, the sweepers. Suds.

She turned left and quickly braked. A car honked at us then whizzed by, splattering a pool of dirty water onto our windows. I couldn't see and was sure Lena couldn't either. I watched her face while gripping the leather handle at my door for life. I watched the dent in her head wiggle and squirm with the tension in her face. I reached and turned the music up. Acted like everything was okay, would be okay, and her body eased.

I just can't get over losing you, and so if I seem broken and blue . . .

We turned into the store lot and parked. Lena breathed heavily. I saw her chest moving and wondered why she felt it so important that we do this.

In the store, she picked up squash, a bag of rice and some bone-less, skinless chicken breasts. I followed behind her with nervous feet. She walked slowly, evaluating every item as though unsure, she'd read its ingredients twice before dropping it in the buggy. And so I moved slowly, thankful for her pace. Still sore and sleepy. Afraid I would never be truly rested. Not here. Not with these responsibilities, whatever they were. My grief and fears. Whatever they were. I focused on Lena to keep from floating away.

When she asked if I wanted something, no matter how obscure or random, I shook my head, yes. When she picked up the Mexican candles. Mother Mary on one, white Jesus on the other, I shrugged. When she picked up a blue then red candle and placed them inside the buggy, I looked at her and rubbed my jaw. I stood behind her in the checkout. She paid, said gracias to the cashier and we ran to the car with heavy feet. Her thighs and heart aching, my everything doing the same.

Once inside the car, we listened to the motor hum and watched the rain. She didn't move. She stared ahead at nothing and I wondered what she saw. Thought maybe what she saw was different but also there.

Water. Blues. Ghosts.

"What you makin tonight?" I asked, genuinely curious. Afraid.

She closed her eyes and took a deep breath.

"Shit," she said, opening her eyes. "I guess whatever tastes good with a seance." She shifted the rearview mirror and moved slowly out of the parking lot. And I watched her eyes, her face, her thighs the entire way home. But she never said another word and neither did I.

Shit, Mama Eloise wasn't playing.

Or if this was a game, she intended to win.

Seance.

We put the groceries up, and Lena picked up the phone and ordered a pizza. She looked at me and said, quick, hurried, "If you go past the pool, you'll see a door. It leads to the basement. You'll find some more candles there. Red. Blue. White. Get as many as you can."

I looked at her but she resumed moving. Fast. Hurried. She turned the water on in the sink and washed the chicken parts, the black hole in her head expanding. It was growing with a depth I never expected.

I watched her for a moment, a new mystery.

Then did as I was told.

I wanted a nap before dinner. I figured pizza could wait; like fried chicken it was one of the few cooked foods that actually tastes good cold.

But my mama had once again found an energy I forgot she was capable of and when she moved towards me in the bed, when she sat beside me and shook my shoulders and said, "Wake up! Wake up!" it felt pleasant to me. I loved any sign of her still being there. Awake. Caring about the moment in ways that could be shown, drawn or sketched.

If she were a commercial, I imagined her sounds were loud. Persuasive. Unwilling to let a person turn the channel. She wouldn't be ignored and for a moment I was willing to buy whatever she was selling.

I looked at her. Took in the image of her alive and smiled. Felt peaceful. Finally.

She'd had her last cigarette of the day with Nettie though it was not bedtime and they had both felt emboldened by the break in routine.

"Did you put this idea of a *seance* into my mama's head?"

My mama.

There it was again. That accusing. That exclusion. My smile receded. I rubbed my eyes, feigning confusion, only it was real because I couldn't figure out when Mama Eloise had all these conversations about a subject I wouldn't know how to approach, much less speak of to anyone aloud.

"Seance?"

Mama narrowed her eyes like, *Don't fuckin play with me!*

I straightened up, familiar with her version of stern. No pinch was needed in this scene of our lives, her pitch was enough.

My mama.

"A water ritual!" she screamed. "Don't act like you don't know what I'm talmbout!"

Water ritual? I liked the sound of that much more. I smiled, involuntarily, until I caught myself and stopped. I tried to remain confused, stoic but my face had never been my friend. It told all my secrets.

"Whose idea was this?" she asked.

I looked at her.

"You know we don't play with God in our house!"

I looked at her. The room was near dark. If not for the pale light, turquoise and shimmering from the window, I wouldn't have been able to see her at all.

Water ritual.

I was confused. Genuinely. And I looked at my mama unable to conceal the fact because how could she not know Mama Eloise wasn't a woman who needed nor could ever be persuaded of something against her might? Her will? Her own thoughts and actions were in my mind more than the world had ever seen. She stood tall even while sitting in her chair. She walked, stomped around the house. Her presence was pervasive and we all bent to her level, still feeling smaller than her even while on our knees.

Any inclination she possessed had been done long before the thought was born.

She was there. She was here. She was that kind of power. She was that kind of strong.

I bit my lip. Looked towards the window for any blue I could find.

"What y'all been doin with that woman in her room?" she asked.

I kept my eyes focused. Open.

Shrugged.

"Living, I guess," I said.

"Living?" Her voice trembled with anger.

"Yes, ma'am," I said. "While you was sleeping."

And I felt her eyes bear down. Tear into my skin. The skin she gave me. I felt the heat of her anger. Pain.

She took a deep breath. I watched her shoulders move up and

down. Her round belly inched forward and fell away. The flowers on her gown leaned towards me. They wanted to grow.

I took my mother's hand. She took a deep breath, her face a maze of yellow and red skin. Beautiful and well-rested flesh that was afraid. I noticed it. Felt it in her touch.

"What she think we supposed to get outta this?"

I was quiet. Watched the turquoise outside disappear. It faded. Blue. Green then black.

The room went dark.

I held her hand.

"I dunno," I said. And I meant it.

I smiled. Looked into the darkness and said, "I trust God. I trust Mama Eloise."

Mama was quiet. The darkness grew but I could still see her. Her body beneath the flowers, her mother's flowers reaching out towards me and I reached back.

"Same thing," Mama said. And her body breathed, deep, strong, full breaths. In. Out. In. Out.

I held her hand. Felt her pulse.

"A lil sun," I said. "A lil water ain't ever hurt nothin."

Mama opened her brown eyes. Stared down at me and said, "But where the sun at?"

She reached for my arm, the one that knew her touch, her pinch best. She squeezed.

"With Sonny?" she asked.

Heat and water. Fire and blue. Who knows what the combination of both can do? Heat. Fire. Rain so blue. The blackness. The color of our hue.

Anything is possible, so say the elders.

When combined, in the mind. When working together, harmoniously? Where there is balance, a restoration is possible. Able.

God's favored son.

Sunny.

We missed the sun.

Never thought about it much until left without its heat. The rays. Our sun.

We women were afraid and brave. Ready to burn it all down and drown. Prepared to grow and age had no say in the matter. Time nonexistent, a concept that only mattered when paid attention to because we lived. We stretched out. We raised our limbs towards the sky no matter what it gave. And guess what?

It gave back. Each and every time.

We believed. We had faith. Where we lacked faith, we had the blues and it was enough. Had always been enough. So we bloomed in spite of our pain.

But we wanted the sun. Longed for the sun. Remembered it in our bones. The frail skeletal system that held our bodies when we wept, or couldn't cry because our bodies had forgotten how. When you think too much, it becomes something choreographed. So that when it's time to perform, you miss the beat. Your natural rhythm is found lacking. The mind plays tricks like that. Until you see.

We had to see, Mama Eloise said. We had to swim. Learn how to swim and be brave against the waters. Or else how could we continue, even knowing what we knew? That life was pain. Beauty. Exquisite beauty that was so powerful that it hurt. It had to hurt because how else could we appreciate it?

We had to use the water. Better yet, she said. We had to recognize the water was us. Our sadness. Our tears. And once no longer frightened of our image, perhaps. Just maybe we could move on. Commune. Let go. Release our ghosts.

Be free.

And it made sense.

Lena, Mama, Beatrice, Mama Eloise, all the parts of me. We sat at the kitchen table, a five-pointed star. All the candles lit—red, white, and blue. They sat atop the table, across the counters, and on the floor like flowers glistening, moving waves of fire.

Marcel walked across the den, ignoring us, hoping we didn't see him or his body. He picked something up from the table and from my peripheral vision he appeared a ghost.

Was he still living? Is he what Lena saw? I rubbed my eyes and looked to my mama for assurance, but when she didn't react to him, I was unsure.

And I was afraid.

"So what we need to do?" I asked again.

Mama Eloise looked at us and her face was the labyrinth we were all stuck within. Dizzy. Spinning in circles to please her. But then she looked at me and asked, "What you think we ought to do?"

"You're older than all of us," she said.

And I flinched at the reminder that only my soul knew. I felt the heat of their eyes upon me and they were the sun. My flowers were waiting to bud and be born. Be something new.

The chicken Lena bought was soaked in apple cider vinegar held inside a teal porcelain bowl placed in the middle of us. Its smooth round breasts were aglow in the flame of the candles' light and I wondered again of its purpose.

Hoodoo was such an old concept. So new. Sometimes the newest improvisation based on an old adage, belief, or thought created something different.

The stench of the vinegar burned the insides of my nose when I answered, "I dunno."

And it was the truth. And because it was the truth it was good. More than sufficient.

Mama E laughed, gently and Aunt Bee joined her.

"This chicken represents the breast of a woman which nurtures the child," Lena said. "The chicken has wings but can't fly very high, much less too far, or maybe it's too afraid and simply chooses not to," she continued and Mama Eloise smiled at her.

She'd remembered.

Lena sighed, looking into the face of a red candle dancing against her face, and she too was a maze. Something beautiful and complex. A mystery.

"I guess we seeking to make another choice," she said and Mama Eloise grunted in agreement.

"Yes," she whispered and the light of the candles blurred before me until it was one flame, one light, a fire.

The rain poured and we listened.

We were making a choice. And beyond that we were re-creating the choices we never had, believed we never had as though options didn't exist for us.

The road splintered in many directions. Which way would we go if given the opportunity again?

"So how do we let go?" I asked, reaching for my mama who sat quiet. She hadn't made a move or sound since the ritual's commencement and when I looked at her, I squeezed her hand but she was gone now, her eyes transfixed by the candles' glare, the rain a hypnosis. I squeezed again and she offered no response, so I pinched, I squeezed until I saw her.

Outside the rain fell and it was a black hole filled, completed with water.

Mama's head hung low, she was hanging from a tree branch, her neck weak. She swung, back and forth.

What do we need to let go?

Ghosts. Our ghosts. Ourselves of the past. Generational pain.

"Mama," I whispered and she said nothing.

"We have to use this moment to cleanse," Mama Eloise said. And there was no lightning. No fire in the sky. Even the rain went quiet.

I cried. I couldn't help it. My shoulders trembled and I was the tree. This exquisite tree my mama had hung from. And I cried, remembering watching her body, like a small child, swing. Back and forth. Back and forth. She made no sound. There was no sound except for the rattle of my branches. My limbs. How could I forget?

Her pain was as old as myself.

And I reached for her, afraid. This was all happening too fast.

The rain fell. Hard. Heavy. It moved at my whim with my tears.

Mama Eloise looked at me with recognition.

Goddess. The worst kind of goddess. One who's afraid of her own creations.

"Water is ancient. The oldest form of anything there ever was, even word. The word was born of the water," she said. "The water moved, swayed, danced and gave birth to sound. From the sound we received word."

Lena shifted in her seat. Moved her sore thighs in recognition.

And when I looked at her I saw her as a child, walking on wobbly feet beside the ocean's lips towards me. It's OK, I cooed to her. It's OK, come to Mami and she did. She walked, her smile a loopy grin that her facial muscles didn't quite know what to do with and I hugged her tight until she was no longer a baby in my arms but a girl. A girl with a man who picked at her body as though choosing fruit. Between her legs, fruit. Bruised. Red. Her small breasts, fruit. He picked and sucked and pulled and pushed himself into her. I watched him until I couldn't stand the sight any longer and looked away.

I cried, watching Lena release.

We were seated at the kitchen table. There was no light except for the candles that burned.

Red. White. Blues.

Yellow and orange flames. The fire reached up, stretched up. Fell down and tried again.

My mama shifted in her seat. Sniffled. I looked at her and saw her face, so beautiful, so luminous within the glow. Her nose was pink. That innocent pink. I wanted to hand her some tissue, some comfort but there was nothing there save for the rain. The flame. Us.

Were we enough?

Mama Eloise was quiet. She was remembering her own body of water, where she was a wave. Gentle. Giant. A tsunami. She quaked. She settled. She was tired. She was a girl who'd been born a woman with a woman's responsibilities. Taking care of everyone but herself. So she was no longer a self. She was a body. A piece of water that dripped. Fell. Caused erosion beneath and inside a house, and from that she drew power. As tired as she was.

And she was exhausted.

In the soft glow of the flame her truth came forward and through my tears I could see her clearly, even while she peered at my mama while wondering what she'd done wrong. How she'd failed. Her gray eyes faded, rescinded into the fact that she too was afraid. Scared of everything, bravery was a notion she hated because she'd stopped believing in it long before she entered the world in her current form. She'd lived many lives and hoped this one would send her home.

Finally.

Daylight come? The sun was coming? She wasn't sure.

Wisdom was the key. But Mama Eloise was still afraid, though no one noticed. Still flawed and everyone noticed. She knew the answers but not the questions.

She was.

She was.

I was. I saw it all.

I saw Aunt Bee rise up from her chair and push her face into the light of the red candle before her. She looked at it. Saw herself inside its reflection and realized the reflection originated from her eyes. She smiled.

"Join hands," she said.

And because we were quiet, each recalling a past that was present and future, we listened. We reached and touched one another. Our fingers joined, recoiled at the heat then moved forward. Binded. Took root.

A seed was planted at her word and it was good.

"Water is old. But even water comes from somethin," she said. "Somewhere."

The blue candles leapt, jumped at the memory and her words.

"There is a place. A darkness within us all," she said. "It neither needs nor wants not. It simply is."

She peered into a blue candle.

The room was quiet. Still.

The theater room was at intermission. Actors taking a well-needed break.

"But within that darkness, we are," she continued. "And it's ourselves that we fear. Deep. Dark. Hidden."

Mama Eloise looked at Beatrice and said, "But it's only through that darkness that we find the light. Find ourselves and when we do, nothing else is necessary."

Aunt Bee smiled, her face aglow.

Lena looked at Bee, tears streaming down her face, like rain, like water, as though seeing Aunt Bee for the first time.

Aunt Bee was not drunk. She was not medicated. She was not scared, crying, reaching out for comfort against a ghost she loved and hated.

"The water is the door," Aunt Bee said. She smiled and paused. "The watery death, the entrance and exit that takes us home, to ourselves."

The candles' flames stirred. Waved. Not feeling threatened or intimidated by an idea that conceded their weakness; they celebrated in agreement and our faces lit up with their joy.

My mama smiled, recognizing their bliss. And I smiled, happy she was there in this moment, understanding.

I squeezed her hand and she squeezed back; her grip strong. Alive. *Moi.*

"We die to live," Mama Eloise said. "We live to love. Through the water we ascend to the fire. To the fire we burn away our grief." She looked at my mama. She looked at Lena. She looked at me and then herself inside the flame. The white candle swayed its hips. Met her face, her eyes, her tears. Leapt in recognition.

"And even though we're not ready to let go," Aunt Bee said. She sniffled and her tears were blooming and flowering; her face becoming a flower.

"We must," she said, shaking her head, the shadow of her bouncing head drawing waves against the wall that fell and rose, bowing down before rising again. Triumphantly.

My mama sniffled. She looked at the flames, red white blue. Looked out the window. Looked at the rainfall. All the colors.

"Maybe we should all say what we givin' up," she said.

She sniffled again and I saw her tears and they were real tears, so strong even medication couldn't hold them back. "Maybe we should speak it," she said, and reached for a napkin within the butterflies to catch her stream. "Let it come from the water."

Mama Eloise smiled through her tears.

"Yes," she said.

I squeezed Mama's hand and she squeezed back.

"I'll start," I said, wanting deeply to support my mama, to help in any way release her from the tree. I walked to her body at its trunk, reached my hands out and caught its girth. Stopped its movement and held her until tempered. Until still. At peace.

"I release my fear," I said. "I let go of my anger and grief. I let go of expectations of something bigger than myself. Of hating myself for what I think I'm not because I can't see what I am."

I stopped. Looked at the blue and red flames until I could no longer recognize them through my tears. It was a waterfall and volcano combined, and there I was. All parts. So scary, so powerful that I laughed through my tears and my mama squeezed my hand. She looked at me as though she saw me. Recognized me. Had seen me all along.

She squeezed me again, her warmth reminding of the gentle body from which I'd emerged.

She cried. Soft tears.

"And I," Lena started, but she stopped before she could fully start. Tears, hurried and quick, spilled down her pale face. Her wig shook with her shoulders and Aunt Bee reached over, rubbed her back. Rubbed her face with a thick, clumsy palm and Lena calmed. Continued.

"And I, I give up tryin to save no-good, triflin-ass niggas!"

Mama Eloise looked up, raised a gnarled hand and lifted her neck to direct her consternation at her baby sister. "Now wait a minute, Lena!"

Lena looked Eloise in the eyes, her face red, shoulders trembling. Aunt Bee moved her palm inside the small of her back and Lena closed her eyes. Opened them again and looked at her sister Eloise, across the flames, the fire and said, "Especially the one who hurt me."

And Eloise sat back. Looked at her sister. Looked down at her gnarled hands. Remembering the tub of water and Lena's tiny body. Her tiny breasts. Her big eyes.

He hurt me.

And though she was quiet, not saying a word beyond her own tears that fell inside the same pool where Lena's gathered, Eloise told herself, she told the Goddess that she too forgave herself for not protecting Lena. Not protecting her brother. Her son.

The flames swam. They lit up the room with their mercy. Outside the water seemed to greet their small bodies; washed them down with redemption. Bent and bowed to their power knowing though small now, they possessed a great might. A great will.

"I let go of the boy!" I blurted it out. Quick. Hurried. "I wish him the best and all my love." Tears stopped my words, the water too strong. My throat yielded. Mama rubbed my back, arms, and shoulders. "I wish I had been better," I said. "I wish my father had been better too."

I felt my mama tense. Her body went stiff, then cold.

I reached for her, and tried to make sure she wasn't a ghost. A blue or red lingering; blending into itself.

But she was quiet. Tired of swinging. Tired of sleeping. Tired of the closet. I mistook her silence and fatigue for rejection, when it was nothing like that. It was more. She was more. I looked at her darkness against the walls, against our faces, her shadow waved and moved. I felt her heat. Her pinch. Her squeeze.

"I wish I'd been better too. For him," she said. "And for you."

Tears.

"I miss my brother," she said. "I miss my daddy." She looked up at me, and her tears caught the flame and glowed. She was golden. Yellow. Red. Orange. Peaches. "I miss my love." She looked down at her hands. Stretched her long fingers inside her lap, watched them grow and recede back into the soft pink of her flesh. "I miss my mama."

"But I'm here, baby," Mama Eloise said. She shook her head. "I'm always here. I'll always be here," she said and reached across the surface of the table. She took Mama's other hand and squeezed with everything she had in her crooked fingers.

Mama looked up, crying. Took Eloise's hand in hers and squeezed back. "I'm sorry," she said.

And Mama Eloise shook her head and said, "Stop! Stop, you have nothing to be sorry for." She looked at my mama in her eyes and said, "You are my strongest child and a mother always knows but you are. And I love you, Peaches. I'm so proud of you, baby."

She squeezed Mama's hand, tried to wrap her fingers around my mama's slender digits but her hand, curled and knotted up, wouldn't cooperate, until Mama released my hand and grabbed Mama Eloise's gnarled hand in both of hers. She watched how the brown met the yellow. Melded. Melted. Joined.

"I love you too, Mama," she said.

"I know you do, and no matter what, just know Mama is always proud of you and everything you are, everything you've done. You're my pride and joy," she said, shaking Mama's hand.

Once again there were tears. Flames. Rain.

"You're my everything, my baby child." Mama Eloise tried to squeeze and though weak, the heat and pressure of her hand was enough.

I watched my mama cry. She squeezed Mama Eloise and then reached for me. Grabbed my hand. Looked at me and I knew, I felt the same. She need not say a word.

I love you too.

"Well shit!" Aunt Bee started. "I guess it's my turn."

And we all looked up at her. Sniffling. Water. Flames. Blue, pink and red. Like babies, like buds. Sweet. Tender. Remembering our cause, we turned to her and loved with our attention.

She looked back. Looked at the candles, then outside where the rain tumbled down, seemingly unaffected by our revelations. It was wet. It was warm. It did its own thing.

Aunt Bee looked at us as though the same. Only I knew she wasn't.

I smiled. Recognized Bee as my reflection. My mimic. My closest ally and enemy. If I moved a hip she responded. If I needed a hip she was not to be counted on. And when push came to shove, quite literally, she might let a nigga down. Tumble down on me like rain. Cry and wait for me to fix her dress. Pull her nightgown down, resolve her situation, tidily. Discreetly as possible. She depended on me. Saw herself in me. Even if I wasn't there. And somehow, I felt obliged to let her. Though she was older. Had walked the Earth in this incarnation far longer; we both knew the truth. I knew she knew. She knew I knew.

It was enough.

She looked at me now. Lowered her gaze beneath that of the flame of the red and blue candles sitting in front of her body, melting. Melding into one color.

"Hmph," she said.

Her eyes scanned the table. She took in Lena. Her small body. Her quick cadence and glossy wig. Soft touch.

Smiled.

She looked at my mama. Saw a child. The child she'd never had in this life and she smiled. Felt soft. Tender. Weak.

She looked at me then shook her head. Thought, *My drankin buddy.*

I smiled back like, *True.*

She looked at Mama Eloise and her eyes went black. Turned brown then gold. The candle's light flickered against her pupils. She teared up. I knew there were tears because they fell and the red candle in front of her frail body caught them all. One drop at a time.

Singular stories told.

Had been waiting to be heard. To be told.

Fables. Tall tales. Myths.

She laughed. Laughed through her tears.

She was real.

Palm trees, beaches, badass students and sad. Her daddy's clock.

Sonny.

She was here.

She laughed.

I smirked. Moved my hips. She laughed more.

"Shit!" she said. "I guess I give up the nigga."

Mama frowned. "*The* nigga?"

And Bee nodded and laughed. She reached for a glass but found nothing there but the heat of a candle. Red. Hot. Glass.

She shook her small head, her mushroom hair flowering, waving, moving, dancing.

"Well hell," she said. "I feel like any dead man who cause all this gotta be *the* nigga."

Mama Eloise frowned. Lena dropped her head into her hands, held it there. Mama looked at me and opened her mouth and laughed hard. Laughed harder than I'd ever heard her. So I looked at her, shook my head and laughed too.

Her sound was too persuasive. If she were a commercial she guaranteed only good things. Her 1-800 number assuredly a good thing.

I called. She picked up. She laughed hard.

I said, *Hello? Hello?*

Laughed.

Said, *I'm so happy to hear from you. Finally.*

But she only laughed. Held her belly. Laughed.

And then Aunt Bee looked at me and smiled. Winked.

Meanwhile, Mama Eloise took a glass of warm water and poured it gently into the mouths of each candle along the table. She whispered with a bent neck, "With love and gratitude, we set you free. With love and gratitude, we be free."

To the chickens, she whispered. "Fly!"

The candles shivered and shuttered down.

Outside, the rain bended, finally yielded. Bowed to us.

Said, "Ashe."

Inside, Marcel's voice called, "Lena? When we eatin tonight? What you waitin on?"

But Lena only looked at us, smiled then rolled her eyes. "In a minute, Marcel, can't you tell I'm busy?" she called back and her wig shook, shivered and cheered for her.

Mama Eloise said, "He gon be mad when he find it's only pizza."

Lena rose from the table, gently blowing out the candles settled on the floor and across the countertops. She paused, looked inside a blue candle, and watching its flame she said, "He'll be awright."

Then blew it out. Quick. Hurried.

"Well I'll be damned!"

I smiled. Pulled from my pipe and my mama made no judgments. She watched the smoke and looked up. We both watched the sun. Shine. Shine. Shine.

I smiled.

Lena peeped her head outside the patio door and looked up.

"You mean the rain done finally stopped?"

I smiled. Nodded my head.

Ashe.

Mama smiled. Pulled from her cigarette and there was a breeze. On the patio we stood, our hair flying. Up up and away.

Lena's wig wiggled. Her dent, the black hole closed some though we couldn't see its movement. The gap decreased and she shook her head in agreement. She stepped outside the door, and peered into the sun's rays.

"Weatherman said the rain wasn't 'posed to stop till next week."

"Mmhmm," Mama Eloise hummed. "I know."

She poked her feet out, those hickory legs, thick tree branches capable of holding the heaviest of bodies. See 'em through until the end. And she let the heat of the sun warm her. She longed for a tan, but not because she hated her color or lack thereof. She reached out with pale limbs for more because she wanted it. Deserved it and that was enough.

She smiled and spit into her cup.

Mama looked at her and said, "Now, Mama . . ."

But Eloise raised her hand and it wasn't bent. Wasn't curled. And my mama remembered what that meant so she stopped herself and smiled. Happy to see her mama here. In the moment.

Aunt Bee was quiet. She looked at the sun and smiled. She looked across the stretch of the backyard, watched the green grass dripping with dew. Refreshed. She took in the flies, the butterflies that swam and swarmed towards her body. They circled her chair and one landed on her lap. It was brown, black, yellow. It waved its wings. It stuttered and swam away and her heart leapt.

She giggled.

She was sober. She was honest about who she was.

Sonny was gone on home. She knew it. Felt it deep in her gut where the ultimate truths could be found.

She was authentic and no one pretended not to know who Bee was. Her mind was right and strong. Had been strong even at her weakest.

Still, she leaned forward in her chair when she looked at me, then looked at the sun, eyeing my pipe.

"Say! Lemme hit that," she said.

And I looked at her in the chair, a mountain, a rock of brown flesh. Laughed and stuffed my pipe with more green. I took a toke. Watched the green turn red. Watched the smoke escape and twist from my mouth like a lost spirit trying to find its way home. Then reached over to Bee, coughed and said,

"Here."

Acknowledgments

As always and with most things, I'd like to thank my mother. She brought me into this world, has threatened to take me out with much sincerity and still continued to love me patiently, gently and ferociously. The true definition of a mama bear she is, and there is no one else whose body I'd rather come from into this world. I love you so much for carrying me in all ways. Always and forever.

I'm incredibly grateful for my agent, PJ Mark, whose patience, faith in me and honesty is truly a gift. Sometimes when we're a little lucky the universe rearranges itself to align souls for a special purpose and I truly feel your presence is divine.

I'd like to thank my editor Maria Goldverg and publisher Lisa Lucas for believing so deeply in this work and sending it into the world. Likewise, so much gratitude for all those at Pantheon who've championed this novel.

Many thanks to the Iowa Writers' Workshop and Lan Samantha Chang without whose support I may not have had the confidence to keep going. Special thanks to Jan Zenisek and Deb West for all you do, both seen and unseen. Thanks as well to the Jeff and Vicki Edwards fellowship for your financial support that made so much of this project all the more achievable.

There are so many friends to thank: Jennie Linn, whose enthusiasm and encouragement has kept me afloat more than she knows. Thank you to Jamel Brinkley and Madeline Carey for your kindness and warmth at the best possible moments. Thank you to Kimberly Wise, who pushed me every day for many years to believe in myself. Thank you to Kristina Johnson for her sweet late-night company and technical prowess that allowed many applications to be properly formatted and submitted. So much love to Chris Hill, Daryl Rosborough, Tyrese Coleman, Donald Quist, Derek Nnuro, Mgbechi Erondu, and Maleda Belilgne, who've all held me down and lifted me up at various points.

Matthew Weiss, you made the cold days and nights of Iowa worthwhile, if only to cross paths with you!

Thanks to Camille Kraeplin for her grace and advocacy and for being one of the best teachers ever. Thanks to Dean Baquet and Dylan Landis, who were early cheerleaders for my fiction writing. And I'll always be grateful to Warren Leary, a great man of the stars, whom I was blessed to have had both scold and gently guide me towards my soul's purpose.

I'd like to express immense gratitude to the Callaloo Creative Writing Workshop which proved to be a pivotal moment in my life. It was there I began to believe this might truly be possible. Ravi Howard, Angie Cruz and Elizabeth Brunazzi dedicated so much of their time and provided countless recommendations along this journey. You have no idea how much you've meant to me.

Ernestine Lampkin, I love you. You come to my dreams often and I'm so appreciative of your continued presence in my life. I spray perfume in all the right places, as you taught me, and eventually I'll get my nails consistently together too because I know you're watching.

Clarence Bailey is the only father I've ever known, and he walks with me still. He never raised his voice. He never lost his patience. He taught me what gentleness looks like in a man, no matter his flaws or mistakes. He was truly love personified.

And finally, this book would not exist without the lives and spirits of the Black women I've known. This is a picture. This is a moment. This is a homage to all we were while here. This is my love everlasting for you.

A NOTE ABOUT THE AUTHOR

LAKIESHA CARR graduated from Southern Methodist University in Dallas, Texas, and received her MFA at the Iowa Writers' Workshop, where she was awarded a Maytag Fellowship for Excellence in Fiction and a Jeff and Vicki Edwards Post-graduate Fellowship in Fiction. A journalist and writer from East Texas, she has held various editorial and production positions with CNN, *The New York Times*, and other media. Her writing has received support from the Bread Loaf Writers' Conference, the Callaloo Creative Writing Workshop, the DC Commission on Arts & Humanities for nonfiction writing, and the Kimbilio Fellowship for fiction writing.

A NOTE ON THE TYPE

This book was set in a type called Baskerville. The face itself is a fac-simile reproduction of types cast from the molds made for John Basker-ville (1706–1775) from his designs. Baskerville's original face was one of the forerunners of the type style known to printers as "modern face"—a "modern" of the period A.D. 1800.

Typeset by Scribe,
Philadelphia, Pennsylvania

Printed and bound by Berryville Graphics,
Berryville, Virginia

Designed by Cassandra J. Pappas